Amulet Books
New York

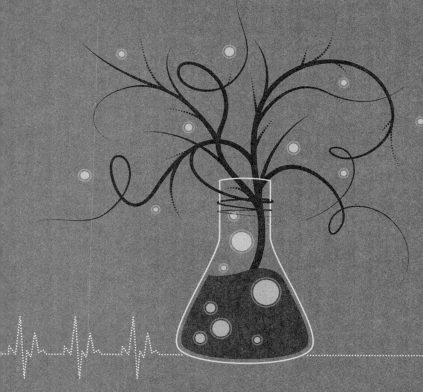

POISON
MOST VIAL

A Mystery by
BENEDICT CAREY

Library of Congress Cataloging-in-Publication Data

Carey, Benedict.
Poison most vial : a mystery / by Benedict Carey.
p. cm.
Summary: "When a famous forensic scientist turns up dead and Ruby's father becomes the prime suspect, Ruby must marshal everyone she can to help solve the mystery and prove her father didn't poison his boss"
—Provided by publisher.
ISBN 978-1-4197-0031-6 (hardback)
[1. Mystery and detective stories. 2. Murder—Fiction. 3. Neighbors—Fiction. 4. Fathers and daughters—Fiction.] I. Title.
PZ7.C2122Poi 2012
[Fic]—dc23
2011038222

Text copyright © 2012 Benedict Carey
Book design by Maria T. Middleton

Printed and bound in the U.S.A.
10 9 8 7 6 5 4 3 2 1

Amulet Books are available at special discounts when purchased in quantity for premiums and promotions as well as fundraising or educational use. Special editions can also be created to specification. For details, contact specialsales@abramsbooks.com or the address below.

ABRAMS
THE ART OF BOOKS SINCE 1949
115 West 18th Street
New York, NY 10011
www.abramsbooks.com

For
Gorda and Bay

CONTENTS

COURTYARD

ALLEY

Rama's
Office

FIRE
DOOR

WINDOWS

Work
Counters

KITCHEN AREA

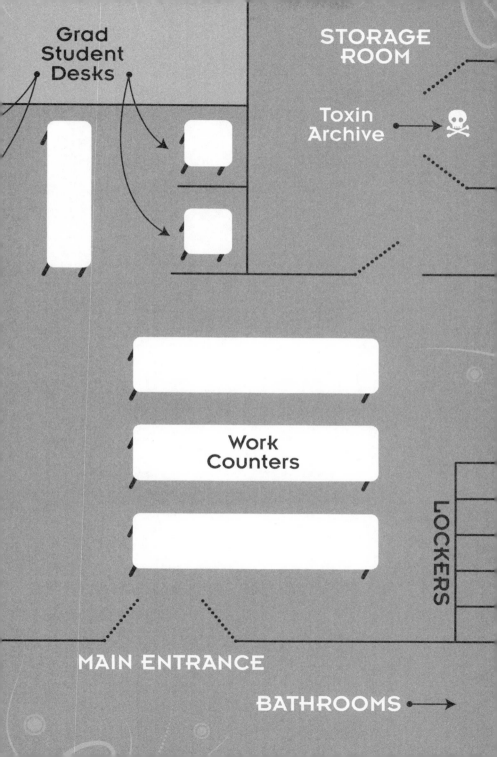

STATEMENT TO THE COURT

CASE 156724-1801: V. S. Ramachandran Murder

Let the record reflect that this statement was taken over four hours on 11/4 and 11/5 at the home of Mrs. Clara Whitmore, the Garden Terrace Apartments, 1575 College Ave.

Video deposition: Det. R. A. Cullen, interviewer

INT: All right, ma'am. The tape is running. You may proceed. Please state your name first, for the record.

SUBJ: Clara Orfila Whitmore.

INT: Your age and occupation, please.

SUBJ: (long delay) I am seventy years old, young man. Retired. I was a toxicologist. A forensic scientist, and I . . . I am retired.

INT: You understand that you are under no suspicion in this case?

SUBJ: Oh heavens, of course not.

INT: You have waived your right to an attorney, is that correct?

SUBJ: I have no need of an attorney, detective.

INT: OK. Now, please explain how it is that you knew the two children involved in this case. Start by stating how you met the girl. The court is very interested in the girl. Where were you when you met her?

SUBJ: (barely audible) I was dead when I met Ruby Rose.

INT: I'm sorry?

SUBJ: Oh, I don't mean *dead* dead, detective. I mean numb. Numb, like you feel when a good friend turns away and you don't know why. Cut off. Left behind, just . . . I don't know. Playing out my days. That's where I was when I met Ruby.

INT: No, I meant—

SUBJ: I laugh at it now, I do. At all the little girl did. How she and her friend Rex solved a murder case—the famous Ramachandran case, no less! But you cannot begin to understand how that happened, detective, without knowing why. You see, this girl had no choice. None.

Her father was headed for jail, and he was all she had. She was cornered. Trapped.

I have come to believe, over my many years, that the only time we face a problem directly and ruthlessly is when all other doors are closed. When there is no other way out. When our doubts about ourselves shrink in the shadow of some larger threat.

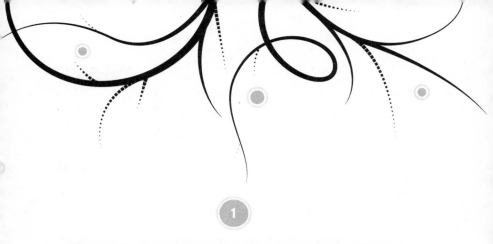

1

THE POISON FLOWER

Squirming her shoulders like a penguin, head down under a spray of yellow hair, Ruby Rose pushed through the tangle of legs, arms, and backpacks at the door and tripped down the steps of DeWitt Lab School, annoyed about something but not sure what it was.

Which only made things worse.

"School's out, Ruby. Why you always want to be staring at the ground like that?"

No need to look up. Rex. She could almost *hear* the lunatic smile on his huge face; he probably grinned in his sleep.

"What do you mean *always*?" Ruby asked, studying her purple boots and keeping them in rhythm for luck: three regular steps and one long stride, three plus one, three plus one, three and one . . .

"I mean, you're so busy counting your steps that you're about to miss Simon and his briefcase. Pick up your head and check this."

The briefcase—that was it: the annoying thing.

Simon Buscombe, spidery with damp hair and a fake limp, strode along in front of them, carrying a briefcase that he'd recently started bringing to school instead of a backpack. A briefcase, for eighth grade! Simon being Simon, he'd been all pompous and secretive, making sure no one peeked inside the briefcase when he opened it in class and carefully removed a piece of paper.

"Look. He got that thing handcuffed to his wrist!" Rex said. "Like he's carrying nuclear secrets in there, CIA documents and whatnot. Don't that beat all? And you know all's he got in there is a bunch of them grimy headbands he wears."

"Hey, you do not want terrorists getting their hands on those," Ruby said.

"Aww, no, you do not, now. Drop one of those into the water supply, paralyze the whole city. Toxic onion rings. Weapons of mass putrification."

Ruby started to smile when a hissing sound came from behind and someone said, "Lookit there, the poison girl. Who're you and your dad going to take out next?"

Rex turned, his surprise hardening into a cold stare. He

searched the scattering crowd: some high schoolers, others younger, too many kids chuckling and smirking to tell who it was. Another voice called out, "The Poison Rose!"

Ruby clenched her fists. *What a place,* she thought. DeWitt Lab School, all these young geniuses, the sons and daughters of professors: "the little gods," Rex called them. Didn't even know you existed until they learned that your dad worked in the lab where a crime happened.

What a crime, though! Dr. Ramachandran, the great genius of DeWitt Polytechnic University (which contained the Lab School), poisoned and dead on campus. *Murdered.* Right there in his office in the forensics laboratory where Ruby had been a hundred times, doing homework. The little gods should be begging her for details about the lab if they were half as smart as they thought they were.

"Rex, c'mon, forget it," she said, turning her friend around. "Let's pull out of here."

Ruby started counting steps again. Oh, to describe all this to a real friend—to Lillian from back in Spring Valley, Arkansas, where Ruby used to live. Rex and Spider Simon with his briefcase and the little gods: Lillian would scream out loud.

Three plus one, three and one . . . The street from school—she'd describe that, too. College Avenue got stickier and dirtier as it approached their neighborhood, College

Gardens, aka "the Gardens," with its Caribbean stores, nail shops, wig shops, moldy bars with moldy people in them all the time. And here, smack in the middle, Garden Terrace Apartments, "the Terraces," the rotting brick-pile tower where she lived.

"What's she always looking at?" said Ruby.

Rex glanced up to the ninth floor where a woman's head was barely visible behind the glare of a window.

"The Window Lady?" Rex shrugged and turned to dash up the steps. "Maybe she got no TV—more later, Ruby."

The first thing Ruby heard when she pushed through the door of her apartment was a rhythmic sound. Pacing. Her father, in front of the table in their small living room. Pacing, serious, holding a letter, his face squeezed up.

"Dad," she said. "What?"

"Nothing, Ru," Mr. Rose said, folding and unfolding the letter, looking for a moment like a little boy, ten-year-old James Rose seeing his first bad report card.

"Ruby, I need to tell you something," he said.

She waited. She could see the DeWitt crest on the letter. That couldn't be good.

"You know about Dr. Ramachandran, of course," Mr. Rose began. He was her dad again. "And you know I was working that night, like normal. Well, Ruby, I'm—" His shoulders fell, and he turned away. "I have to go in for more questioning by the police."

Ruby had to force her words out. "Can't you, you know, find out what really happened?"

"How, Ru? I have to get a lawyer. I don't even know how to do that."

"Well, can't you investigate? Ask people at the lab, like they do on TV? You work there."

"Not anymore, Ruby. Not anymore. My security card was taken away. I can't even get back into the lab. No one who worked there can. I need to talk to someone, I just—I don't know. There's a lawyer comes into Biddy's a lot."

Ruby did not want her father going down to Biddy Runyan's, not now. Biddy's was one of the bars on College Avenue where the older neighborhood people went. Not the best place on earth to look for a lawyer. Her father often went there when he was upset and was worse when he returned.

Ruby picked up the *DeWitt Echo* and reread the newspaper's story on the Ramachandran murder. Found in his office at a minute before 8 o'clock last Friday. The only people there, other than her dad, were the school's dean, a publicity person, and four graduate students—all of whom Ruby knew.

The university police suspected that the professor had died "from the effects of a monkshood cocktail," the article said. Some help that was. Ruby sneaked another look at her dad, who now seemed to be talking mostly to himself.

"I don't believe it," Mr. Rose was saying. "These people at the university, they really think . . ."

2

THE WINDOW LADY

She left him alone. Put a hand on his shoulder, then slipped out into the corridor to get some air, to move, to do something. In her old house in the country, Ruby could have wandered the fields out back, maybe found some empty dirt path, sat there with her sketch pad, and drawn until dark. Or walked the mile over to Lillian's.

Not here; there were only hallways and the constant need to watch for older kids, the dropouts and users, the kids who might come after you. In moments Ruby was up four floors, knocking on apartment 1113. A radio was on, voices and cooking smells radiated through the door.

"Ruby, what you doing?" said Rex, holding the door half-open.

"Rex, you coming out?" If she didn't get him out in one

second, his mom or dad would come to the door and she'd be invited into the chaos of that apartment, with Rex's twenty brothers and sisters and Aunt Esther and Uncle Neville talking and eating and talking; it would be winter before she made her way out. "C'mon, quick."

Rex shouted something over his shoulder and escaped into the hall. "OK, OK, why you all dialed up?"

"Need to talk to you for a second. Not here."

He led her down the hall, around one bend and another, up some stairs to a landing between floors thirteen and fourteen that had a view east over the city and was usually off-limits; a gang of older kids played cards and smoked on this landing most days. "Don't you worry, they won't be back up here till later," Rex said. "What's up, now?"

"Trouble, that's what," Ruby answered. "My dad, I mean. I think they think it's him. The university police—that he's guilty. I never seen him so scared."

"But he didn't do it—the police will find out, that's their job. He just needs to tell the truth."

"I don't know, though," said Ruby. "He already talked to them once. I mean, what if you tell the truth and nobody believes you? My dad's not exactly . . . He's a janitor. They don't really care what he says."

Rex put a hand on her arm. "Aww, now, don't you look like that. It's gonna be all right. Hey, wait. You know what?

You should figure out what happened. Who really killed Dr. Rama. Do it your own self. You know everybody who works there, right?"

Ruby was taking deep breaths. "I—yes, I do, but—Investigate how? I'm a kid; how do I even start?"

"You're asking me? I never had a good idea in my life. Seriously, not a one. But you could maybe—well, no, maybe not."

"What?"

"Nothing."

"No, really, what?"

"It wasn't a good idea."

"I don't care, it's something—tell me already."

"You could talk to the Window Lady, that's all I was thinking. I heard she used to work as some crime investigator type of thing. A long time ago."

"What—how come you never told me?"

"I just did. Besides, I'm not sure it's even true. And I can't—I probably shouldn't go with you."

"What? We'll just talk to her, that's it."

Rex looked away. "Nah, it's OK. You should do it, though."

"Huh?" Ruby studied him for a moment. "You scared? You are. I can tell. She's, like, ninety. You worried she's gonna ram you with her wheelchair or what?"

"Look, Ruby, I never should've said anything. It's nothing.

I just heard she got a fake eye, that's all. Like a marble up in there. I can't be around that."

"What—where'd you hear that?"

"Jimmy said it."

Jimmy, the youngest of the three Woods brothers. The Minister of Information, he called himself. Jimmy's older (and much scarier) brothers were the Minister of Defense and the Prime Minister. Kids believed everything Jimmy Woods said, for some reason.

"Rex, c'mon. *Jimmy?*"

"I mean, Ruby, what if she sneezes or something? I don't want to be there when that cue ball is rolling around on the floor . . ."

"Rex! Stop—this is serious."

Ruby paced in a circle, counting three and one, three plus one. Unbelievable. A fake eyeball. It's something Rex himself would have made up. She pulled her sketch pad out of her back pocket and wrote something down.

"OK, ninja warrior, I have a plan," she said. "We'll ask the Window Lady for help, and you don't have to meet her. You won't even have to see her if you don't want to."

"Like how?"

A minute later, kneeling beside Rex outside the door of apartment 925, Ruby wondered if she'd ever had a worse plan. She pushed a note under the door, knocked twice softly, and fled behind Rex down the hall to the stairwell.

Peeking back around the corner, Ruby saw a light under the door blink once, twice; the note disappeared. "I feel like I'm in kindergarten," she whispered.

"Seriously," Rex said. "I'm gonna jet up these stairs if she comes out."

But she didn't. *Strange,* Ruby thought. You spend all day watching people from on high and don't even look when someone knocks on your door. Maybe the Window Lady was scared of something, too.

"Let's walk past, all casual," Ruby said, moving out into the hallway.

She had a strong urge to knock again, harder. This lady was her only lead, her only hope right now, and—maybe it was just impatience for a stroke of luck on a bad day—she stopped and pounded on the door: one, two, three.

Ruby turned to Rex—"There, that should wake her up"— as the door swept open and a man with no shirt and a long white beard towered over them.

"Mr. Nelson, Mr. Nelson, we don't mean nothing, sir!" Rex said. "We playing, is all."

Ruby couldn't move or speak. The Medicine Man, people called him, the tallest, darkest, most savage-looking human she'd ever seen.

"You play outside, not in the corridor. There's people living in here, boy," the man said. He gave them a wild, frowning stare, slammed the door, and turned the lock.

"OK, Mr. Terraces Expert, that's good work," Ruby said when her breath returned. "So she lives in 925, huh?"

"Yeah, I probably mighta got that wrong."

"Probably mighta? You almost got us eaten. Man probably drinks chicken blood in there."

"You sicker than I am, Ruby. I forgot about this here ninth floor; the apartment numbers don't line up with the other floors."

"Good to know. Is there a door we can try where a native healer doesn't pop out like a jack-in-the-box?"

"I'm counting the windows in my head right now," Rex said. "Don't say anything to mess me up . . . It's 921. Right down there."

"Oh no," said Ruby. "You mean the one with the Do Not Disturb sign on it?"

3

FRIAR'S CAP

Disturbed Already, Ruby wanted to write beneath that sign.

The Window Lady never responded to the note Ruby slipped under her door. The two of them had moseyed by the door dozens of times over the weekend, and it didn't ever seem like anyone was home.

"No sound, no movement, not even any light that I could see," said Ruby as she and Rex ate in the school cafeteria on the following Wednesday. "Maybe she's one of those fake people, you know? What're they called—"

"A femmebot?"

"No, you know, like you see in stores—"

"Avatar?"

"No, I mean—"

"Pod. Pod-person, alien pod, like in that invasion movie, with the exploding heads—"

"Stop, no. Forget it."

"Femmebots, though, usually they're not old ladies. I never seen that."

Ruby opened her mouth to answer and stopped. There, swinging from a bench across from where she and Rex sat, were the most severely annoying things in all of DeWitt Lab School.

Laces. *Shoelaces!*

Sharon Hughes, long black hair, gliding walk, and precious boots with paint splashed on them, all designerlike. Sharon and her laces. Two colors today, wound together and woven in a fancy macramé pattern that every kid would be trying to imitate by next week. Each day a new color, a new pattern: the most showy, prima-donna, trivial thing.

Why do I even care? Ruby thought. *Big deal, the girl is a footwear artist. The Shakespeare of shoelaces, the Van Gogh of high-tops. There are much bigger things to worry about.* "Probably spent three hours on those things this morning," Ruby heard herself say out loud.

"What things?" Rex said, following her gaze. "Oh yeah, Sharon. Girl brought it all in today, how 'bout those laces? Skills. She got skills, a true fact."

Ruby rolled her eyes. What did he know? He liked

practically everything, smiling with his tiny mouth and huge head. Rex the Jolly Jamaican Giant; T. Rex, everyone called him, short for Theodore Rexford and because of his size and short arms. He hated it, but it totally fit.

The rest of the school day took forever, and with every endless minute in class Ruby became more convinced: She would have to knock on the Window Lady's door tonight. At least make sure she got the note, if nothing else. The worst that could happen was that she'd be mean, or just say no. But she had to be less scary than the Medicine Man.

"Moment of truth," Ruby said to Rex; the two were making a last pass by 921 before dinnertime. "Let's see if she's still alive," she said, raising her hand to knock.

"Oh, Ruby?"

She held up. "Oh yes, Theodore?"

He was holding a slip of paper in his hand. A note! She grabbed for it. Rex held it out of reach—"'Scuse me, but who found it?"—and bolted toward the stairs.

Ruby chased him all the way back up to the landing near thirteen, where Rex collapsed to the floor, laughing like it was all a fun prank.

Ruby snagged the note and spread it open on the floor. There was her question—*What is a monkshood cocktail?*—and below it an answer, typed on an old typewriter.

Monkshood is a tall plant with blue blossoms. Aconitum napellus *to the botanist. Also called Friar's cap or garden wolfsbane. Deadly poisonous, especially the leaves. "Cocktail" simply means that it was mixed with other things.*

I have been following this case, too. Get the coroner's report. You may e-mail my friend at the coroner's, Grady Funk (gradyf1138@tkko.com) and use my name. He will send it to you. Print it out and bring it to me.

Sincerely yours,
Clara Orfila Whitmore

Ruby read through the note again, Rex now peering over her shoulder, panting like some huge hound. She turned the note over slowly, as if expecting it to self-destruct, and looked up at Rex. He took a step back.

"We're gonna have to go to the DeWitt Library," Ruby said, "unless you've got a printer that works."

Rex shook his head. "Grady Funk. Now, how's a man gonna live with a name like that? *Grady's* bad enough, but you'd have to shower twice a day if—"

"Rex, please. She wrote us back. And just look at this. She's for real. You know what this means?"

"Uh-oh."

"You've now had one good idea. How does that feel, Mr. Funk?"

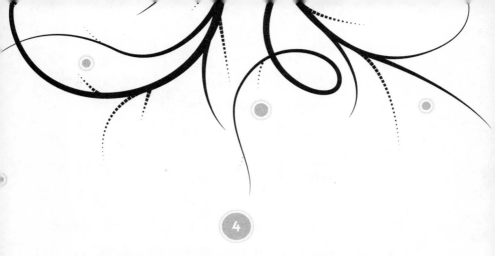

4

THE VIALS IN THE LOCKER

The DeWitt Science Library looked like some medieval fortress, and to Ruby the computer terminals, video booths, and digital scanners inside seemed tacked on, artificial, like a face-lift on an old dragon.

She moved quickly to one of the open computers and clicked through to her e-mail. Mr. Funk, whoever he was (and however he might smell), had replied to her the night before, attaching the coroner's report.

"Whoa, he sent it to you right away? Lookit you, Mr. G-Funk," said Rex.

"I told you she was for real, the lady," Ruby said. "Now, let's see what this thing looks like."

"Excuse me, you really mean *I* told *you*."

"'Scuse *me*, *you* nearly wet yourself walking by her door. OK, here it is."

The screen blinked, filled, and the two of them took a half step back. There it was, in black and white.

CASE 156724-1801
NAME: Ramachandran, Vijay Sanjit

Below were his address, his age, his medical conditions. Something about prescriptions he was taking for type 1 diabetes, for arthritis. Another page described tests run on the kidney, liver, brain; then more about the body being dissected and analyzed.

"I'm sorry, but that right there is a horror movie," Rex said. "*The Toolbox Murderer, Part II.* Seriously, I don't know how people want to do all that to a body."

"Is *The Toolbox Murderer* the only movie you ever saw?" Ruby replied. "It's the only one you ever talk about. Look, they're forensic experts. It's their job."

"Just be glad you never seen it, is my advice to you."

Rex ransacked his pockets and Ruby hers, finding just enough change to print out the eight pages of the report. Rex pulled the pages out of the machine, peering over his shoulder as if he were worried about being caught. He handed the report to Ruby—"Here, you hold these for a sec"—and turned to go.

"Slow down, where you going?" Ruby said.

"Bushes," he said, using his word for the bathroom.

"You're kidding—*now?*"

Rex found the men's room on the main floor locked, with an OUT OF ORDER sign on the door. He found a librarian and asked if there were any alternatives. "Elevator three levels down, dear," she replied, "then go left, and left again, then right, than angle left, finally right again. Can you remember that?"

"Thank you, ma'am," Rex said, without really listening.

Ruby followed him down. She did not want Rex getting lost beneath the library now that they had the coroner's report and someone waiting to read it. And he would have, she saw that right away. The subbasement was a world removed from above. Dim hallways, exposed pipes along the walls, no signs or arrows pointing the way. From somewhere close came the *drip-drip* of leaking liquid.

"Left and left again, and then right, and then . . . What did she say?" said Rex.

"I'm not the one who talked to her," Ruby answered.

Some of the bulbs were out, and Ruby moved close behind Rex. The two left turns were quick and seemed obvious. The right turn was not. The hallway forked before one intersection and it was not clear whether they should take a hard right or the slanted one.

"Oh no, three minutes and we're lost," Ruby said. "That's got to be a record, even for you."

"Well, one of us is lost and in need. I'm about to get whatyoucallit, when scuba divers come up outta the water too fast—"

"The bends."

"—my back teeth already floating."

Another turn, another dim hallway.

"We're gonna end up in the morgue, with bodies tumbling all over us," Ruby said. According to DeWitt rumor, whispered by older kids to younger ones, the morgue was a cavern under the library where the forensics department stacked bodies.

"Ruby, you take that back right now," Rex ordered. "You're gonna put a hex on us down here."

Finally, Ruby saw it: pretty much a hole in the wall with a male/female sign on the door. Hard to believe any librarian would send two kids down to this ruined-looking place. The woman must have messed up her directions. Or Rex had.

Ruby waited as Rex bumped around inside like a chubby rooster trapped in a crate. "Looks like nobody cleans in here, Ruby. There's toothpaste and things all over in here," he called through the door.

"Would you hurry up?" Ruby wanted to drop off the

coroner's report to the Window Lady, and fast. She wandered a little ways down the hallway, three steps and one, then noticed a heavy door marked EXIT.

She stopped. To where? Where were they, exactly?

"Ruby, where'd you go? Let's get out of here," came Rex's voice from behind her.

"How? You have any idea where we are?"

"I been counting right and left turns, so yeah, pretty much."

"You mean like you figured out where the Window Lady lived? No way we can get back. I think we should just go out here. It says *exit*. Can you see anything through that hall window up there?"

On his tiptoes, craning his neck, Rex peered up through a small barred window near the hallway ceiling. "I don't know," he said. "It's outside, it goes outside; looks like there's a tree out there. I can't tell."

"One way to find out." Ruby pushed on the door—a fire exit, she saw—that opened easily to a flight of crumbling concrete stairs that went up and out of the building. She propped the door open, crept up the stairs for a better look— and stiffened.

She called to Rex in a low voice.

Underground hallways ran under the entire campus (or so Ruby had heard), connecting the library, the university buildings, the Lab School, all of it. And the forensics building, where her dad worked, was next to the science library.

The crumbling steps led to a narrow alleyway between two buildings. To the left was what looked like a small courtyard; Ruby saw a couple of old flowerpots and a wooden bench. To the right, just a few steps down, was a thick window that Ruby knew very well from the inside: the main forensics lab.

The crime scene.

She moved to get a closer look. Rex wedged a stick between the door and the wall so they could get back in and followed.

Through the thick window, the lab looked like it always did. Refrigerated cabinets banking the walls. Rows of work counters piled with the tools of forensics: racks of test tubes, circular centrifuges used to purify substances, pipettes; the hulking chromatographs, instruments that separated chemicals. There were lockers, too, where people hung their jackets and stored their lunches, and—straining now, looking at a steep angle through the glass—Ruby could make out the Toxin Archive, the large glass cabinet containing hundreds of poisons for research.

She leaned forward to get a better look at it—and ducked.

Occupied! Two men with thin latex gloves suddenly stood and came into view. Not regular police, either; older, much more serious-looking. Rex was down on the ground, staring up. *What now?*

Ruby instinctively pulled her sketchbook out of her back pocket and opened to a blank page. She sketched the lab from memory.

She counted three and one in her head several times, then peeked at Rex, who nodded. The two lifted their heads and had another look. The men had their backs to the window now. They appeared to be searching through a locker on the back wall that looked like it could be her dad's.

"Oh no," Ruby whispered.

The men's movements seemed to slow down: They had found something, something small, and were handling it with their gloves; Ruby strained to see what. And then she knew. A glimpse of red between pale-green gloved fingers told her all she needed to know. Two of the small, red-tinted vials from the Toxin Archive.

Ruby turned away. She assumed that the killer had gotten the poisons from the archive cabinet, and now these detectives, or whatever they were, had found two of them. In her dad's locker? Now, why on earth would—

"Ruby, they left—the men—in a hurry," whispered Rex. She sensed rather than heard footsteps.

"Move," she said.

Rex took three long steps and pulled on the door into the library. "Uh-oh," he said. Hadn't he propped it open? He looked down. The stick had fallen out.

"You there!" came a man's voice.

This was crazy, Ruby thought. Busted before they ever got started, all because the rooster had to find the bushes.

Rex pulled again, harder. The door swung open.

Into the subbasement hallways, half running, staying in the shadows close to the walls. One left turn, another, then right and left again, and through a door well before they looked back. Nothing. Waiting. Listening. Only that steady dripping noise and their own breath.

Casual now, like a couple of kids goofing off, Ruby and Rex wandered back in the direction of the elevator. Hours it seemed, strolling, moseying, wanting to run; and then there it was. Dumb luck, nothing else. Both took a step back when the doors opened, as if a policeman would lunge out. But it was empty, like most of the main library, yawning and sleepy as always.

Neither felt safe until their feet were back on College Avenue and they had passed Trevor's Tropical Corner Store, the two wig shops (House of Wig, and House of Wigs, plural), and the Orbit Room bar, and were stopped out front of Sister Paulette's Bakery, where most everyone in the Terraces seemed to spend some part of their day.

It was a miracle Rex did not stick his head into every one of those places, even the wig shops. He actually looked like—

what was it?—like he was in a hurry. "This thing will take care of it," he said.

"What thing?"

"The report. The lady's gonna solve the crime so we can get our normal livelihoods back."

"Normal livelihoods? You mean, making fun of Simon and trying on orange wigs at the wig shops?"

"They're burnt orange. And you can hate the man, but why you want to go and hate a man's livelihood?"

"'Cuz that's who I am," said Ruby, now staring up at the window of 921, a mirror of gray light. "I just wonder who she is."

Looking through the other side of that window, a step back from her usual spot to avoid being seen, Mrs. Whitmore wished for a moment that she hadn't responded to the children's note. It was impulsive, with no thought of the possible consequences: very unlike her.

Too late now; the children were almost back.

"Why must they all walk in the middle of the street?" she said aloud, turning from the window.

She removed an advertisement from her bulletin board— *Emmet Sloane and Bernie Diaz, Attorneys at Law*—and made a phone call. A recorded voice answered, followed by a tone.

"Is this recording? Oh dear, I guess so. Bernie? Why, hello. It's me, Clara. Clara Whitmore. I do hope you'll forgive my dropping in on you like this after so many years. I so hope you are well. But I'm calling to send you a client. It's someone who—"

Beep. The machine cut her off.

She redialed. "I am sending you a client, Bernie; I hope you don't mind. You will know who it is the minute he walks in the door, and I can pay for your time, if needed. I hope we can catch up very soon."

She hung up. Not much time. She folded the ad in half, wrote *For Ruby* on it, and pushed it under the door. It disappeared instantly, replaced by a sheaf of papers coming the other direction—the coroner's report.

She swept the report off the floor and abruptly stood. She faced the door, light-headed. What was it? Nothing; nerves, maybe. They were kids, for heaven's sakes. She had seen them a hundred times. They seemed perfectly nice, if a little scruffy. Surely she would think of something to say as soon as they knocked.

But the knock never came.

5

SUSPECTS

The office of Sloane and Diaz was in an old building downtown, a half-hour ride on the bus, during which Ruby studied
her father while pretending to daydream. He looked pale,
drained of all his humor. Dazed.

He didn't even argue when she'd shown him the ad; only
asked where it came from, who the Window Lady was. Then
he nodded and made the call—"The woman said to come in
now; the office is open"—and off they went.

The place sure didn't look open. A grimy turnstile pushed
into an empty lobby steeped in wasted brown light. No
doorman, no information person, nothing but a stack of
boxes in a corner. An old directory on the wall read LAW
OFFICES #601.

"Fat guy with a hat and a cigar," Mr. Rose said on the

way up in the elevator. "Chewed cigar, food stains on his tie."

"No—skinny, crooked glasses, stooped over," said Ruby. "Mole on his forehead, hair coming out."

"You mean, pants pulled way up, that kind of guy? Let's hope not."

Bernie Diaz was not a he but a she, a squat, dark woman with brown lipstick set off by a black outline. She was seated behind a large metal desk heaped with paper. Ruby couldn't believe this woman was a lawyer at all. Didn't lawyers look like—well, she didn't know. Not like this.

"Mr. Rose, I guess?" the woman said, coming from behind the desk. "I am Bernie Diaz."

The two shook hands, and Ms. Diaz turned to Ruby. "And this young lady is . . ."

"My daughter, Ruby," Mr. Rose said. "She'll make sure I don't forget anything important."

Ms. Diaz looked ready to say something but only nodded, resting her flat eyes on Ruby for a moment. Ruby held out her hand stiffly. How could this goat of a woman with moles on her forehead possibly help her dad?

"All right, have a seat, Mr. Rose," the woman said. "Young lady, I'll ask you to take a chair in the room next door and not to interrupt us. This is a confidential conversation. Do you understand that?"

Ruby gulped. She found a hard wooden chair in the small

room adjoining Ms. Diaz's office, opened her sketchbook, and let her thoughts wander for a second. An early-morning scene filled her head: wooden fence, hardened by age, still damp. A footpath there, just behind a stile. A figure down the path, someone friendly: her pal Lillian, maybe?

Ruby studied the scene, shaded each detail. She drew until her ears froze her hand. She looked up.

"Describe, sir, your own relationship with the victim," the woman was saying to Ruby's dad in a soft voice, her face impassive.

Ruby could see and hear the whole thing through the open door between the two offices. She closed her eyes, her ears warming. She had been afraid to ask her dad about this directly, afraid he'd think that she doubted him. She peeked at him over her sketchbook, saw her father nodding, shifting in his chair.

"Our relationship?" Mr. Rose said. "Not good. I mean, Rama was such a total—ah, I mean, he was, you know, formal. Cold. That's just how he was. That's who he was. What I didn't like was . . . well, Rama didn't notice people. It was like we were invisible, all of us, even the grad students. Then he'd blow up at some little thing out of nowhere."

Ms. Diaz held her pen over her pad but had not taken her eyes off of the client. "Mr. Rose," she said coldly, "did you poison Dr. Ramachandran?"

Ruby saw her father sit up, tip forward on his chair. He looked somehow bigger. "No. No, ma'am, I did not."

Ruby breathed again. Of course he hadn't. Ms. Diaz seemed satisfied, too. She nodded slowly and sat back in her chair. "Well, someone sure did. Someone in that lab, almost certainly. If it wasn't you, then who?"

Mr. Rose did not have an answer. Ruby, her head down now, wished her dad could say something. Anything.

"OK," Ms. Diaz said. She sighed heavily. "Mr. Rose, tell me about everyone who came into the lab that night, starting with yourself. The times people came and went, as you remember it all."

"Right," said Mr. Rose, glancing over his shoulder at Ruby. She pretended to draw but began taking notes.

"Well, I got there just about six o'clock in the evening, like always. I can tell you the exact times. I already been through all this with the police." Her father stated his routine, which now seemed much less boring to Ruby than it usually did. Punch in with security card (6:02 P.M.). Hang jacket in locker, put sandwich in fridge (6:05 P.M.). Make sure lab instruments are clean, well supplied (6:10 P.M.).

"And then I made Rama a pot of tea, because Lydia was busy, I guess." he said. "I took it in to him at about 6:15 or just after, I'd say."

"Stop there," said Ms. Diaz, still engrossed in her notepad. "You usually made his tea, or you did it this once?"

"Well, this once. Lydia—she's a grad student—she usually made it."

"And she asked you to do it this time?"

"That's right."

"A change in routine. No wonder you're a prime suspect. I wonder what they found in that tea. We'll have to find that out, and soon."

Ruby felt an urge to mention the red vials but swallowed it. She wasn't even supposed to be listening; and how would she explain knowing about that?

"OK, keep going. What else?" Ms. Diaz said.

Her dad said that Rama had a taped TV interview scheduled for 8:15 p.m. Nothing unusual there. Dr. Ramachandran often commented on cases and evidence as an outside forensics expert and, Mr. Rose said, he was expected that night to say something about the Robert Pelham case. Pelham was a prominent investor with ties to the university. He'd been cleared of an alleged plot to kill a business partner as a result of problems with the handling of evidence.

"You know, the rich guy who went free because the evidence fell apart—"

"Of course I am very familiar with that case; when Pelham's company went bankrupt, people all over the city were trying to get their money back," Ms. Diaz said. She made a note, circled it. "Go on."

"Well, you may not know that DeWitt Forensics did the lab work while Rama was gone on vacation. I don't know the details, but someone made a mistake there, at DeWitt, handling or testing the evidence. Rama took it personally, even though he wasn't around. He couldn't let it go."

Ms. Diaz raised her eyebrows. "Hmm. Did he blame anyone in particular?"

"No idea. He kept his opinions to himself."

"All right. What was the next thing you remember from that night?"

At 7:59 P.M., the dean and a DeWitt publicity person knocked on Dr. Ramachandran's office door to make sure he was ready. No answer. After repeated knocks and calling his name, they entered.

"Dean? You mean Earl Touhy, dean of forensics, correct?" Ms. Diaz said.

"Sorry—yes, that's right."

A minute later the entire lab was gathered around Rama's body, awestruck. "And there he was, right on the floor near his chair."

"You heard nothing before that?"

"Nope."

"You didn't even hear him fall?"

"The lab can be a noisy place, and the door was closed."

"OK. You said the entire lab gathered around, huh?" Ms. Diaz said, again lost in her notepad. "How many people total in that group? In fact, tell me how many people total entered the lab that day. As far as you know."

Mr. Rose looked up at the ceiling. "Right. Including me? Seven. Four grad students. Me. The dean, and Miriam— that's the public affairs lady."

Ms. Diaz squinted at her nails. "Let's hear about every last one of 'em," she said. "Including the dean. And the publicity person. Everyone. Everything about them and anyone who regularly enters that lab."

Mr. Rose dropped his head and put a fist to his mouth. Ruby badly wanted to get a drink but didn't dare move. "I feel like I'm ratting people out here, and I don't like it," her father said finally. "But I guess there's no choice."

Ms. Diaz tipped her head and gave him a look that said, *Uh, no.*

"Right, OK. Well, let's see. Regularly entered. Well, there's Roman Kapucinsky, the day janitor. His shift starts at about 10 A.M. or so, goes till about 6 P.M., when I start. Older guy, barely speaks English. Kind of angry, in a quiet way. Not the smartest kid in class. I'm not saying I'm a genius, either, but Roman sometimes has this slack-jawed look, like a lost peahen. Almost retired, I think. I can't imagine him doing something like this. He doesn't have the energy, at least I don't think—"

"OK, good. Who else?"

Ruby wrote in her book: *Roman, day janitor, quiet, angry, tired.* She'd seen Roman dozens of times but had never thought about him much.

"All right," her dad was saying. "Well, I don't know if it matters, but Dean Paul Touhy was always in there. You seen the dean. Big boy, sometimes on TV with Rama, commenting on crime stuff."

"If he was there, he's a suspect," Ms. Diaz said.

"Yeah, I agree, he should be. Dean and Rama got on OK, but Dean's job depended on Rama totally, and I don't think he liked that. You know, having to manage this superstar and all. Then again, he'd be crazy to take out Rama; it would be impossible to replace him. And Dean completely lost it when we found the body. Fell to the ground on top of the body, all that. I don't know. Maybe they were closer friends than I thought."

Ruby wrote: *Dean Tubby.* That's what the grad students all called him behind his back. Big, jolly fella, reminded her of Rex a little, the way he laughed a lot at almost everything. He was nothing like Rama or the other important people over there. Dean Touhy knew who Ruby was and actually greeted her, asked about school. Random adult chatter, but it was more than she ever got from the little gods.

"Who else, Mr. Rose? What about students? Don't forget a single person."

"Yeah, there's a bunch of students. Or fellows, or, uh, postdocs, or whatever. Some's all right, others I don't like so much. Sit there studying for ten hours and never say boo to anyone. I mean, I guess—"

"Names."

"Right. Victor Ng. From China. Still learning English, but jokes most of the time. Victor is half clown. The other half is all business, though. He kind of turns it on and off, like he has a switch. Victor liked to take charge at times when Rama was out. That was strange. No one liked that at all."

Ms. Diaz nodded, made some notes to herself. So did Ruby. "Go on," the lawyer said.

"All right, let's see. Grace Fleming. She's from Boston or somewhere around there. Friendly but very, I don't know, fragile. *Stressed* is the word people use. But it's more than that, I think. She's the daughter of some big shot, not sure who. I personally think that—well, not my business really."

"Tell me."

A moment passed before he answered. "Drugs. It's a hunch, that's all. I have seen her with those little prescription bottles, and I don't know. I just got this feeling about it."

Ruby, taking notes, wrote exclamation points in the margins where the descriptions rang true to her. She saw instantly that her father's description of these people matched some of her own vague impressions of them. If only she'd paid more attention, she'd have known them all so much better and, being a kid, maybe learned stuff about them that her dad never could.

She leaned forward to catch every word.

"Lydia, the one who usually made the tea. Lydia Tretiak is her name—"

"Yes, let's hear about Lydia."

"Grad student, like I said. Russian or Ukrainian or something: I mean, really Russian, from over there. Intense, almost desperate, for some reason. I don't think she has much money. I mean, I don't know anything about her situation. I just know that look."

Mr. Rose also described Wade Charles, from Colorado, the other grad student regular. Easygoing wise guy Wade, who reminded Ruby and her dad so much of characters from back home in Arkansas. Wade was good to have around, a cool breeze in this hothouse of work-crazy egos. Maybe a little too cool. He was out drinking at all hours, and Mr. Rose mentioned that he'd seen Wade at Biddy's (*pathetic*, thought Ruby) and even once coming out of the Orbit Room (*insane*).

Mr. Rose knew very little about Miriam, the publicity

person. She was new and hadn't met Rama before that night.

Ruby wrote down every word that she could catch, working until her hand froze with a cramp. She now had a list of suspects.

"That's it? No one else came into the lab?" Ms. Diaz said.

"Those were the regulars, and the ones who were there when we found Rama that night," Mr. Rose said. "Bigwigs came in, too, once in a while. City officials. Dr. Childress, the university president. That kind of thing. Rama was always working on these big cases. But no one like that came in that night."

The lawyer shot a look over at Ruby. "Are you taking notes on this case, too, young lady?"

"Huh?" Ruby said, as if startled from a nap. "Drawing." She turned her book to reveal an intricately detailed horse, drawn the previous day.

Ms. Diaz gave her a brief, knowing look—almost like a wink—before turning back to her own pad.

"OK, Mr. Rose," she said abruptly, pushing her chair back and coming out from behind her desk. "This is a start. Here, take my card." She handed him a Post-it with a number on it. "We'll speak in a few days."

Ruby's dad, standing now, made for his wallet.

The lawyer put a hand on his arm. "Not yet. No talk about money until we get further along. I'll have an expert pull the coroner's report, and we'll begin reviewing witnesses' statements as soon as possible because"—Bernie Diaz turned to Ruby in midsentence and held out her hand—"if your father didn't do this, we need to come up with some theory of what happened, so talking to suspects is particularly important."

Ruby took the lawyer's hand and bowed abruptly, wondering why it felt like the woman was asking her to do something. Interview suspects? No way on earth a kid could possibly get access to the very people who— Oh.

Take that back.

6

REGULAR HONORS

"Another day at the Regular Ranch, where the wild animals roam," Rex said, arriving in class. "Now, what's this secret plan you're talking about?"

"You'll see, you'll see," Ruby said, glancing around the familiar room. Regular Honors was where DeWitt teachers dumped any student who wasn't identified as High Honors or otherwise didn't fit in with the little gods. Ruby was moved in the middle of seventh grade ("student highly distractible," for drawing in class) and met Rex ("anger issues," for sitting on an older boy who had started a fight).

"All you have to do is get a hall pass and follow me to the library when I leave after this period," Ruby told Rex. "Let's hope this lesson goes fast."

Their teacher, Mrs. Patterson, arrived a minute later,

and without a word slashed out on the blackboard, in huge letters, *What is a criminal?*

Mrs. Patterson turned, opened her book, and tapped her knuckles on the desk. "All right, now, all eyes here, the day has started. I trust that everyone's done the reading." She scanned blank faces. "Miss Rose?" So much for fast.

Rex whispered, "Incoming."

"Yes, Mr. Rexford?" Mrs. Patterson said. Ruby took a breath. "You have something you'd like to tell the class?"

"Uh—no, ma'am. Nope, sorry, I'm good."

"Then maybe you would like to begin the reading. Please open to page— Excuse me. Yes, Simon?"

Simon Buscombe, briefcase boy, who usually spent class time drawing intricate mazes, had his hand up. "A disturber of the peace," he said in his deep, formal-sounding voice.

"Come again?" said Mrs. Patterson.

"Who is a criminal. Outsiders, castoffs, disturbers of the peace. Those who don't fit into the accepted power structure."

"Sounds like Regular Honors," Rex said.

Mrs. Patterson gave him a look. "There happen to be some very gifted children in this— Why, yes, Danielle?"

"Simon's confused, as usual," said Danielle Mays, who objected strongly to almost everything (which was why she was here). "How about the person who poisoned Mr. Rama?"

Ruby flinched. She knew it would come to this.

"He killed someone," Danielle continued. "Doesn't matter to me if he's an outcast or whatever Simon's little theory is. He did it—period. He's guilty. He's a criminal."

"How do you know it was a he, Danielle? You know something the police don't?"

Ruby turned. Sharon Hughes ("character issues," for hacking into the school computer), the laces girl, was doing her nails in the back of the class. "Have you solved the crime already? Go ahead, tell us who did it, then. A criminal is the person who looks most guilty, that's who it is."

"Yeah, you should talk, Sharon."

Sharon glared at Danielle.

"Those two about to go criminal on each other," Rex said.

"Theodore, no more comments from the peanut gallery," the teacher said. "Raise your hand if— Yes, Kevin?"

So it went, for longer than Ruby could stand, until Mrs. Patterson finally put her hands up. "OK, OK. That's enough. I think everyone gets the idea. It's not always so simple as people assume. Why don't we take a break, a short study period. Let's everyone calm down."

Ruby took the cue and approached Mrs. Patterson for permission to leave class (the one good thing about having a father involved in a murder investigation was that you always had a ready excuse for a hall pass). The teacher seemed too happy to hand out the pass, maybe because she felt embarrassed, too.

Minutes later Rex joined Ruby in the science library, a short walk through an enclosed passageway from the Regular class. "How about that Sharon? I never seen that before."

Ruby put a hand up. "Stop. Forget your true love Sharon for one second. Look who's here. Just what I thought, too. I knew they must be meeting somewhere, and that's their table. All hidden back there."

"My true love always been myself. Who's here?"

"Shh. Way back there by the copying machines. That first table. Those are the grad students who worked in the lab—stop staring, will you?"

"Grad students? Looks like some metal band. Tattoos all over that one girl's neck. Now, why do people want to go do that? That's worse than those maroon wigs they got at the House of Wig."

"Wigs. House of Wigs, plural. They're henna, not maroon. And if that's a band, it's the Suspects. Someone over there knows something. I'm going over."

"Nah, you're right, House of Wigs plural's got those maroon— Hey, you're going now?"

"You just hang back and cover me if something happens, OK?"

"You be careful, now. They gonna be as suspicious as they look."

At first it seemed like the opposite. Victor stood up and smiled wide as Ruby approached the table.

"Ruby. Oh, hello!" Victor actually gave her a hug, the way some older adults did to say hello. "We are so very sorry about your father; we don't think he did this at all," he said, and blushed and half bowed to her.

"I, uh, thanks, Victor," Ruby said. All of the others were there: Wade, Grace, Lydia.

Ruby learned in no time that these four, Rama's chosen grad students, had been meeting regularly at this back table in the forensics section, trying to figure out how and where to carry on their work. And she could tell by the looks on their faces that they were talking about the case.

"How are you holding up?" Grace Fleming, her voice more fragile than ever. "We are devastated. The lab work is probably over. None of us can leave town because of the case. We think it must have been one of the other university people who were in and . . ." Grace stopped and the group exchanged looks. Nobody spoke for a moment. Silent signals were flying between them, Ruby sensed.

Wade opened a book and began reading. Not like him

at all. Lydia squinted out the window as if the secrets of the universe were inscribed in tiny print out there. Grace turned to Victor, who nodded slightly.

"Ruby," Victor said finally. No longer a friend, now the lab leader. "Listen. If you need anything, please don't hesitate to ask any of us. But we're really not supposed to discuss this case, because the investigation is ongoing. We shouldn't be meeting at all, to be honest."

Ruby took a step back. "But . . ." She was confused. She had so much to ask them. They were witnesses as well as suspects. How come they got to discuss the case, but she and her dad were excluded?

"It's really for your own sake more than anything," Victor was saying.

"But so, I can call you?" Ruby asked. "Can I have your number then, or e-mail? I mean, my dad, you all know him." She lowered her voice. "You've got to help us."

"Well, ah, we've been coming in here, so . . ." said Victor. "And I've been keeping my phone off." He glanced back at the others. "We're really not supposed to be in touch with anyone about this."

Keeping his phone off? Not Victor. He was asking her to leave, that's what was happening. Unbelievable. Ganging up like this. What had she expected? One of these four was likely guilty, maybe all four.

Turning to go, Ruby heard one of them whisper, "Maybe ask about the red vials?"

"Ruby." Victor again.

"What?"

"Um, could you—well. Could you ask your dad about the red vials? You know, the ones from the Toxin Archive?"

Ruby got home from school just as her father was about to go out. She had no idea what he was doing with his days; the papers now called him a "person of interest" in the case, which seemed to mean that Mr. Rose was the prime suspect but hadn't been arrested. Yet.

"Dad."

"Ruby."

"One question for you."

"Uh, OK. I was heading out to Biddy's. Can it wait?"

"Biddy's? Really? Now?"

"Uh, yes, really. I need a break, Ruby. To laugh a little. I'm not a flight risk—I'm too slow on my feet, especially when trying not to spill a beer. And the Biddy's gang don't care whether I'm a suspect or not."

"Why, because they've all been in jail, too?"

His eyes widened, and then he laughed like his old self. "Exactly, that's why they look up to me. Now, what's your question?"

"Tell me about the red vials."

"That's a question, is it? You sound like a lawyer. Back in Spring Valley, you used to ask me why crickets made that sound, whether the chickens slept lying down or sitting up. Which vials exactly?"

"You know, those ones they kept in that archive cabinet, the little red ones—"

"Yeah yeah, of course, that's where the murderer got the poison, it looks like; and the police are very interested in those."

"Right, but I'm asking about the ones they found in your locker. Two of 'em."

Mr. Rose sat down at the small table where they ate and looked at his daughter. "Ruby, how do you know about that?"

She gulped. "OK . . . oh yeah . . . well . . ."

"Yes?"

Ruby explained about the coroner's report and the library, how she and Rex stumbled on the lab scene, making it sound even more accidental than it was. "You know Rex. We got lost."

Her father put a hand to his forehead, stared at the table, and shook his head. Finally, he smiled. "OK, detective. Let us assume you are telling the truth about that. Yes, someone dropped a couple of those red vials from the Poison Archive into my locker. The police are all over me about it."

"When? That night?"

"Must have happened between about 6:02, when I came in, futzed around, put stuff away, made the tea, and 7:59, when we found the body. Or maybe just after that, before the police came."

"Well, that narrows it down."

Mr. Rose stared at the ceiling. "Wait, take that back. I got some money out of the locker at around 7:15 to buy a pop and didn't see anything. I would have seen something in there, I'm sure."

"So?" Ruby said.

"So whoever it was, they did what they did to Rama sometime after 6:15, when I brought in the fresh tea. And they stashed the vials in my locker after 7:15. My best guess is they planted them right then, at 7:15, when I got the pop, because I wasn't gone out of the lab other than that."

Ruby began to study her father, who was now by the window, as if she were going to draw him. "Well," she said, "that main door was the only way into Rama's office, right? You must have seen who went in."

Mr. Rose shook his head. "No, no, no. No. Rama had French doors installed last year that opened out back into a small courtyard. He has a little veranda out there—or had—you never saw that? That's where the murderer had to come from."

Father and daughter looked across the room at each other for a long moment. "We're not in Spring Valley anymore, are we, Ru?"

Ruby felt a stabbing ache about Lillian, who was avoiding her e-mails and texts. Mr. Rose gave her a hug, told her to think about her homework for now, and took himself out to Biddy's. "I'll say hello to the ex-cons for you, Ru."

The red vials. She knew about them only by accident. Her dad knew from the police. But how did the grad students know? How could they, unless one had a connection to the police—or to the crime?

It was time to visit a real crime investigator.

7

MRS. WHITMORE

"Why, hello," said Mrs. Whitmore, opening her door.

The young faces looked so different up close, she thought, and it seemed that the boy was more then merely anxious. He was searching her face so intently that she averted her eyes.

"Welcome," she said, stepping aside. "Do come in."

The untied sneakers, the shuffling way they walked, the shifting eyes; like no one had taught these children the proper way to carry themselves.

"I made some cakes," Mrs. Whitmore said abruptly. "Pudding cakes. Would you like some?"

She disappeared into the kitchen and overheard the boy whisper, "It's the left one, see how it bulges a little?"

"No more than your big bug-eyes are right now," the girl replied. "Jimmy's pulling your chain. He's got no idea."

Jimmy?

"Ruby," the boy said, "why do you think they call him the Minister of Information if— Oh, hello."

Mrs. Whitmore marched back in with a tray from the kitchen and nearly dropped it on the coffee table in front of the couch. A piece of cake tumbled to the floor and the boy—Tex, was it?—made to lunge for it and then recoiled, glancing oddly at her face and turning away, moving back toward the window.

"This is real nice," he said in an alto voice that surprised her. "You can see all the way past DeWitt through here."

"Yes, it's quite a view," Mrs. Whitmore said.

"Yeah," he said. "It's a good view."

Silence held them in place until the girl—Ruby, with that pile of golden hair—said, "This is so much bigger than our little window. It's like there's a whole village down there."

Mrs. Whitmore smiled and felt the air return to the room. "So there is, dear, so there is. I see people come and go. The children, walking to school. The mothers, in Sister Paulette's Bakery. The men who hang around Barber Neville's. The shops, the people going into the bars at night. Sometimes I see them stumbling home in the morning, the poor souls. I see all of it."

"Ruby Rose," said the girl, all business now, holding out her hand. "Apartment 723. Two floors below you."

"I'm pleased to know you, Ruby. I am Clara Whitmore. And you, young man?"

"Yes, hello, ma'am," said Rex, still standing at a distance. "I'm Theodore. Theodore Rexford, 1113. You could call me Rex, though. Everybody does."

"My pleasure, Rex," the woman said. "Now do sit down, please, both of you."

By the time Mrs. Whitmore brought tea out from the kitchen and retrieved her copy of the coroner's report, the two children were parked on the couch—Ruby on the edge like an eager student, Rex pushed way back—and the cakes were almost gone.

"Are you . . . Were you . . . You're a detective, or crime investigator, right?" Ruby said, between bites of cake that seemed far larger than her mouth could hold.

"I was a forensic toxicologist, dear," Mrs. Whitmore replied, settling in a chair opposite the couch. "I worked with crime scene investigation teams, the same as you see on TV. I'm the person in the lab who determined what people had in their systems. Usually it was alcohol or drugs; those are the most common companions of crime, you know. But sometimes we got a real poison case, like this one."

"So, uh, you can tell who did it, who killed Dr. Rama?" Rex said.

"Oh, I wish I could, dear. I wish I could. But no. Toxicology tells you what's in a person's blood, nothing more. On its own it can't even tell you how much of the poison the person ingested."

Ruby's chin dropped. "That's all? I mean, we already know what Rama took, right?"

"Yeah, they put all that in the newspaper," Rex said. "Long as the paper got that stuff right."

"Yes, Rex," said Mrs. Whitmore, pulling papers out of a manila folder and placing one on the coffee table. "It appears from the coroner's report that the campus newspaper has reported correctly."

She pushed the coroner's report toward them with a portion of the text circled.

Toxicology studies show metabolites for several substances:

a) monkshood (aconite)
b) chokecherry (amygdalin)
c) deadly nightshade (atropine)

Cause of death appears to be accumulation of toxins (see full toxicology study).

Rex shifted heavily on the couch. "The studies show metabo-what?"

"Metabolites," Mrs. Whitmore said. "Metabolites are what's left after metabolism, which is the process in which the body breaks down what it consumes into chemical pieces. Food. Alcohol. Aspirin. That pudding cake you just ate. Metabolites are the chemical pieces. Breakdown products, some people call them. And we can detect them in the blood hours, days, even weeks later for some toxins."

"Then what are those words in parentheses?"

"The chemical names of the active toxins. Monkshood, chokecherry, and deadly nightshade are the plants. DeWitt, as you may know, is renowned for its specialty in plant toxins, so the lab would have had all these toxins on hand."

Ruby shook her head. "But so what? That's not telling us anything new, right? Besides, they found only two red vials."

"Who, dear? What vials?"

"You don't know about— Oops." Ruby glanced at Rex, who was covered in crumbs, still averting his eyes from the conversation.

"I'm listening," Mrs. Whitmore said.

After Ruby explained what she and Rex saw at the crime scene, Mrs. Whitmore sat back, took off her reading glasses, and looked them over. "Well, now," she said. "That's very good work. Very good. I daresay, that changes everything."

"How?" asked Ruby.

"Listen carefully," Mrs. Whitmore answered. "Toxicology

tells you what toxins are in the blood. But if we know *how much* poison the person took, we can determine *when* it was taken—when the poisoning took place. Think about that for a second."

Mrs. Whitmore could all but hear the wheels turning in the girl's mind. No one knew for sure exactly when Rama ingested the toxins. It might have happened before Mr. Rose ever got to work, absolving him of the crime.

"Uh-oh, I know what that means for us," Rex said. "Don't tell me please we got to go down in there and find out how much poison was in those red vials. Unless you or your dad knows, Ruby."

"No, no way, he won't know," she said. "But there's a big book where it's all written down, right there on top of the Toxin Archive."

"You'll never get in there, not now," Mrs. Whitmore said. "And even if you do, you would be tampering with evidence, a crime to which I would then be an accomplice. No, I don't think so." Give explanations, not assignments, she told herself.

"No?" The girl's voice changed. "What do you mean?"

"I mean that it's one thing to think through a case based on the evidence that's legally available. It's altogether another to insert oneself into an ongoing investigation. That's a gray area, and I could get us all into trouble."

"But—but—we already are in trouble," Ruby said. "I sure am, anyway. They took my dad away yesterday. Arrested him."

"What?" Rex stood, staring. "When? You didn't tell me that. He's in jail?"

"Yesterday, I just said. After school. I had to go down to the police station. That lawyer, Ms. Diaz, she got him out. She said they didn't have enough evidence to hold him. Yet, anyway."

"Bernie? Why, I've heard nothing from her." Mrs. Whitmore stood up to think. She paced to the window and back. The poison vials found in Mr. Rose's locker: Yes, those were incriminating enough to make an arrest. It was a wonder Bernie got the man released so quickly; did she have to bail him out? "But, child, if he was picked up, where would you have . . . ?" she started, but stopped herself.

Mrs. Whitmore sat back down and folded her hands. "Never mind all that. Listen for a moment. Here's what I think: The records for the Toxin Archive must be stored electronically; everything is these days. The numbers will be on a computer file somewhere. In the lab's database, accessible to anyone doing scientific work there."

"Not my dad, you mean," said Ruby.

"No," Mrs. Whitmore replied. "But the students, yes. You don't happen to know any of their passwords, do you?"

The woman let that sink in. Questions, not assignments; that was the only way. Let the children move the investigation, see how determined they really were. She stood to get more tea, got a chill, and sneezed suddenly.

Pandemonium. The coffee table flipped over, and the boy dove to the floor, scrambling to the far end of the room near the window.

Mrs. Whitmore gasped. "What on earth—"

"Rex!" Ruby cried. "Jimmy doesn't know anything. He's pulling your chain! Stop it."

The three of them glanced around the room at one another, then at their feet. Mrs. Whitmore put a hand to her head. Invite two strangers into your apartment and this is what you get. What was happening?

"I'll explain later," Ruby whispered, and glared at her friend, who was now staring intently down into the street. The boy clearly needed help, maybe medication, Mrs. Whitmore thought.

"Whoa—Ruby, come over here," Rex said. "That Russian girl, the grad student—is that her? What's she doing in the Gardens?"

Ruby squinted out the window. Was it? It was. Lydia Tretiak, walking stiffly along College Avenue, very much out of place among the regulars, who moved around like ducks on a pond.

"What, if you please, is going on?" Mrs. Whitmore said.

"It's a suspect," Ruby said. "Walking right by here, way, way out of place."

"Well, then"—the older woman's voice changed, Ruby noticed—"what are you doing up here? Are you investigating this crime or not?"

8

DAVENPORT TOWERS

Down they went, down the abandoned freight elevator at the back of the Terraces, down to the ground in about twenty seconds. Across the courtyard, through the lobby, over the front stairs so quickly that one of the Woods brothers half stood in surprise, fumbling his cell phone. "Dammit, Raoul, watch yourself!" (The Woods brothers called everyone Raoul, for some reason.)

Lydia was still visible, barely. Ruby saw her lean figure just turn off the street, heading north, a half block past the wig shops. The only thing over that way was the James Davenport Towers, which most residents approached from the other side.

"She's taking the back way to the Davenport, looks like," Ruby said, jogging with Rex just behind her.

Though plainly visible from the Terraces, the Davenport was a foreign land. No one wandered over there, Ruby knew. No reason to, and plenty of reason to stay clear. The young men who sat out on the steps of the Davenport were wiry and hard, tattoo-covered chain-smokers every one, who whispered to one another in some unknown dialect.

"OK, we just crossed Elinor," Rex said.

"Who?" Ruby said.

"Elinor Street. The border. We're in barbarian country now, not healthy for us civilized tribes."

Ruby knew what he meant: She might wander in Davenport country unnoticed for a while, but Rex, dark as he was, could not. She begged him to go back.

"No, uh-uh, no way you're coming in here alone," he said.

The pair kept their distance, staying about a block behind Lydia, who marched, head down, without looking around. All concentration and forward motion, she slipped in the back of Davenport Towers, into the courtyard area.

"OK, you stay here, out of sight. We'll meet right by this tree," Ruby said, turning to cross the street.

"Don't you worry about me," said Rex. "And you better don't spend too much time in there, or I'm coming in."

At the back entrance, the guardians of Davenport were nowhere to be seen. Still, Ruby sensed that someone was watching, and she moved quickly through the narrow pathway between the towers and into the courtyard. Same as the Terraces: paved, picnic tables, graffiti; a few high school–aged kids were draped over one of the tables, smoking.

Ruby slid by, doing the Davenport walk: hands in pockets and head down. She ducked through the nearest tower door before stopping for air, three normal breaths and one deep one.

The place appeared identical to the Terraces on the inside, too, only dirtier. Empty soda cans huddled in one doorway; coffee cups full of cigarette ashes lined the hall between candy wrappers and pizza crusts. Mossy yellow light bled through the windows, and for a moment Ruby thought about the early evening summer light in Spring Valley; how she and Lillian, after a day playing in the fields, would head toward home at dusk, racing the darkness.

From the fields of Arkansas to the wilds of Davenport. How on Earth was she going to find Lydia in here?

A low mumble of voices and daytime TV filled the hallway. One voice seemed to rise above the rest, and Ruby moved toward it. Loud, angry. An argument down the hall. Her ears strained to hear. The angry voice seemed somehow familiar. She moved toward it, and the voice became louder, then fainter, then louder. Ruby stood in front of each door that she encountered, listening. The voice always seemed to be coming from the next apartment.

Upstairs maybe? She knew that at the Terraces, sound from one apartment sometimes traveled back and forth in the hallways below. She had to risk it. She slipped into the stairwell at the end of the hall and, as Rex would have, put a hand on the steel frame of the stairs to feel for activity on the landing. All clear.

Up on the second floor she heard the voices again, this time more distinctly. Again the sound rose and fell, seemed to travel. And then, just like that, the voices went silent.

Ruby moved against the wall. She could not keep listening at people's doorways much longer. Had she been heard already? Was that possible?

No. The argument was back in the air, and after passing a half-dozen doors, Ruby stopped at apartment 247. She put her ear to the door. Now she recognized the voice: Lydia, barking away in Russian or whatever it was. The other voice was a man's. Who could Lydia possibly know in Davenport Towers?

Ruby was about to peer through the peephole when the stairwell door clanged open and a flashbulb shot of sunlight swept the hallway. A dark figure moved through the glare toward her, and Ruby turned to run. Nothing happened. She couldn't feel her legs for some reason.

"Um, hello," she said.

The shadowy figure came closer and closer, until Ruby's

eyes adjusted to the changing light and settled on a hunched older woman, who gave Ruby a toothless grin and a pat on the shoulder before limping slowly by.

From the apartment, the sounds of the argument returned, softer now. The conversation on the other side of the door, whatever it was about, seemed to be winding down.

So was her time. News of an unknown girl in the hallway would spread as fast here as in the Terraces, and sounds came from the courtyard below; something was stirring there. *Time to bail,* Ruby told herself. She headed back the way she came, praying that the landing was still empty. It was, and in seconds she was down, into the basement stairs (identical to the Terraces'), through the laundry room, and out a basement door.

In the open air, a floating sensation crept up her neck as she trotted across the street to meet Rex. Ruby's vision was off, too narrow, like somehow she was peering through holes in her head. What was happening?

Rex wasn't there. She looked behind one tree, and another, and another. She weaved in and around parked cars. He would not have left her here. Ruby swung her head around to see as much as possible.

"Rex," she called out softly. "Rex, where'd you go?" She circled the big tree where they had agreed to meet and sat against the trunk, staring at the broken pavement for a few moments. Even that looked foreign to her, dry and pockmarked, not sticky like College Avenue.

Ruby's hand moved to her back pocket for the sketch pad. Still there. She needed to move. She needed to hide. She needed to get back to the Gardens, and fast.

But where was Rex?

A rustling of leaves made her stifle a scream—and there he was, barely visible, behind a hedge in a small front yard a few parked cars away. "Ruby," he whispered. "We need to go. *Now.* Those Davenport boys are out round here, and they saw me."

The first shouts seemed far away. Not loud, not too crazy, nobody in sight. Like chatter from a distant basketball game. The sound of sneakers squeaking over pavement was different: This was no game. Rex motioned Ruby to come toward him and stay low.

The two crawled along the hedge back alongside the apartment house. A window lifted open somewhere above; in the distance an elevated train rumbled and screeched. Rex was in a low crouch, running, Ruby behind, into a small backyard.

Not a good move. A shoulder-high chain-link fence, no gate, an old skeleton of a man sitting like a statue on the back stairs outside. The man hissed something and Rex threw a garbage can against the fence, jumped on top, and was over the fence, Ruby right behind.

A howl went up and every dog in the neighborhood seemed to start barking. Ruby glanced back and saw the Davenport kids breaking for the yard.

"Rex, they're one yard away!"

Rex cut to the right in the alley behind the fence, past one garage and another, left through a gate, Ruby still behind. Across another yard, Rex wove to dodge a dog on a chain, the pair barging through a hedge. Out to another street, people watching now, Rex cut to the left, fast as he'd ever moved, between parked cars.

A horn. Someone was blasting a horn. The street was unfamiliar, strange—they could be anywhere, Ruby thought.

Into another yard now and Rex ripped a plank out of a wood fence and ran into another alley. Nowhere left to go. Bags of garbage. A huge mound of leaves. A stack of long, rusted metal poles. High fences in front, footsteps coming right, left, and center.

No time now—"Ruby, follow me!"—and Rex dove into the leaf pile, Ruby, too. And there they sat, side by side under the big pile of leaves against a cinder-block wall. Longing for air but breathing through their mouths silently, barely.

Quiet for a second, maybe more, even the barking faded. But the alley was filling up. Shoes on gravel, heavy breathing, someone kicked a pop can. And that smell, the tang of stale cigarette smoke. No running now.

"Come out, come on out. Where you are, little children?" one boy said.

He said it again.

Another voice, angrier. "You still around here? You stay away Mr. Rome. Understand?"

Ruby took a tiny breath. Leaves in her mouth, that sweet dirt smell. Mr. Rome?

"Come out to here! Where you are? We like to talk to you."

"They not in here, Ronny." A girl's voice. "Why don't you leave it alone?"

"Yeah, we scare them enough." A boy. Maybe there was some hope. Some of these kids sounded OK.

"Shut up, you. They are here. Close. I feel this."

More mumbling. Somebody swore. Chuckling. A clinking of metal. Quiet again.

What now?

A grunt, a whisper of leaves, and a clang, metal on stone—a small explosion right next to Ruby's shoulder. Was it a bullet? They had a gun? Now another grunt and a hiss: a grinding thud, neck high, between Rex and Ruby.

The poles. The steel poles.

Rex was stirring. Ruby felt it. And after more laughing in the alley, another pole flew in; and another, which caromed off the ground and grazed the bottom of Ruby's shoe. The leaf pile must look like a giant pincushion from the outside. How on earth were they missing?

"Nobody in there, I told you," came one voice.

"They are lost," said another.

"Lost us. They've lost us," said someone else, the girl again. "Learn the language."

"You are the lost one," said the first voice, and they were all joking now in Davenport-ese. Only—could it be?—there was that clinking sound again. Another pole was coming.

Rex lost his mind.

He roared and grabbed the pole between them and raged out of the leaves, swinging wildly. The sound made Ruby jump and scramble.

The light was suddenly different, darker, and the sight of Rex was terrible even from behind, holding that pole in the center and whirling like some crashing helicopter. The skinny tattoo kids scattered, some fell, and Rex and Ruby flew down the alley.

Out into the middle of the street now, left between cars and right, everything streaming by fast—but was it fast enough? She allowed herself a swivel to check: not good. Davenport kids pouring between the parked cars just behind them. Ruby cried out. Stumbled down onto the pavement, rolled herself into a ball, and waited.

Waited.

Eyes closed, she heard breathing again, heavy, the voices of the gang. That's all. Nothing happened.

Ruby opened her eyes. There was Rex, leaning on a car, a tiny smile on his face. She pushed up to her knees and saw that the Davenports—six or seven kids, a couple of them girls—had stopped and were glaring at something behind her.

She turned to see the three Woods brothers. The ministers, big and fat, sideburns, half-asleep-looking, in those big jackets with the hoods. The Prime Minister himself was there.

Elinor Street! The border between College Gardens and Davenport.

How Rex had managed to get them across, Ruby had no idea. But they were back on the Gardens side now. Not a chance the Davenports would take on the Woods brothers, not here.

Ruby leaned down and touched her cheek to the ground. Safe.

"You got an issue here, Raoul?" Woods #2, Eddie (the Minister of Defense) was saying, arms crossed, staring at the Davenport group. Woods #1, Earl, was leaning on a car, clipping his nails. The Prime Minister never said much of anything, as far as Ruby could tell.

"Why not to come over here talking to me?" said one

of their pursuers, maybe Ronny. But the boy's heart was not in it.

"How about you take an English class first, Raoul? America's full. Go back home," said Jimmy Woods.

The Davenport boy spat on the ground, a wad fat and juicy as a slug, and flicked a hand in dismissal. His friends took the cue, peeled off, turning to shoot a death stare once or twice, and were gone.

Eddie turned to Rex, now on his feet, brushing off his pants, and said, "That you who broke out the primal rage with that pole?" The three brothers chuckled. "T. Rex and all. You got some skill set. You come see us when you're ready to talk about a career, little big man."

"Nah, I'm all good," said Rex. "Glad to run into the extended Woods brotherhood right about now. Eddie. Jimmy. Earl. You know Ruby, right?"

"What, you don't think we read the papers?" Woods #1 said, still clipping his nails. He stopped and looked up. "Pass on regards to your dad, understand?"

"Uh, OK," Ruby said, surprised at how soft his voice was and sure she would never pass on anything from the Woodses to her dad. "Thanks."

Ruby and Rex turned and headed back down College Avenue toward the Terraces. Ruby kept her eyes on the ground, that sweet sticky urban pavement. "How?" she asked. "How do people keep living in this lunatic gangster place?"

"You want to go back down on the farm, huh?"

Ruby lifted her head. "Uh, yeah."

"Take me with you, then," said Rex. "I'm good with the chickens."

That image made Ruby nearly stumble. "They'd peck your fingernails off if you ever got close enough," she said. "You know, I think you made that one boy swallow his cigarette, he was so scared."

Rex smiled so big that his eyes glistened. "Just expressing my ninja side. I owe so much to them ninjas, their traditions and all."

"Thank them for me. We now got two more prime suspects, don't you think? Lydia and Mr. Rome."

"Mister who?"

"Roman. The day janitor. Didn't you hear those Davenport kids warning us away from him?" Ruby told Rex about the argument she'd overheard. "That was Roman in the apartment arguing with Lydia, I'm sure of it. They're up to something. You know what's next, right?"

"A milkshake for me. Best thing on this planet for mental stress, of which I have a modest case right now."

"A malt for me. Then we're gonna go swipe ourselves a password."

"To what?"

"To get into the Toxin Archive."

9

PASSWORD HUNTING

It might even be easy, she thought. Wade probably wrote his password down on the cover of his forensics textbook. Lydia was always borrowing other students' logins; she probably had a half dozen of them written all over her stuff.

The problem was, none of them was in the library that week, at least not during the period that Ruby and Rex had free.

"Forget it," Ruby said, counting steps along College Avenue on the way to school on Friday. "We're running out of time. I'm just—I'm going down and just grabbing that stupid record book off the archive cabinet."

"Good luck. That lab is crawling with police," Rex said. He circled an old car, gaping like it was an alien spacecraft. "Dodge Dart Swinger is what we got right here," he said.

"Says *Swinger* right on the side, too—that just kills me, I'm sorry."

Ruby snorted. Old cars. Wig jokes. Fake eyes. She needed one girl conversation, and Lillian sure didn't seem to want to talk anymore. "Would you for once— Rex, watch out!"

A passing car slowed just enough for the kid in the passenger seat to yell out, "Hey, it's Fat Boy and Poison Rosey—the twisted twins!"

Rex chased them for three steps and stopped. He stood there for a while, staring, breathing hard. "Why do I miss my ninja pole right about now?"

"I'll tell you what: If today's class is about 'Who is a criminal?' I'm going to go get the ninja pole."

"Money," Mrs. Patterson said, once the class was settled. "I want you to think about what this author is saying about money as we read. You are all familiar with this story now. Paris, why don't you start?"

Silence. Paris, tall with long red hair and pinprick eyes, never said a word. Everyone in class kept their distance. Mrs. Patterson almost always called on him first, maybe on the off chance he would make a sound.

"He's gonna go off and firebomb the school, you watch," Rex said. "Only question is when."

"All right, Paris, we'll come back to you," Mrs. Patterson said. "Bruce, please begin."

Ruby gave a silent scream. Bruce, worst out-loud reader on the continent, was breathing heavily as he began: "*My mother—taught me—never to speak about—money—when there was—a shirtful—*what's a *shirtful,* Mrs. Patterson?"

"What do you think it means, Bruce?"

More silence. A rubber band flew by Bruce's head.

"A lot," said a deep voice. Simon. Suddenly, he was Mr. Participation. "Don't talk about money when you got a lot; it doesn't look good. Reveals your true greedy nature. Much better to be smug about it."

"High Honors smug?" Ruby said.

Simon actually smiled at that, and now Sharon had her hand up.

"What's wrong with having money?" she said. "You know you'd all rather have it than not."

"Why, so we can buy eighteen pairs of boots?" someone yelled.

"You wouldn't know how," said Sharon.

"Now, now, everyone take a breath," Mrs. Patterson said. "The point of this story—and I want everyone to think about this—is how attitudes about money can drive almost anyone to commit a crime."

"Anyone?"

"Almost anyone," she said.

• • •

It was near lunchtime before the class got a break and Ruby and Rex could slip away to the library.

"Oh no," said Ruby when she saw from across the room that there was no one sitting back in the forensics corner. "Where are they?"

Rex walked over to look more closely and whispered, "Uh, Ruby? Come look at this."

An abandoned campsite: backpacks on the floor, books stacked in the cubicles, papers everywhere. Even a couple of security ID cards, draped over chairs. The grad students were here, all right, either taking a break together or meeting somewhere else.

"But where?" Ruby said under her breath. "You keep a lookout; I think I know where they are."

Ruby took her sketchbook and turned into the stacks, threading her way toward the far wall of the library where there was a bank of conference rooms. Sure enough, the light was on in the first one, and Victor's profile was unmistakable through the frosted glass door. She heard voices raised and moved in closer to see if she could hear anything.

Not much; the door was too heavy. Scraps of conversation, but that was all. She scampered back, motioning Rex into the stacks to watch the conference room. *Time to get some real evidence,* Ruby said to herself. *Should've done this a long time ago.*

Where to start?

Wade's cubicle was neat, the books stacked by size, notebooks labeled. Victor's had his boxes of exotic tea, his packs of gum, his index cards full of tiny scrawl.

Take something.

Grace's books and notebooks were busy with doodles, her pens chewed. Lydia's space was by far the messiest, with empty diet soda cans, candy wrappers. Among the debris she found little except two exams stuffed into a textbook, both marked *Unsatisfactory*. One of the exams had a note in green pen—Rama's writing—that said, *Please come see me.*

Ruby noted all this in her sketchbook, feeling like she was sneaking around someone's home.

Lydia's backpack was lying there, practically asking to be unzipped. Ruby reached for it, stopped herself, looked up. She saw Rex circling a finger in the air. "Like *now*," he whispered. "Hurry up, they're almost done in there."

She had thirty seconds, maybe twenty. Her heart was doing cartwheels. This was it, surely her last chance at these unattended backpacks and books.

She collected anything with numbers on it: a sheet of Grace's doodles, the numbers from two ID cards (she wrote them down), several Post-its; Rex mumbled, "Time's up," and Ruby's hand reflexively reached out and grabbed one more thing before she darted into the stacks.

She found Rex on all fours, peering through the books at the grad students' legs now headed toward the cubicle area.

"That was too close. Here they are," he said. "I hope you got something good."

Ruby peered through the books back at the cubicles. "You know, I got pretty much nothing. The problem is—*aaaagh!*"

A face pushed through the space between the books: Lydia!

Ruby fell backward, hitting her head against the shelves behind her, and Lydia's big face now loomed above her. "What you doing in here?" asked the older girl. Lydia shot a disgusted glance at Rex, who was still struggling to his knees, and looked back at Ruby. "Answer to me. I saw you near to the desks. I'm asking you now."

"OK, right," said Ruby, light-headed, reaching for her backpack to retrieve the things she'd pilfered. "It wasn't hardly anything."

Rex stood and moved between the two girls, his face close to Lydia's. "We're in the library. This is our library, too— what are *you* doing here?" he asked.

"This is the forensics section," Lydia said. "This is for the graduate forensics students—"

"So you're the owner?" Rex said, his shoulders rising and falling, and now Ruby had a hand on his shoulder, talking in his ear: "Rex, Rex, Rex . . ." She had to calm him, or he'd end up sitting on Lydia and bringing down a pile of books. That would be the end of their library privileges.

"How much you pay for this shack?" Rex continued, same tone, a little quieter.

"Rex, third period—c'mon, third period," Ruby said. "Let's get back. She's done bothering us."

And she was. Lydia, pointing at Ruby, in retreat now, her face colored with—what? Fear. Not just of Rex's anger, either. Lydia had to be involved somehow. If not, why would she care so much about their snooping?

Ruby had no chance to talk it over with Rex. The two had to hustle back to class to beat the bell between periods.

"Now, now, no running in the hallways, please," came a voice from behind. "Oh, it's Miss Rose. And her friend."

Ruby turned to see Dean Touhy. The dean; he'd been there that night, too. Another suspect. He looked terrible, Ruby thought, haggard and even heavier than usual. The entire forensics department had been shut down by the murder investigation, and no one knew when it was coming back.

"Ruby," Dean Touhy said, "I do hope you are holding up, and I am sorry for everything."

"It's OK," said Ruby. "We're just trying to get back to class."

"Please tell your father that when all this is settled and he is cleared—and I fully expect that to happen—he is welcome back here in his old position," the man said. "He must be in a state. Please pass on my best to him, would you?"

"He'll be cleared?" Ruby asked. The dean, now walking them toward class, nodded distractedly and said, "I have reason to believe so, and soon."

Ruby's head swirled. "What? Why? Then who did it?"

But that was all she got. Dean Touhy, arriving at the door of the Regular class, signaled to Mrs. Patterson—and with a wink to Ruby, he was gone, down the hall.

Cleared? She peeked at Rex, who shook his head in confusion. How could she possibly tell her dad that without knowing more?

"All right, Theodore, please continue reading where we left off," Mrs. Patterson said.

Relief. Rex was a smooth reader, and the story was getting kind of interesting. It was about a man living in a nice house with a pool who needed money so badly that he sneaked into the house next door—his friend's house—and took money from his neighbor's wallet.

Rex was reading: *"In the dimness I could see the bed and a pair of pants and a jacket hung over the back of a chair. Moving swiftly I stepped into the room and took a big billfold from the inside of the coat and started back to the hall."*

Half listening, Ruby slipped from under her arm the last thing she'd grabbed from the cubicles, the lining of a garbage can under Lydia's desk. She almost laughed out loud when she saw what it contained. Victor's tea bags. Pages with Grace's doodles. Gum wrappers, two empty energy-drink cans, tissues (disgusting). Garbage. She thought of passing it all to Rex with a meaningful look on her face, just to see him claw through it.

She found a Post-it note stuck in the folds of the plastic bag. *Come see me about this exam at your earliest convenience. Bring your ID.* Rama's writing, his signature in green pen.

Bring your ID. Ruby had a feeling about what that meant. Her dad had told her that Rama's students did not last long if they couldn't master the material. The scores of Lydia's two tests were 62/100 and 49/100. Not so good, those. Now he was asking for her ID?

Rex stopped reading. "Now, why do you want to be taking cash money from your friends?" he said. "For real, now. Creeping around in their house, while they're in there sleeping? The man lives next door. You can't ask for a loan? I'm sorry, that's just desperate."

Desperate. Lydia Tretiak seemed to be failing out. She was broke, Ruby's dad said. All those late nights, working on the weekends—only to be failing. Was that really enough to make you want to kill someone? Lydia was crazy, in her way (they all were, Ruby thought). But was she really so desperate?

Ruby had no way to know. The other grad students had motives, too. Victor clearly saw himself as capable of running the lab, and Rama never really let him. Grace was so anxious, maybe there was a drug problem. And Wade—he despised Rama's rules, his coldness, the way he demanded that the students come in even on weekends.

Too many possibilities. She let it go. The ID numbers she'd copied down—hmm, nothing much there.

Now she sensed something else, not related to the evidence. What? A chill.

She was being watched.

Ruby looked around.

Sharon. Sharon Hughes, the laces artist. The girl was watching her intently. Openly.

Uh-oh. What's *her* problem?

10

BADGE NUMBERS

The note must have been there for a little while. On the edge of Ruby's desk, a piece of torn paper folded in half, lost amid the scraps she'd taken from the library.

She glanced up at Mrs. Patterson, who was listing vocabulary words on the whiteboard. All clear there.

Ruby opened the note, written in Sharon's purple pen: *I want to help.* She looked at the other side; that was it.

Ruby glanced back at its author again, who nodded almost imperceptibly.

"What the . . . ?" The rumor was that Sharon landed in Regular after she'd hacked into the school's computers and . . . what? Ruby didn't know the full story.

The girl wanted to help how, exactly?

Mrs. Patterson's lesson ended, finally. The class broke,

with an audible collective sigh, for a half hour of free time. Ruby, Rex, and Sharon gathered at a table by the window by themselves.

"What do you mean, you want to help?" Ruby whispered.

Sharon swept a strand of hair from her face (*Everything she does is like some shampoo model,* Ruby thought). "I mean," Sharon said, "I know what you're doing. I think. I've seen you in the library."

"But what do you care?" Rex said. "Don't you tell me you been spying on us."

"I care because—well, you know. Because the school accused me of stuff, too, stuff I didn't do, I'd never do. They accused me of hacking into the mainframe, of changing my grades." (*So that was it!* Ruby thought.) "They said it, and now everyone believes it, and nothing I can do. Kinda like what's happening with your dad, Ruby."

Ruby winced. She hoped that maybe not *everyone* believed that her dad was guilty.

"But, like, how are you going to help?" Ruby said. Those worked-up laces and that prima-donna way of swinging her hair. "We don't—we really don't have anything for you to do. Rex?"

He shrugged. "I don't know. Something, maybe."

Oh no: He wants her in? Does Rex like Sharon?

"Nothing?" said Sharon. "You got absolutely nothing

I can check out or work with? No school documents, no numbers?"

"Just this," Ruby said.

Ruby wrote down in her notebook an equation that she saw all over the grad students' notebooks: $Ln(2)/T\text{-}1/2$. She had no idea what it meant. *Good luck with that,* Ruby thought, not sure whether she wanted the girl to succeed or fail.

Sharon's face went slack at the sight of the equation, and she turned the page around. "No idea on this thing." She looked up at the two of them. "But I can bring in someone who might know. Is that all?"

"Nope," said Ruby, and she felt of twinge of something— jealousy, maybe—that Princess Sharon was casually asking for items that Ruby had taken big risks to get. "Uh, let's see. I wrote down the ID numbers from a couple security badges. But I'm not even sure whose they are."

Ruby thought she saw a flare pass through Sharon's eyes. "Security badge numbers, did you say? Uh, yeah, I'm familiar with those. Let me show you what we can do with 'em. Meet in the library after school?"

Ruby stalled for a half second, stole a glance at Rex. He was smiling, of course. "All right."

Ruby arrived first and checked the forensics cluster. Empty, and thank goodness; no need for another run-in with Lydia, not now.

She staked out a table near the computers and flattened her lab diagram on the table just as Sharon and Rex were arriving.

"Hey," Sharon said, putting her backpack on the table.

Ruby nodded, glancing at Rex.

"Go ahead, Ruby, you tell it," he said.

She recited most of what they knew. The timing of the murder. The poisons used. The red vials. The grad students, with quick descriptions. And the layout of the lab. She did not mention Mrs. Whitmore.

Sharon was nodding impatiently by the end. "So, OK, OK," she said, tipping forward in her chair. "Now, let's see those security card numbers again."

"Oh, right." Ruby copied them on a piece of paper and handed it to Sharon.

"Perfecto," she said. "Now watch this."

She led them to one of the library computers and went to work, with Ruby peering over one shoulder and Rex over the other. She pulled up the DeWitt campus security page from the school's website.

"You're not gonna get us in trouble, are you?" Rex said.

"No, no," Sharon replied. "Should be fine, no problem. I'm just going to see what happens when I put these badge numbers into the site."

"How you know how to get in that site, anyway?" Rex said.

Sharon gave a half smile. "Login and password, all it ever takes. Now let's just see what this tells us about where those ID cards were used."

Ruby thought of something. "Just a second. Are we—can you get into the lab's files now?"

"Probably. At least the general files, not personal ones. Why?"

"Search for the Toxin Archive," Ruby said. "Just try it; there may be a file there somewhere that tells us how much poison was in those vials."

Two clicks and there was the lab's internal homepage, with *Toxin Archive* right there in the left margin. Sharon clicked on it—*ACCESS DENIED* flashed on the screen. "Oh, I hate that," she said. "I always take it personally."

"Police probably blocked it," Rex said. "Anyone else gonna have that file, Ruby?"

"Wade," she said, slapping her head. Better than that, she thought: Wade ran those sensitive detection machines, and he kept better records than Grace, who was in charge of the archive cabinet. "Wade Charles. Let's go get his personal web page."

"Hello, Mr. Wade," said Sharon, who now had the page on her screen. "Now, what are we looking for?"

Ruby smiled to herself. "Try *cocktail lounge*. That's what Wade calls the cabinet."

"How's this?" Sharon said, pushing back from the screen, which had filled with a long list. There were deadly nightshade, monkshood, chokecherry—all of them. The archive.

"Amazing," Ruby said. She printed out the list and stashed it in her backpack.

"OK," Sharon said. "You ready to see who was there?"

"You mean in the lab?" Ruby said, moving closer. "Of course. How?"

"You watch."

Sharon opened a page called *Badge Tracking*. In a badge number search space, she typed the first number: 011-9865.

She hit the Enter button. The screen filled with a list of numbers and dates. Sharon scrolled down to September 20, the day of the murder. She pushed back from the screen, so they could see.

D12 1650
D7 1651
D5 1653
D17 1752
D5 1753
D8 1853

D17 1855
D5 1956

"Uh, OK," said Ruby, feeling a stirring in her stomach.

"What do the *D*s mean?" Rex said.

"They're doors," Sharon said. "Places where you have to use your security card to buzz yourself through."

"And the numbers?"

"Times. Military times, counting up from noon. So, noon is 1200, one o'clock is 1300, two is 1400, and so on. See that?"

Ruby felt her temples warming. This was more information than she ever imagined having for that evening.

"It looks like you buzz through these doors just one way, from the outside," Sharon said.

"Yeah, that's right, most are like that," Ruby said. "Except the main front door of the building. You have to use your card to get out, too. Same goes for a few other rooms."

Rex said, "D12 must be the main building door, then."

Ruby pulled out her sketchbook and flipped to the diagram of the lab. "Exactly, here's what we have."

Ruby pulled a chair closer to the computer and began numbering doors to her diagram as Sharon read them off. "Remember, this is one person's badge we're following," Sharon said.

"Right, OK, here they are coming in, through D12," Ruby said, staring at her diagram. "Then they would have to swipe their card to get the elevator down to the forensics department—that must be D7. And that makes D5, the next door, the one into the lab itself."

"Whoever it is," Rex said, "they're going out and coming back in D5, with D17 in between there—and once, D8."

Ruby put her head back and imagined the hallway outside the lab. Only two ways to go: through the door on the left to the kitchen area with the microwave, candy machine, sink, and coffeemaker. Or through the door on the right to the bathrooms.

"Victor," Ruby said.

The others gave her a blank look.

"One of the grad students. He's always going to that candy machine to get licorice to have with his tea. Like, it's a ritual thing, every hour." Ruby wasn't aware that she picked up this pattern while sitting there doing her homework in the evenings. But now she was sure of it.

So door D17 must be the door to the kitchen area. That meant that door D8 must be the one you had to go through to the bathroom. Ruby filled in her diagram.

Sharon wrote down *Victor?* next to that badge number and plugged in the second number that Ruby had given her. "OK," she said. "This person came into the forensics building at 5:13 P.M. and entered the lab a minute later . . . then, it looks like, they went out to the snack room. Right after they got there."

"Lydia," Ruby said. "Like, 5:13, that's late for a Friday. Everyone else is in there by five o'clock, latest. She always got there late—dropped her stuff and went right out to get a snack. Those nasty jalapeño pretzels."

"Right, well, that's not all she did," Sharon said.

After arriving that night, Lydia came back through D17 and D5 a couple of more times. Runs for diet soda, Ruby told them. The badge also passed through the opposite door in the hallway, D8, three times—for the bathroom.

"Nothing strange there, that looks normal," Sharon said.

"Wait," said Rex. "Go back to that part, around 7:12 or so. The bathroom door one."

"Yep," Sharon said, scrolling back. "There," she said, pointing.

D16 1901
D8 1912
D5 1912

"D16?" Rex said. "Where's that door?"

Ruby made a guess. "On the other side of the bathroom there's a tech room off the hallway. I was in there once;

there's a back door that leads to some stairs that go—I don't know where. But I've never seen anyone else from the lab go in there."

"You have now," Rex said. "That's more than ten minutes before she comes back through the hallway door. What's she doing in that little tech room that long? I go in the bathroom fifteen seconds at home there's someone at the door."

"That's because you got twenty people in that place," said Ruby.

"Nine. And you be quiet. Least we don't hang boxer shorts out the window to dry, like your dad do."

"Yeah, well, if you guys didn't tie up the dryers for five hours every day—"

"Wait," said Sharon. "Think. Keep your heads in the problem. What is Lydia doing over there for so long? Could be no big deal. But it's a great question."

Ruby checked the library clock and saw that they hadn't been at the computer for much more than ten minutes. Eleven minutes was a long absence at that lab. She was surprised that her father hadn't mentioned it.

"Huh," Ruby said. "Is there any way to check if someone else was in there? I mean, it seems weird that Lydia's just there by herself. Doing what?"

"Let me try something," Sharon said. She clicked on the D16 door symbol, waited a moment, and sat up with smile.

"Excellent. Click on the door and it gives you the badges that went through, with the times. And the answer is yes—there was someone else in there with her."

"Another badge?"

"Yup," Sharon said. "Look for yourself—number 015-4007, whoever that is."

Ruby shook her head. "No idea."

"Hmm," said Sharon, dropping her head in thought. She clicked and scrolled some more. "OK, check this out. This person who met with Lydia—if it is Lydia—whoever it was, they didn't go back to the main lab or leave through the building's main door. This record goes all the way to midnight."

"Will you look at that? Somebody's up to something," Rex said. "Ruby, you got no ideas?"

"I—I don't know," she said. All signs had been pointing to Lydia, and now—well, what? Could that be Wade in there? Or Grace? Hard to imagine. Nothing made sense.

"The mystery person," Rex said. "Double-O Seven."

Sharon said. "Hmm. What do you notice about that mystery number? I mean, compared to the others."

Rex saw it first. "Well, those two grad student numbers start with 011, and this one starts with 015."

"Exactly right," said Sharon.

"But so—so what?" Ruby said.

"So, uh, you know," Sharon said. "These school security badges have different categories, usually in the first few digits. So if 011 is a graduate student, then 015 may be some other type of person—an employee, say."

Ruby held her breath. "You mean . . ."

Sharon did not answer. She and Rex continued to study the computer screen as if searching for a hidden code.

"You mean, like a janitor."

11

GRILLING DAD

Ruby dropped her backpack near the door, headed into the kitchen, and fixed a bowl of cereal. Make that two bowls, she thought, for stability.

"Dad?"

"Ru, is that you?" Her father was in the bedroom, sprawled on a chair, listening to baseball on the radio. "I didn't hear you come in."

"Um, yeah, OK. It's me . . . um."

"*Um.* Yes, I've heard that before. *Um* meaning what?"

"Well, so. One thing is, I have a question."

"Another one, huh?" he said from the bedroom. "That's all I get anymore."

"You know your security ID badge?"

"Of course. Couldn't go anywhere without that thing. Why?"

"Do you still have it?"

"No, no. They took that away, that very same night. The cops did. I told you that a while ago. Why do you ask now?"

She tried to sound casual. "Well, do you happen to remember the number on it?"

Mr. Rose leaned over, pulled out a pencil and a pad out of a nightstand drawer, and wrote it down. He handed the paper to her. "Anything else, officer?"

Ruby stared unseeing at the number for several seconds before seeing the same 015 as the mystery person's number. She blinked at the last four digits and saw with a wave of relief that it was 4003. Her dad wasn't Double-O Seven.

"Dad," she said, her voice closer to normal, "one more quick thing."

"Yes, Ruby. What's going on?"

"Well, you said that Roman, the other janitor, would not poison Dr. Rama, right? That he was about to retire and all."

"That's right. He had no reason to do it and plenty not to. He was a pretty sour old coot. Rarely saw the man laugh at life. But he also had a pension coming and no reason to make trouble and lose that."

"What coming?"

"A pension. That's where your employer pays you a certain

amount every year after you retire. But why are you asking about Roman?"

"I mean, why do you think?"

"Ruby, you and Rex aren't interfering in any of this investigation, are you? I know you're trying to help, and I know you've done a lot already. Just be careful you don't make it worse."

Ruby widened her eyes. "Dad, you're the prime suspect! They're about to charge you. How could it be worse?"

Mr. Rose held up a hand. "I know. Believe me. I just keep thinking, you know, they'll find something that shows I didn't do it. Ms. Diaz has been working hard on this, I know that."

"Well, at least . . ." Ruby wanted to tell her father what Dean Touhy had said, but she stopped herself. Cleared? Did the dean mean, like, free? How did he even know that? And why would he tell her? Maybe it was all random, just talk to make her feel better, or— What did the dean actually say? Ruby wasn't so sure anymore. "Just let's not wait around to be rescued—isn't that what you always say to me?"

"It sure is, Ruby."

"OK, then listen," she said. "We know that Lydia met Roman for about ten minutes before the body was found, around 7:30."

"How do you know that?"

"Never mind. Just listen for one second."

Mr. Rose narrowed his eyes. "All right."

"Well, Rex and me, we followed Lydia the other day," Ruby continued. "She walked right through the Gardens on her way to Davenport."

"You—what? Davenport? Ruby, please tell me you didn't go over there."

"She met someone in there, Dad. Roman, I think. No, I'm sure. Mr. Rome, they called him. This was just last week. They were arguing, Lydia and Roman, loud. He sounded scared."

Mr. Rose nodded slowly. "Huh," he said. "Roman lives in Davenport, yes. And I always wondered . . ."

"What?"

"Well, whether he and Lydia are related. Just the way he looks at her, like she's a daughter. Can't be, of course. He's too old. But I know his younger sister has a daughter."

"Is it Lydia, you think?"

"No idea. But let's assume it is. So what?"

"Well, what if she was flunking out? Lydia, I mean. If Rama was about to drop her from the program."

Mr. Rose got up from the table and went into the kitchen, returning with a root beer. "Ruby, what are you asking me?"

"If Lydia was flunking out, and she was Roman's niece or whatever—how would that affect him, knowing about it?"

"He couldn't possibly know. Rama kept those kinds of decisions strictly to himself, as far as I know. And Lydia—I can't imagine her telling anyone that she was struggling. If she was. Least of all her uncle."

"She was struggling," Ruby said. But her dad was right. How would Roman possibly know what Rama was planning to do?

"Hypothetically," her dad was saying, "I can see what you're thinking. Although I don't—well, let's see."

"What?"

"If she really is his niece, his one and only in this country . . . You work so hard to get a chance. I know what that feels like, all those long hours and taking orders to get a chance not for yourself but for someone you love. But still."

"Still what?"

"I don't buy it. One, Roman never showed his face that night. And two, no way he dreams this up himself. Not a chance, take my word for it. And that's assuming he knew that Lydia was failing."

"OK. Maybe . . . uh, I don't know. What if someone told him and put him up to it?"

Ruby's father took a long draw on his drink and shook his head. "Well, that's a whole bunch of hunches based on hunches, detective."

"Well, that's what detectives do, right?"

Mr. Rose finished the root beer and set the can down gently. "Yes. And yes again if Roman is involved in this at all, someone else got him to do it."

12

WHITMORE LAB

Saturday morning, a quarter to nine, warm for late fall. Mrs. Whitmore, in a dark blue skirt and red cardigan, stood at the kitchen counter with a cup of coffee and a copy of the *DeWitt Echo*—and there it was.

Deep in a story about the ongoing investigation into the Ramachandran murder was a quote from "an unidentified federal investigator." The FBI was involved.

"That explains it," she said out loud. Agents from Washington, D.C., were involved in the case, almost certainly because the city police and DeWitt Forensics were such close partners. More detectives meant more delay, which had to be why the police hadn't filed formal charges against the girl's father yet.

She clipped the article and was placing it in a manila folder that said *Rama Jr.* on it when a knock came on the door.

"Coming," Mrs. Whitmore called from the kitchen. She cleared dishes from the table, smoothed her hair in the small mirror in the hall, and opened the door.

"Why, hello again." Had it been only a week since she last saw them? It seemed far longer. "Please, make yourselves at home."

The girl looked eager; the boy, nervous again. She wondered if he had attention disorder, or whatever it was that so many young boys were supposed to have.

"Roman," Ruby said suddenly. "We think Roman did it. With Lydia's help. And maybe someone else, too."

"Whoa there, Nellie." Mrs. Whitmore smiled, beckoned the two of them to the table, and opened a tin of brownies. "Tell me more," she said.

Ruby explained how Lydia was failing Rama's program. Rex told how they tracked her security card. Ruby said they thought Roman was Lydia's uncle. Rex said Lydia met with Roman just after seven o'clock, plenty of time to grab the vials and stash them in Mr. Rose's locker..

"Very good, very good," Mrs. Whitmore said. "Yes, yes. I am inclined to agree with you about Roman and Lydia. And it explains something about the timing. Why didn't Lydia bring Rama his next cup of tea at 7:15? The answer, apparently, is that she was still busy."

"How do you know about Roman?" Rex said.

"You've just told me about him, for one," she said. "But I have read the news accounts, I know who was in the lab that night. Remember, young man—Rex—that I am, I was, in forensics myself for many years."

"Oh right, I knew that," Rex said.

"Look, we need to go tell the police about Roman, like, now," Ruby said.

"Easy now, dear, there will be time for that. When we have a clear idea of what happened and evidence to back it up. As it is, we don't even know how much poison Dr. Rama swallowed that night and when. That's critical information, and only the toxicology will tell us that."

Ruby opened her sketchbook, pulled out a piece of paper, and pushed it across the table. "OK, well, look at this," she said. "This is the list of poisons in the cabinet, with all the amounts. You were right: There was a computer file."

Mrs. Whitmore straightened her glasses and studied. "Oh my," she said. "The toxin quantities. How on earth did you manage to . . . ?"

She pulled a page from her manila folder and put the two pieces of paper side by side. A long silence; the woman was a statue of concentration. Ruby shrugged at Rex. Now what?

Mrs. Whitmore stood abruptly, strode across the room to

the window, turned. "Well, now," the woman said. "Well, well, well."

"What?" said Rex.

"We have something here, is what." Mrs. Whitmore returned to the table. She picked up a pen and circled a number on the archive list. "Take a look at that number right there."

"So?" Ruby said. It read *1 milligram.*

"That's the amount of the deadly nightshade that was in the red vial, according to Wade's file. See that?"

"Yeah, I do."

The woman circled a number on the toxicology report: 2 ng/mL. "Two nanograms per milliliter. Ignore the big words for now: That's the concentration of deadly nightshade in Rama's blood at the time of autopsy," she said. "Well, technically, it's the toxic compound in nightshade—atropine; that's what we look for."

"OK."

"Well, the half-life of atropine—of nightshade—is two to three hours. That means that, after two hours, we should see one half of the amount that was absorbed into the blood. And we do—there it is, the two nanograms per milliliter on the toxicology report."

"So what's the problem?" Rex said.

"None. Yet," Mrs. Whitmore replied. She circled the same

two numbers for the chokecherry. "Here again, the numbers make sense. After two hours, almost all of the toxin would be eliminated, and that is what we see here: only a trace amount in the blood."

"So I don't get why—"

Mrs. Whitmore put a finger up. "But have a look at the monkshood numbers. And remember, the active toxin in monkshood is called aconite."

The amount of the monkshood in the red vial was 0.5 milligrams, according to Wade's file. The amount in Rama's blood was 6 ng/mL—six nanograms per milliliter. "That's way too high, if the murder occurred the way the police are saying," Mrs. Whitmore said.

"What do you mean, too high?" Rex asked, now leaning forward in his chair.

"Well," the older woman replied. "Only a fraction of an ingested substance is absorbed into the blood. That fraction may be as high as 70 percent, depending on the substance. But it's not higher than that. Organs like the liver and kidneys metabolize some of the substance, and some is tied up in the mucosal linings of the mouth and the digestive system. Once you subtract that, you should have only one to two nanograms per milliliter after two hours."

"And that's lower than what they found," Ruby said.

"Significantly lower, dear. Now, why would that be?"

Rex said, "Maybe he drank the monkshood after the others?"

"Good," Mrs. Whitmore said. "That's one possibility. But it would have to be more than an hour afterward to see this big of a difference. And it doesn't really add up; all three poisons were found in that same teacup."

"Well, huh. Then maybe this printout we got is wrong," Rex said.

Ruby shook her head. "No, no way. Wade was crazy about this kind of stuff. It's right."

"Extraordinary." Mrs. Whitmore was on her feet again. She had forgotten what this work was like; it had been far too long. "If Dr. Rama had this much poison in his blood at autopsy, then I think we can conclude—for now—that he drank more than was in the red vial from the Toxin Archive."

"Meaning what, though?"

"We don't know that, Ruby. To me, it supports what your dad told you—that someone else was involved. If indeed Roman dosed Dr. Rama's tea, he would have grabbed the red vials and dumped them in. Period. I doubt from what you've told me that he would know where to get more of this rather exotic toxin."

"So someone else in the lab . . . ," said Ruby. "But wouldn't the police know all this by now?"

"No, dear, not necessarily. The only way to know that the

blood level was high is to check the contents in the red vial. Right now, the police are far more focused on the suspects: where they were, what they did, what they said. So the police may not be ahead of us on this."

"What now?" Ruby said.

"My instinct," said Mrs. Whitmore, who noticed she was twirling a pen in her fingers like she did back when she was working a hunch in her lab days, "tells me that whoever was involved with Roman would have met him that Friday, the day of, to make sure the crime was in motion."

Ruby smiled. "The badges again."

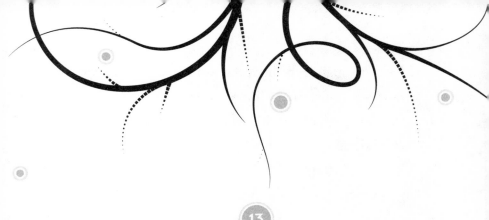

13

SIMON

Rex said, "My guess is Paris."

"Yeah?" said Ruby, arranging her drawings, copies of the toxin levels, and other notes on the large table in the science library that had become their base of operations.

"Probably making a pipe bomb right now to help us out. Or Bruce, to do the reading for us—you think?"

"I sure do. What are you talking about?"

"The person she said she was bringing to help. Sharon. Remember?"

"Oh yeah, right. The someone. Watch it be Simon."

"Long as he hasn't handcuffed himself to another piece of luggage for national securit— Uh-oh."

Ruby turned to look. Sharon was approaching their table

with . . . *Simon Buscombe.* Rex leaned back in his chair and closed his eyes. Ruby blinked in disbelief.

"Hey, remember I said I had someone?" Sharon said.

All elbows and dirty blond hair, Simon slid into a chair across from Rex without a word. He adjusted his headband, carefully pulled a plastic wrapper off of a giant cinnamon roll, opened a bottle of cream soda, and plunged his face into the roll.

"Uh, I just lost my appetite, and that's saying something," Rex said. "What you think that pastry made of, Simon?"

Simon ignored him, demolishing the cinnamon roll in three bites. "I understand my services are needed," he said in that deep voice that surprised Ruby every time she heard it in class. He had to be faking it.

"Yeah," said Ruby, glancing over at Rex. His services, thank you so much. "We, uh, we've been looking into this case . . ."

"I am aware of your pursuits," came the deep voice. "I have eyes and ears." He glanced at Sharon. "And I have associates who keep me informed." He then cleared his throat, took a long hit on the soda, burped, and said, "Half-life."

"Huh?" Rex said.

"In your equation. *T-1/2* means *half-life*," replied Simon. "It's pharmacokinetics. The study of what a body does to substances, how it breaks down and gets rid of them. The half-life is the amount of time it takes the body to eliminate half of a substance. Different times for different substances."

"Gracias, Einstein, we already know all that," Rex said.

"Then perhaps our business is done," said Simon, whipping out a cell phone and slouching in his chair. It looked to Ruby like he had some video game going.

"Perhaps not," Sharon said. She turned to Ruby. "Look, he knows a bunch about the buildings, don't ask me how. Can we just, I don't know, see how it goes for a while?"

Ruby scanned the others' faces: Rex exasperated, Sharon impatient, Simon pretending he wasn't listening. "A while," she said. "Get me back into the badge tracking system."

She explained their hunch: that someone was helping Roman, and if so probably met him sometime the day of the murder.

In moments Sharon was into the system, the others peering over her shoulders at the nearest library desktop. The familiar door numbers scrolled by on the screen, and again Ruby felt light-headed. "Go down farther, earlier," she said. "And we're looking for Double-O Seven, remember."

"Is that a joke?" said Simon.

"No, it's the number—Roman's number," Ruby said.

And there was 007 Roman, coming back from the men's room at around 4 o'clock; and before that, from the kitchen;

and at his lunchtime, he went up to the ground floor to his locker area to have lunch. All normal.

"Wait. Back it up. D16 again, see it?" Rex seemed to have memorized all the door numbers.

"Where is it—oh yeah, there, he goes in there at, ooh, at 1:21," Sharon said. "And then at 1:38 he's going back into the kitchen."

"Same room where he met Lydia later," Rex said. "Right, Ruby?"

She had to check her notes. "Yeah, same one. Any other numbers going in there?"

Sharon scrolled up and down. "Oh no, not one. Nothing . . . Simon?"

"You called." He was standing right behind her, squinting at the screen.

"Make yourself useful," Sharon continued. "This door we're looking at goes into a small tech room down the hall and around the corner from the kitchen. You're the map guy. Tell me whether there's another entrance."

Simon was studying what looked like one of his mazes, rubbing his chin. He probably had a pipe at home, Ruby thought.

"Yes," he said finally. "The small tech room has another door that goes out to this little courtyard out back. According to my layout, which is accurate."

"Arg," said Sharon. "If there was someone in there with Roman, he or she could have come in and out through that back door, not using a badge at all."

Ruby tried to imagine it. A person crossing that courtyard behind Rama's office twice, in the middle of the day. "No, I don't think so. Do one thing: Check the front door and elevator just before Roman went in there—right around 1:20."

"You mean— Oh, look," said Sharon. Someone had come in, right through the front door and down the elevator, just after 1:20. Roman could have let the person into the tech room. It was a number that started with 222—and whoever it was exited the building not long after Roman left the small room.

"Ruby Rose, look at you," said Rex. "Now, what d'you know about that number, Sharon? Is that a student, or what?"

"Oh no, shoot, I don't know. It looks like a miscellaneous number. Could be anyone's." Sharon was working the computer. "Wait, I see. It's a general passkey. The kind they give to visitors, totally anonymous. Of course. This person is not stupid."

"Well, it means something already," Rex said. "We know it's not Lydia and it's not Victor; we can scratch them off. If our theory is true, anyway."

Sharon pulled her chair closer to the computer and said,

"No reason I can't search the whole system for this number"—when the screen froze.

The girl clicked and clicked, but there was a humming sound; Ruby peeked at the other screens in the cluster just as they all went black.

"How extraordinary," Simon said. "All the computers in this whole library seem to have simultaneously—"

"Pick up everything, now, they on us like white on rice," Rex said. "Time to move our getaway sticks."

"Our what?" said Sharon.

"Legs—let's go!" Ruby said.

Ruby made sure their table was clear before leading everybody along the wall toward the main lobby. She had no interest in going the other direction toward the hallways leading to the main school. Still dead quiet, and they were into the stacks now, under some cover, close to the doorway leading out to the main library lobby.

"Listen," Ruby said. "For one second."

The mumble of heavy soles on the stone floor, a whispered voice behind them, everyone down now, near the floor. Between the shelves Ruby and the others saw legs swarming around the computer cluster, now fanning out. "Follow me," Rex said. "Look natural."

He stood and slipped through the door to the lobby, just a student with his books under his arm. The others trailed, smiling hello to the woman in the main information booth near the door. Briskly now, across the lobby—other kids were coming through, and teachers; it was busy—and here was an entire High Honors group coming down the stairs.

"Everyone, excuse me, your attention, please." A voice over the intercom.

Campus police officers were slipping into the lobby behind them, two moving quickly toward the main door, another to the information lady. "Excuse me. Everyone in the library please gather in the lobby. Everyone, please. Campus police are searching for a lost child in the building."

"So let's get lost," Ruby said. She led the others through the stirring crowd of students, across the lobby, and into the far wing, history and literature. The back of that wing was under construction—she could see the workers from the second-floor window of the Regular Ranch. There must be a way out.

"C'mon," Ruby said; there were students strolling in the opposite direction, some college students, and then the lights went up—way bright—and a red light blinked somewhere up high.

"Whoa, are you kidding?" Rex said. "When'd they get these lights? Ruby, someone wants us bad."

"Quiet, quiet. Let's find that construction area," she said.

There it was, in the back: a wall of plywood, a door cut in

the middle with *Men Working* in orange spray paint across it. Ruby turned the handle: locked. Rex grabbed it and turned with all his might.

"Are you absolutely sure that this is our best—" Simon was saying when Rex said, "Outta the way," and threw his shoulder into the door. It snapped open and Rex landed on the floor on the other side, covered with white dust.

"Look, the Pillsbury Doughboy," Simon said, but there was no time. Ruby yelled, "Go, go," put her head down, and banged into a giant blue tarp, which shuddered and lifted. They were outside, in back of the library.

The gang split in two.

Fall, Ruby thought as she and Rex plunged into the bushes and leaves that ringed the library building, everything orangey and earth-smelling. Why was she thinking about the season now? "Where you think they went?"

"I don't know," answered Rex. "Across that way, the other side of the campus, the Manor, whatever they call that nice neighborhood."

"They live over there, in those big houses?"

"Simon and Sharon? Where you think they live . . . in Davenport with Ronny?"

Ruby got on her knees and peeked through the bushes. They crawled along the base of the building and turned the corner. In the failing light she could make out the DeWitt front gate and beyond that a few lights in the familiar silhouettes of the brick apartments along College Avenue. Blue-red tracers swept the area, lights from a campus police car, maybe two.

Some memory came of a campout or fireworks back home. She shivered. "What now?"

"Dark soon," Rex said. "When it's night, we'll mosey out right through the main gate like a couple of students. Which we are, in fact."

Down low, knees damp and cold, they inched closer to the library main entrance to get a better look. They stopped just this side of one of the science library's broad windows, still glowing with the turned-up lights. Waited.

"Looks like cops are letting people out one at a time," said Rex, up on his knees, peering over the bushes. "Some of them coming up this way, too; a little darker and we can just step out and walk."

Restless, Ruby turned, pushed herself up, and peeked through one of the library windows. She sat back down suddenly.

"Oh no," she said.

"What happened?" Rex said.

"Nothing. But have a look in there."

Rex looked and then sat back down, eyes wide. "What's *she* doing in there?"

Ruby felt like crying but couldn't. "Mrs. Whitmore, Mrs. Whitmore . . . We've never even seen her come out of her apartment, and now she's in the forensics library with the campus police?"

14

THE PAST

The newspaper article was more than thirty years old and so yellow, it was hard to read. But one line near the end was clear enough: "Mrs. Clara Whitmore, a forensic assistant in the office of chief toxicologist Dr. R. J. Ramachandran, said the driver's blood contained traces of narcotics, as well as alcohol."

Ruby read it again. Dr. R. J. Ramachandran? Could there be two people with that name?

She reached over and punched Rex, who was fast asleep, his head resting on an open folder of old newspaper clippings.

"Huh . . . Where am I?"

"Downtown library. You've been asleep for an hour. Wake up and look at this."

"I'm taking a break from libraries after this, that's one

thing." Rex blinked, stretched his shoulders, rubbed his eyes. "OK, I'm looking; so what?"

"Near the end."

"Oh, there she is." The boy shook his head. "And another Rama name? Maybe it's his dad. Or mom. But I don't see why you had to wake me up; we already knew Mrs. W. worked in forensics."

"Yeah, but she's up to something," said Ruby. "Why else would she be snooping around the library, in the forensics section, too?"

"Maybe she was there to help us, do some research on her own."

"And not say anything? And the campus police just let her stay. Maybe she's in with them, too."

"Nah, Ruby, now you're seeing things. I do wonder, though, about that apartment."

"Whose apartment?"

"Hers. Mrs. Whitmore. A scientist, in the beat-up old Terraces? I never heard of that. Most people with those kind of jobs, they're too scared to even come down College Avenue, much less live in the Terraces. At least since me and my Jamaican brothers arrived."

"What about those Woods brothers? They're whiter than I am."

"I consider them partially Jamaican."

"Yeah, right. They hate the islanders."

"They hate everyone. They're equality-based, deep down."

"Deep down, you're disturbed." But Rex was right about Mrs. Whitmore in the Terraces, and now Ruby wasn't so sure of anything. You'd think an old woman who never left her apartment would be—what? Nice and helpful? Not so complicated?

"Huh, I wonder if this is the same one, too," Rex said, squinting at the old newspaper article. "Diaz. That's the name of your dad's lawyer, right?"

"What?" Ruby grabbed the old article from him and saw the name. "'The defendant's attorney, Bernice Diaz, charged that the city's toxicology analysis was incomplete . . .' This couldn't be the same— Wait. Maybe it is. No— It is, has to be."

"So?"

"So they knew each other—that's why Mrs. Whitmore told us to go see Diaz. They knew each other, and they knew this other Ramachandran guy, and so, so—so I don't know. Arg! I thought it would be a good idea to research Rama and Whitmore, but this is just confusing."

"Easy, Ruby, you gonna wake up all these other researchers," said Rex, as an older man in a chair across from them stirred in his sleep. "There's got to be some explanation; you just got to ask someone. Like whatshername—Diaz. She's your dad's lawyer; she's supposed to be working for you."

Ruby closed her eyes, took a breath. Smiled. "Yes, she is."

"Well, now, will you look at Mr. T-Bone Big Rooster Funky Rex. I just had my second good idea. Your dad must have Mrs. Diaz's number up there on the fridge, where he keeps everything."

"No need. We can walk there. Her office is about three blocks away. I saw it on the bus ride over. Let's see if she's there."

Rex rattled the door when he knocked, and there was no answer. He tried again—a light was on in the office—and this time a voice came from inside.

"Go away!"

Ruby knocked the third time, more politely, and they heard, "No one home! This is my writing day, OK?"

"Writing day?" said Rex. "She's a writer, too? How many jobs this lady got?"

"Too many to see us, I guess," Ruby said. "Maybe we should come back when—"

"No more Girl Scout Cookies, please!" The door was open; Ms. Diaz was standing in it, hands on hips, in a gold-and-purple sweat suit. "Oh—is that—Ms. Rose, is that you?"

"Yes, hello. This is my friend Rex."

Ms. Diaz looked Rex up and down and shook her head. "OK, c'mon in, make it quick. What's up?"

The office was different. Messier, an ashtray full of cigarette butts on the desk next to two empty diet soda cans, opera playing on the radio. Ruby wondered if it had something to do with it being a writing day.

"I have a question, Rex and I do—just something to ask, if you don't mind," Ruby said.

"Ask it already, and I'll tell you if I mind."

Ruby's heart was pounding up in her neck for some reason. "Do you know Mrs. Whitmore? I mean, Clara Whitmore, this old lady—I mean, elderly, you know, at the Terraces, a woman?"

"I'm not sure that's a question, but the answer is yes, I know Clara. And she's certainly an old lady. She's at least ten years older than me, and I'm a dinosaur."

"You known her a long time?" Rex said.

Ms. Diaz circled around her desk, sat down, and opened another diet soda "Forever and a day, young man." She took a sip. "Clara was one of the city's top toxicologists back when I was a young lawyer. Not that they treated her like one."

"And did she, did you—was there another Ramachandran, like the one who was killed?"

Ms. Diaz, up on her feet again, motioned them into two chairs, like students, and leaned back on her desk like a teacher. She didn't look happy. "I don't know what you're doing here, OK? But you need to know this: I will say not a word about the Ramachandran case to anyone but my client, your father. Understood?"

Ruby swallowed; Rex was nodding manically.

"Right. The answer is yes: R. J. Ramachandran was the father. He's long dead now, but in his day he was as famous as the son was. More so. And, in the end, just as petty. Though you didn't hear that from me, and it will not leave this office."

"So, Mrs. Whitmore was—"

"Clara was a scientist in his office. A toxicologist, a good one. All of this is public information. And what happened in the Plaxton case was—strike that. You want more, you ask Clara."

Ruby peeked at Rex, tipped forward on his chair, who said, "So how you spell *Plaxton*?"

"Look it up. I've said too much."

"Would she want to kill Dr. Rama for some reason?"

Ms. Diaz rocked forward, then back, looked up at the ceiling, and let out a loud whispering cough that Ruby realized was laughter.

"Oh dear me, no," the woman finally said, her face still red. "Clara would not kick a squirrel who came to eat her dinner. That's one reason she disappeared and ended up in those proj—I mean, why she disappeared."

"You got a problem with the Terraces?" Rex asked.

Ms. Diaz took a deep breath. "No, young man, I don't. I grew up in Davenport Towers. First floor, 112, next to the elevators: never a dull moment. But I do have a problem with what happened to Clara Whitmore, and that is all I have to say to you two."

She stood and opened the door. "Please say hello to Clara for me."

"Not one hint?" Rex said. "Like, did it affect one of her eyeballs?"

"Out," Ms. Diaz said, pointing to the door. "Writing day."

15

THE PRESENT

Grady Funk was not picking up his home phone, and she dared not call him at work. Dearest Grady. He was doing nothing more than simple tests at the city's crime lab these days, and he'd surely lose even that job if he was caught informing her about the Rama case.

He'd told her plenty already: that Rama's teacup was empty when they found him; that just two vials of toxin were found; that traces of all three were in the empty cup.

Then again, so what? Was Grady's job worth letting an innocent man go to jail?

Clara Whitmore reached for the phone and froze. A knock rattled the door. "Who is it, please?"

"Us."

"One moment," she said, hanging up the phone. She

wrote herself a note on the front of the Rama Jr. manila folder: *Ask Grady about glass vials.* Underlined it.

"I wasn't expecting you so late on a Saturday," Mrs. Whitmore said. "Please have a seat while I fetch some cookies."

She brought a tin of oatmeal raisin cookies from the kitchen—an old batch; they'd surely eat every last one—and noticed that the children weren't seated. Ruby stood by the couch with her hands in her pockets. Rex was over staring out the window. What was it?

Awkward. Like the very first time they came over. She straightened her sweater. The two of them weren't even looking at her.

"Lookit down there. Mrs. Juliette, that lady with that orange wig?" Rex said, finally breaking the silence. "Now, how you gonna wear something like that? It glows in the dark! It's the color of one of those traffic safety cones, I swear."

Mrs. Whitmore could think of no response.

"Hey, how come you don't go down there more?" At least he was looking at her now. "Down on College? We never see you out."

"I don't move around as well as I would like," Mrs. Whitmore answered. "I am—well, I'm not so young as I once was."

"You're no older than all these ole ladies round here," Rex said. "They're out everywhere, too. I've seen Mrs. Juliette in the bars. Biddy's—she's in there all the time. Even the Orbit Room once."

"You did not see her in the Orbit Room, Rex," Ruby said. "Don't make stuff up."

"I did, too."

Ruby made a dismissive motion with her head and cleared her throat. The girl was about to say something. "But we saw you, ma'am. At the science library. Yesterday."

Ma'am. So formal, with a cold note of Southern detachment in it.

Mrs. Whitmore put a hand on the table to steady herself. She didn't know why she should feel so guilty; what she did on her own time was her business, after all. "I was doing some investigating. On my own. I am not perfectly helpless, you know; I am not just a . . . a . . . ."

"What?"

"A shut-in. That's what people call me, I've heard them. A shut-in."

"We never called you that," Ruby said.

"Look, we almost got caught over in there," Rex said. "By the campus police. They shut down all the computers and searched people like criminals."

"How come they didn't check you?" Ruby said. Like a pair of cops, interrogating, the good one and the bad one. "You're not working with them, are you?"

"Stop! Stop this. I feel like I'm being ambushed. They didn't check me because I'm an old lady, that's why. Did that ever occur to you? Because I'm invisible. 'What can she do—she's so old, she's so nice!'" *Don't let them see you shake,* she thought, *not now.*

"Sorry, sorry," Ruby said. "Maybe let's sit down. You maybe want your cane?"

"No, dear, let the cane rot for all I care; I'll be fine." She would not sit down. This was her apartment. If she could not hold her ground here, she had nothing left. She straightened herself, took an oatmeal raisin cookie from the tin, and strode into the small kitchen to put tea on.

She returned a few minutes later, steadier. "All right," she said.

"Tell us," said Ruby.

Mrs. Whitmore pulled a chair from the table, sat, and straightened her skirt. "I worked for Rama's father, R.J., a greater man than the son in my opinion. Brilliant, rigorous, even approachable. Up to a point."

"What do you mean?" said Ruby, now seated next to Rex at the table, the cookies between them.

"Well," Mrs. Whitmore continued, "forensics is a team sport, that's what I mean. It's people working together to unravel the thread, to run the tape backward—it's important, and mostly it's fun. But team members need to support one another."

"Kinda like we've been doing here, on this case," Rex said.

"Yes, yes, dear," the old woman replied. She removed her glasses, rubbed her eyes, and turned away for a moment. "The three of us are a team."

"So what happened at Rama's father's lab?" Always zeroing in; the girl was made for this.

"Grady. Grady Funk—yes, the same one—he was a young associate under my guidance." Pacing the living room now, head down. "And he made a mistake, or so it appeared. In a poisoning death, like this one; woman named Marie Plaxton. A mistake right there on the official toxicology report, the same kind of analysis we've been reading in the Rama case."

"And the murderer got away?"

"Almost, Ruby, almost. And I had reason to believe that someone had tampered with the data, but I could never prove it. Mostly, though, the episode was an embarrassment for our lab. And I covered for Grady. I was his boss; it was ultimately my responsibility. I thought R.J. valued me enough to forgive the error. I was wrong."

"The tampering, though; didn't you explain?"

"No. I didn't have enough evidence to show it happened. It was more a hunch—and R.J. couldn't tolerate hunches without real evidence."

"You were fired?"

"No, Rex. I was demoted. Pushed aside. Left off the team.

Denied the one thing I loved most. I was no more than a technician. And, eventually, I resigned."

"Couldn't you have complained, or gone to his boss, or something?"

"I ask myself that every day, Ruby. Yes, I could have done something. Yes, I could have fought for my career. My life. People say we regret more deeply the chances we didn't take than the mistakes we made. The more so when it's clear that we knew better at the time."

"Ooh, you musta hated Papa Rama."

"Yes, Rex. And I'm not ashamed to say that I still do. But not enough to want to murder his son. I was researching a more recent case that reminded me of Plaxton—Robert Pelham, the investor, who was tried for the murder of his business partner."

"That's the guy who lost everyone's money, and now they want it back, right?"

"Right, Ruby, including the university, although DeWitt seems to have recovered its losses. But I was interested in what happened to the evidence. There appeared to be the same kind of tampering in this Pelham case as there was in the Plaxton case. I just smelled a connection."

"Well?"

"Well what, Rex?"

"Was there a connection?"

"Yes, I think so," Mrs. Whitmore replied. "Having to do with the chemistry."

"What is it? The connection, I mean," asked Ruby.

"You know—technical stuff. The samples were contaminated, the peaks were too hard to see."

"What do you mean? What peaks?"

"Like I said, it's chemistry stuff. Advanced."

"What, chemists don't speak English?" Rex said. "Tell us exactly what the problem was."

She could detect no mischief on those two faces, only curiosity. "All right then."

Mrs. Whitmore marched into the kitchen and returned with three small glasses, each about half-full of something red. She passed one glass to Ruby, one to Rex, and kept one herself.

"Beads?" Rex said. "They're tiny."

"I have worked with beads since I was a little girl," Mrs. Whitmore said. "Someday I'll show you my work. But for now, it's more important that you tell me if you can see any differences between the beads in the glasses."

After minutes of staring at the tiny plastic spheres, they gave up. "They're too small," Ruby said.

"That's right. And so are molecules, the basic units that define any substance, like a poison. But molecules are real, just like these beads, and they have different weights and different masses, just like these beads do."

"But how can you tell?" Rex said.

"Only by reading the packages, for the beads," Mrs. Whitmore said. "But there is another way, and I'm going to show it to you."

She went to the kitchen and returned with another glass, also full of red beads. "This glass contains a mixture of the beads. It's more like what we see when we analyze blood: There is a mixture of molecules in there, and they're too small to see any difference."

"But we know they're different sizes, right?" Ruby asked.

"Precisely. Now, how would you separate them? I'll take any ideas."

After several minutes, Rex said, "I know. Filter. Filter them, like you do when you sift flour. Small enough filter and only the small ones will get through."

"Good. But not good enough," said Mrs. Whitmore. "Remember, in the blood there are many substances you don't even know are there. Are you going to build some kind of filter for every one? No, there's a better way."

She cleared the table and placed a shiny silver tray in the center. Next to the tray, positioned to blow across the middle from side to side, she put a small fan. "This is a demonstration I used to give to visitors to the lab."

Mrs. Whitmore took a spoonful of the mixed beads, poured them on one end of the tray, and tipped the tray slightly. The beads all rolled to the other side.

"I don't see any difference," Ruby said.

"No, the speed at which they roll down the tray isn't good enough to separate these molecule-beads, either," the woman said. "But watch this."

She gathered the beads into one corner of the tray, turned the fan on, and again tipped the tray. By the time the beads rolled to the other end, they had separated into three clumps. "See that? The wind from the fan pushes the lightest beads farthest, and the heaviest ones the least. It has separated them by size, by mass. We do the same thing chemically to detect substances in the blood, by the masses of the molecules."

"What's that called?"

"The process is called mass chromatography. The instrument that does it is called a mass chromatograph."

"Oh yeah," Ruby said. "I remember those from the lab."

"Well, Ruby, now you know roughly how they work," Mrs. Whitmore said.

"So what's the tampering part? What happened in those cases?"

"Oh. Right. Well, if the blood sample becomes compromised—if I dump a whole bunch of molecule-beads into the glass that are similar to what I'm looking for—then it's very hard to tell what I have. It's too messy."

"And that's what happened in this, whatyoucallit, the Pelham case?"

"Plaxton. Yes, it did. And it appears the same happened in the Pelham one that Rama was investigating. And it was deliberate. The Rama Jr. lab has much more advanced instruments and procedures—someone messed up the samples on purpose."

Ruby slumped. "Plaxton, Pelham—it's— Everything's too confusing. I just want them not to take Dad away."

Mrs. Whitmore looked directly at the girl. "It's confusing because you are trying to see everything at once, child. The murder itself is almost always a very simple act. In fact, let's focus on just one small part of it: *How.* How did Roman, or whoever it was, manage to put the poison in Rama's tea without the man noticing?"

"He came from the outside, from that courtyard," Rex said. "We thought of that."

"But when? Rama was presumably there the whole evening. And your father fixed his tea. Isn't that correct, Ruby?"

"Well, yeah," said Ruby. "But we thought maybe Rama was napping or something. He was always in there late."

"Rama napping? Never. He worked like a man possessed. Like his father. The man wouldn't know how to nap."

"Well, then," Rex said, "how?"

Mrs. Whitmore was pacing again, her face flushed, drumming her fingers against her hip. All the old habits coming back, she thought. "One step at a time, one step at a time," she was saying.

Ruby turned to the page in her sketchbook where she had diagrammed the lab.

"The answer is not there, my dear. It's in here." Mrs. Whitmore placed her hand briefly on Ruby's head. "You are the only one among us who has spent time in that lab. Enough time to know its rhythms, its routines. Something is missing, and you have it."

Ruby's head dropped. "But what? He hardly ever came out of that office. The door was closed. If he didn't nap . . . ?"

"I don't have the answer, Ruby. Not for this. You must discover it, for it is there."

"Think, Ruby," Rex said. "You're gonna get it."

"I have been thinking!" She was surprised at her own reaction and tried to calm herself, if only for Mrs. Whitmore's sake. "I've done more thinking in the last month or so than I ever have. I'm not going to just get it, Rex. Just because you think so."

"Don't force it, dear," Mrs. Whitmore said. "I want you to think in another way. Not logically, as a forensic scientist. You've both been doing that, and it has gotten you far. Now I want you to do something else. Travel back in your memory. Let yourself be in that lab. See every detail. Watch what people are doing. You can do that, can't you? I know you can. I have seen your drawings. The detail there, the power of your memory to bring back your former life. If anyone can do this, it is you."

Ruby flinched and turned away. She hated anyone commenting on her drawings. "That's it? I have to imagine what happened, just like that?"

"Not just like that. Take some time. Pay attention to your remembered observations. Something is off here. There's some very essential thing we are not seeing, and I suspect it is something obvious. Rama Sr., the father, who was as much a detective as a forensic scientist, used to say, 'The only way out is in.' Put yourself there. See the people. See what they're doing. See what they're not doing."

The woman rose from the table, buttoned her sweater, and moved to the window, her perch. "Sleep on it. Because we can't do any more with what we have."

16

LAB MEMORIES

It took her almost a day (and a night) to see it.

Ruby parted with Rex at her door, leaving him to wander College, make his usual rounds. She headed straight down to her room and closed the door.

"Dad, I'm OK," she said when her father knocked to check on her. He knew that meant she wanted to be alone.

Ruby pulled out her favorite sketches, about a dozen in all, and placed them on her bed. She stared at them as if they were so many postage stamps, unfamiliar objects, created by a stranger. All those tar-paper shacks, rusty wire fences, wagon-rutted roads—they seemed to her now to be from a far-distant place, a time long past.

What was happening? She had drawn all those scenes to keep them close—to keep them alive. To remind herself that it was still there, Spring Valley, Arkansas, still a place that existed. A place she'd go back to.

Now the scenes looked distant to her, dead even. McClarty's. She thought of McClarty's, the drugstore on Main Street where she'd gotten caramels and tart cherry ice cream. How she'd felt when it closed. Boards on the windows, like a few of the other places on Main Street. What was there to do around there now in Spring Valley, to get away from the farm work? Anything?

She had an urge to call Sharon and let it pass. She didn't know the girl well enough, and sure could not imagine inviting her over here, to the Garden Terrace Apartments. The *projects*. That's what they were. Just say so: housing projects. She had moved from a dying Southern farm town to the projects. She had more in common with Rex, or even Mrs. Whitmore, than she did with any of the kids she knew back home, or even the little gods at DeWitt.

Ruby swept the drawings off the bed and turned away. Sat at her desk, did the only thing she could think of. She began to draw.

At first she did not think much about her subject. It was a face, she knew that, a person. She stayed focused on the small things, the shadows around the lips, the slight indentation above the nose, the shape of the eyes. If the eyes looked too oval, or too symmetrical, they looked unreal. After a long while she looked up and let herself consider the whole picture. It was a simple portrait. A girl's face, kind and open, tilted slightly, with a trace of self-mockery, or something like it, around the eyes.

Lillian Walter, her former friend.

Lillian had hardly called or e-mailed at all in the past year, and her absence lingered in Ruby's head like some important and unfinished thought. Ruby and her dad had never talked much about it, for the same reason that people often leave things unsaid: There was never a good time to bring it up. It was embarrassing and painful for both of them. Now Lillian had her own page in Ruby's illustrated history of Spring Valley.

When she finished, she lay on her bed, on top of her country sketches, and fell into a deep sleep. Her father crept in later, saw the drawing, and sat beside the bed for a while. Around dinnertime, he left a plate of lasagna and a ginger ale on Ruby's bedside table, but let her sleep.

She didn't wake up until early the next morning, before dawn. After a cold lasagna breakfast, she tiptoed out to the living room, careful not to wake her father, and pulled a chair to the window facing DeWitt. The DeWitt Lab School was not going away, and neither was she. It was her school. The little gods were not really a pack of spoiled rats. She didn't know any of them well enough to say so, one way or the other. She hadn't made much of an effort.

And the Gardens was just the Gardens, a place. A place with wig shops and an empty lot and old people who wanted to stop and talk to you. Sister Paulette's was the best bakery she'd ever known, that was a fact. Trevor's Tropical had ginger drops that were spicy and cheap. Even the Woods brothers, the Ministers, had actually saved her skin. The Prime Minister of the Garden Terrace Apartments on College Avenue knew who she was.

She lived here. The Terraces was her apartment building. College was her street. The Gardens her neighborhood. She laughed out loud at that.

Sitting there with her ginger ale, Ruby studied the science library's spires as if they were objects to be drawn, nothing more. Details. The shadows from the eaves. The red-gray of the stone. A stray cord or wire hanging from one tower, now dark and visible against the pearly sky. A tiny bird landing on the tip of a tower, perching for a while, stone still, then flying off.

A window below flared in the rising dawn light, and the sight of it ignited a familiar burn in her gut, the worry for her father, still dangling by a thread despite all her efforts. A note posted on the fridge read, *Keep me as the apple of your eye, hide me in the shadow of your wing*—something from the Bible her dad had been repeating to himself.

She finished her ginger ale, turned the chair sideways,

faced a wall, and let her mind travel deep inside that building. To the lab. How many evenings had she spent there doing homework? Fifty? A hundred? It didn't matter; it was enough. She saw the place now.

There was Wade in the far corner on his computer, running computer analysis of chemicals, looking for tiny differences in line graphs; texting his friends, too, every few minutes. Victor, with his textbooks lying open around him, running off to get his licorice every hour. Lydia, intense, working most nights to purify chemicals needed to run the tests. She also seemed to write in a journal or something when she took breaks.

Could that be something?

No, not that Ruby could see. She let it go. That's what Mrs. Whitmore had said. Let it come; don't force it.

Grace. What did Grace do? Ruby realized that she didn't really know. Chemical stains, maybe; some facet of forensics that Ruby now wished that she had taken the time to understand. All that time hanging around the most famous forensics lab in the country and she'd made little effort to learn what was going on there.

Grace. Very cute, very snobby, and . . . well, there wasn't a lot more Ruby could think of about her. But she noticed that her heart picked up a beat.

What was it? Grace Fleming. Grace, who was so worried

about her looks that she went to "freshen up" in the ladies' room every twenty minutes. She thought about the drug habit that her dad mentioned. She wasn't even sure that was true.

A door behind her groaned, and Mr. Rose shuffled out of his room, interrupting her train of thought. In his slippers, still half asleep, he groped for the coffeemaker, banged around the kitchen. Banged around for what Ruby thought was a very long time.

"Mornin', Ru," he said. After banging around some more, he poured his coffee and cleared his throat.

"Ruby," Mr. Rose said, and for a moment he had a hint of that stricken look he wore the morning when he was named the prime suspect. "I saw the drawing. In your room."

"Oh, that," she said. She got up and opened the windows, just like she'd done that first day; the murmur of College Avenue drifted up from below. So alien then, so familiar now. "It's good, huh?" she said finally, and saw the tension in her father's face vanish instantly.

Mr. Rose smiled in open relief. "You got her," he said. "About to pull off some prank, it looks like."

"Yeah, it was strange. I wasn't even thinking of her when I started drawing. It just sort of happened. I think we've maybe had two conversations the whole year, I don't know what happened. But that's the way I remember her."

"Well, I'm so glad you did. She was a good friend."

Was is right, Ruby thought. "Dad?"

"Yeah."

"We're not going back, are we?"

"No, honey, we're not."

And so Mr. Rose told Ruby some stories about when she and Lillian were toddlers over a long and elaborate breakfast of pancakes, sausages, fried tomatoes, and one chocolate milk shake. It all seemed so easy and natural that Ruby wondered why it had taken so long. She would love to see Lillian again—if it ever should happen. She would happily tell her all about the Gardens, only without any expectation that her old friend would understand the place. It took time to do that.

"Tell me something," Ruby said after bringing her dad up to date on all that she, Rex, and Mrs. Whitmore had reasoned through. "The nights I spent at the lab, doing homework, waiting for you to be done. The grad students had these routines, like Grace going to the ladies' room every fifteen minutes or whatever. Was it like that every night?"

"Yep," he said. "Creatures of habit, all of 'em."

"Rama, too?"

"Him most of all. New pot of tea a quarter after every hour. Same kind, same pot, same cup. He drank it all every time."

"That's a lot of tea."

"He lived on it."

"I never saw him come into or go through the main lab—did he ever?"

"On a normal night, maybe once or twice. He would shove open the door and yell out at us when he wanted to say something. Mostly he holed up in that office, though, with the door closed."

Ruby pushed up from the table, went back to the window. She smiled at the DeWitt campus now, shaking her head slowly.

"I have it," she said, still gazing out the window. "I got it. Oh, it's so stupid, it was right there the whole time. Of course."

"What are you talking about?"

For most of the previous hours, Ruby had been tracking the lab workers in her head, alert for some out-of-the-ordinary act that had slipped under the radar. But what if the crucial act in this case was one so ordinary that people never thought about it at all—except and only when they themselves did it.

"The bushes," she said.

"Come again?"

"That's what Rex calls it. The bathroom. Dad, he had to go. He had to. All that tea. He had to go to the bathroom.

And if he didn't come through the lab, then . . ." She stopped. Snorted. "Oh, I don't believe it."

"What? What are you talking about? Explain yourself, willya?"

She did. The brilliant Dr. V. S. Ramachandran may have been brilliant, but he still had to use the men's room. He didn't cut through the lab and use the ones that everyone else did. He surely didn't water the plants in the courtyard. He must have been using the very bathroom below the library that she and Rex had visited back in August. It was a short walk from his veranda, and the door had opened from the outside. A five-minute visit to the bathroom would have given Roman— or anyone else—plenty of opportunity to spike the tea.

"Ain't that something," Mr. Rose said. "How could I not see that? I guess I bought into all the legend talk about him."

"Legends don't pee," Ruby said.

He smiled. "Hard to look legendary when you got your forehead to the tiles and half of it's going down your pants leg."

"Dad, please."

Her father sighed, shook his head, pushed his chair away from the small breakfast table. "One thing still bothers me, though. I mean, I always thought that those red vials, the poison vials, they were for research, right? I always thought there wasn't enough there to kill someone."

"Yeah, Dad, but you didn't know that for sure; and people react differently to poisons, that's what Mrs. Whitmore says."

"Still—I mean, it can be noisy in that lab, but we heard nothing. I'm not saying he didn't drink some poison; obviously he did. It's just—"

"What?"

"Something's way off, is what. You're telling me Rama didn't call out, didn't make a sound, didn't try to get any help? I know it's Rama and all, but those poisons would not have killed him right away. They would have made him sick. After an hour or so, he had to be feeling terrible—yet he did nothing, as far as we can tell, anyway. It's like he was acting like he had an antidote."

17

THE GLASS VIAL

Coconut pudding, was it? Maybe bananas in there, or whatever you call them—plantains—and with fish, plus some spices?

Ruby always had trouble figuring out what was being served at Rex's place.

"I'm over it, seriously," Rex was saying between forkfuls. "Like the way I see it, this is just an injury, like a peg leg or whatnot, what they call that—a disability. No reason to be prejudiced about things like that, right, Ruby?"

"Exactly," she said as one of the Travises or Justins climbed on her knee.

"I mean, it's not her fault, musta been some kind of accident. Nobody wants to give up a marble just like that, you know."

"Yep, I sure do," Ruby said. "What are you talking about?"

"The fake eye. The technology's so good, you don't notice it. Like when you got a real good wig, you swear that's the person's hair up there, not some furry dish towel like what they got at House of."

"Rex, you still don't think—"

"Travis! Don't you climb on the table," said Rex's mom, Mrs. Prudence, lifting the small boy from Ruby's lap and handing him to Rex's dad, a silent man everyone called Mr. Jeffrey. "I just think it's wonderful that you two are visiting that woman. She never came out of that apartment before, and now I see her down on College sometimes, at the stores, even says hello to you."

"That's something, moving around with a bum eye," said Mr. Rose, who had almost finished the coconut-fish-custard thing. "I've had a patch on, and it's hard to get used to."

"Dad, that's just—"

"What do you three talk about, Ru?" he said. "She's a former forensics person; is she helping us out?"

"Yeah—stuff—not a big deal."

"I just think she's happy to have some company, I really do," Mrs. Prudence said. "Justin—please pass the chicken down this way."

And so it went: more food, more dishes, more adult talk. It was forever before Ruby and Rex could excuse themselves and escape down to College Avenue like freed prisoners. The street was gray and empty, somber-feeling even for a Sunday evening.

"So, one thing," Ruby said, still out of breath. It was getting cold, the leaves mostly gone from the trees, brittle underfoot. "Did you see what she wrote on that folder?"

"Who?"

"Mrs. Whitmore. On that folder she has with *Rama Jr.* written on it. And now we know why it says *Jr.*"

"Yeah we do. And I did see *Ask Grady about glass vials.*" Rex missed nothing, Ruby thought, ever. "What you think that is?"

"I don't know," Ruby answered, "but she underlined it. Another thing. You remember when she said that the teacup was empty? How'd she know that?"

"It wasn't in the reports, you're right. Grady, maybe?"

"Probably. Or her old friend Ms. Diaz." Ruby looked over her shoulder instinctively at the ninth-floor window. She dropped her voice. "Do you trust her, Rex? Mrs. Whitmore?"

Rex stepped forward and kicked a bottle cap toward the opposite curb, watching to see whether it jumped over. It didn't make it, hitting the curb and rolling under a car. His shoulders slumped.

"I do, Ruby. I don't know. She got her own things she's

working out, that's a true fact. But probably so does everyone, you know?"

"Thank you, Freud. And the bottle cap's over there by that tire; I can tell you're working through that right now," Ruby said.

"I am. Need to put at least one of those little suckers over or I won't feel right, psychologically."

Ruby waited while Rex found another cap and kicked it over the opposite curb. "Guess it takes a boy's brain to figure out that little ritual," she said.

"Deep down, we very complex."

"Well, deep down, I'm very superficial, so let's review this case. At 6:15 P.M., my dad sees him alive."

"Check."

"At, let's say, 6:22, the man goes out to that bathroom we found."

"Bushes pit stop."

"Roman's waiting out in the courtyard, hidden. He ducks in there, pours the poisons into the tea—the nightshade and the chokecherry and the more potent one."

"Monkshood."

"Right. Then he slips back into the lab area, passes the red vials to Lydia, who stashes them in my dad's locker either then or later, doesn't matter. Now Rama comes back, drinks his tea, and—that's the problem."

"What?"

"He took no action. And as my dad said, he musta felt real, real sick. If you look up those poisons on the Internet, it says that they usually cause symptoms within the first hour, for sure."

She stopped. They were at the foot of College Avenue, across from DeWitt's main gate; broken leaves swirled around it in the cold, haunted wind. She could see Rama in her mind now, one gulp and another and empty.

"Then what?" she asked out loud. "He goes into that bathroom sometime in there, we have to assume that."

"I sure don't know, Ruby. But say we go down in that bathroom, see if we can find a glass vial. It's all we got. There was all kinds of trash and stuff down in there."

"Any vials?"

"No idea. I wasn't looking, and we got no idea what they look like. You thinking of making a run now?"

Ruby looked up at the great stone dungeon of the science library again. Risky. They'd have to break in. And the truth was that she was not sure they could find the little bathroom again, at least not quickly—or without help.

"We should maybe just see if Sharon's got an idea about it; it's getting dark."

"Or Simon," Rex said. Ruby waited for a crack about Simon, but it didn't come. "Tomorrow, too. Before we start thinking about it too much."

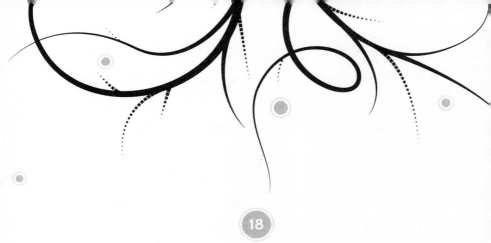

18

THE MAZE MAP

It was a straight-ahead plan that got very twisted, very fast.

In their free period, Ruby and Rex made straight for the library, where Rex again asked a librarian about the spare bathroom. He said the regular one was occupied and he couldn't wait.

"You're going to have to go back into the school then, young man," the librarian said. "Haven't they told you? The entire area under the library has been declared part of the crime scene. Just this morning. The elevator is blocked. You aren't allowed down there."

And that might have been that, except that Ruby did what she wished she'd done first thing in the morning. She asked for help.

"I can get you into the computers, Ruby, but not down

there," whispered Sharon in the middle of the math lesson. "But"—she looked across the class—"I know who can."

At lunch, Simon Buscombe again joined the three of them, bringing his tray to their corner table in the cafeteria. He nodded, said nothing, and immediately bit into a bright orange hot dog with yellow mustard.

"Can't be anything like meat in them dogs; smells like hair spray. How do you eat those things?" Rex said.

Simon shrugged. "I understand my expertise is again in demand."

"Uh, right," Ruby said. "Well, we know you're the maze expert. What we're hoping now is that maybe you know something about the layout underneath the library and the science buildings."

Simon nodded, polished off the hot dog, and took a large swig from a giant cream soda. Burped.

"The catacombs, Simon?" Sharon said.

He nodded impatiently. "Observe," he said, pulling a portfolio out of his briefcase. He cleared a space on the table and leafed through a stack of mazes and drawings, some of buildings, others of cars.

"Whoa, stop," said Rex. "Wait. Lemme see that other drawing, back up, right there. That one. Is that a '69 Cougar XR-7?"

Simon sat stone silent for a moment. He separated the car

drawing and placed it in front of Rex. "How did you know that was a '69?"

"Headlights. See that detail right there?" Rex gawked at the drawing as if it were a real car. He was barely breathing. "Lookit that: '69 is the best year for these. I someday probably might get one."

Simon still looked shaken. "Color?" he said.

"Black cherry."

"Interior?"

"I don't know; between cream and that regular white—"

"Are you kidding me?" Ruby said. "It's a car. All right. A drawing of a car, I mean, and it's good, let's all agree on that. But we're trying to do a job, remember? Simon?"

Simon swung his head around as if he'd forgotten she was there. "Oh yeah. Right. Observe," he said, pushing a fantastically intricate maze to the center of the table. It was all done in red pen, and Simon shooed the others' hands away.

"No touché pas," he said. "This is a map of the catacombs beneath the library. Copied from the original layout, which I found in the architecture section of the library. The original construction is early 1800s, English Gothic, with lines I know and grace notes familiar to the era." The car experience with Rex was long gone; he was back to being his pompous self again.

"Where's our bathroom?" Rex said.

"The modern redesign they did twenty years ago ruined the personality of the place, in my estimation," Simon continued, ignoring the question. "And it screwed up my map; this does not capture every feature. There are blank spots. Dead zones."

Ruby gaped at the drawing, so different from her work and yet she wanted to have it all to herself, just to look at for a while. "This is . . . amazing," she said. "I never knew a mess of dank hallways could look so deadly cool."

"Well, the elevators are blocked, so no way to get down to that mess of hallways now," Rex said.

Simon gave him a fish-eye. "By my calculation, there are seventy-eight entrances to the catacombs. Maybe eighty-one, if you're willing to use the sewers."

"Not happening," Rex said.

"No need for that, young man," Simon said.

Young man!

Ruby, recovering from the hypnotic grip of the drawing, said, "When? We need to go today, before someone beats us to it."

"My schedule has been cleared," said Simon.

"After the bell," said Sharon, sitting back, arms folded on her chest.

"Where we meet, then?" said Rex, reaching for the drawing.

Simon blocked his hand. "No one touches the reconstruction." He looked at Sharon. "I cannot work with people who interfere. This is not a play maze."

"Relax," Sharon said. "No one's gonna mess up your map. Maybe you'd rather not come, Simon. We'll find our way down ourselves."

The long, bony face jerked up, eyes glowing. "No. I'm in."

Sharon again folded her arms. "That's what I thought. Let's meet out in front of the science library."

The four lingered until well after the bell, waiting for most kids to clear out, and then proceeded to the far side of the library building. They followed Simon, squeezing between the stone flank of the science library and the now-dry hedges, the very same ones Ruby and Rex had crawled through days earlier.

"Everyone is prepared, I'm going to assume," Simon said. He was crouching by a small garden-level window with bars, looking back over his shoulder.

Ruby hesitated. Rex shrugged. "Let's not talk about it," he said.

Simon nodded. "Here's our path, very simple," he said, holding the map up to the light and tracing the path with his finger.

"Everyone got that?" Nods all around. "OK."

Simon pulled the bars from the window easily. The bolts

had long ago rotted. He lifted the pane up and slid in. The others followed, Rex last, struggling to fit his large body through.

Ruby recognized the smell from the first time. Damp, swampy, with a machine-oil glaze. Blinking in the darkness, she saw shovels, hoes, a few old lawn mowers, rusting against the far wall. Sacks of something piled in a corner, turning to dust.

They were in.

19

THE UNDERNEATH

"A simple garden shed," Simon said. "At one time it would have opened to the outside. Maybe it still does, through there," he said, nodding toward a thick wooden barn door.

"What's your map say? How far to the bushes?" Ruby said. "I mean, bathroom."

"Easy does it," Simon said. He held his hand out, and Sharon passed him a tiny flashlight. Simon clicked it on and studied the maze drawing. "I will remind you that I have not drawn every corner. I don't know exactly where every hole-in-the-wall whirligig is. I can get us close to the hallway where that bathroom is. I think. Then it's up to you."

"Whirligig?" Ruby said.

Simon led them out through a door and into a stone corridor. Ruby followed, then Sharon, then Rex. All OK so far. The corridor sloped down, turned, and seemed to slope up again. Patches of outside light leaked in, just enough for the four to see their way.

"We going under the library now, I feel that," Rex said.

"Obviously," said Simon.

A clang and hiss of machine noise stopped Simon. He turned the flashlight on the left wall, looking for something. He settled on a small metal door, a half door, no more than waist-high. He pulled it open, and the noise filled the corridor.

"Why don't we just go straight there? Why we want to mess with this?" Rex said over the clanging.

"Because that hallway turns, and by the time you get to the end, you're way under the main school," Simon yelled. "Now, are you following me or not?"

Rex did not want to go through the door. Neither did Ruby, and she peeked over her shoulder to signal that she knew what he was thinking. By the time she turned around Sharon was gone—through the door. Ruby stood aside and let Rex push his way in, headfirst, like some pudgy old dog through a broken fence.

She followed, and the four huddled for a moment on the other side, looking around. Hard to see anything much. A boiler room or something. Huge cylinders, hot to the touch. A tangle of pipes overhead. Nobody in sight.

Simon didn't consult his maze. He seemed to know where he was. He motioned them to follow, around one boiler and then another, hugging the dirty wall, until they'd crossed the room and reached another door.

He put his hand up to stop. "OK. On the other side is where they've modernized. Where we might make visual contact with some random actor. Understood? We'll need to move fast and use door wells, if there's some security or whatever."

Simon dropped to all fours, cracked the door, and stuck his head out. He recoiled, pulling the door shut. "As I anticipated. Occupied. Footsteps out there. Ruby?"

She crept forward on her hands and knees and peeked for herself. Bare bulbs bathed the hallway in wasted yellow light. She blinked once and held her breath. A security person of some kind was down at the right end of the passageway, about forty yards away, where it crossed another hall. Not a city cop, but university security, and now she saw another and another. Had they taken over the investigation?

"Weird," she said when she pulled her head back in.

"What, Ruby?" Rex asked. He was crouched behind the others. He hated being down on the ground.

"Campus security. Lots of 'em. I thought this case was for the real cops."

"Weird is right," said Sharon, moving forward to have a

peek of her own. "At this hour, most of the campus security people are posted outside or in the main lobbies of the buildings, and there aren't that many of 'em working. Now, here's three way down here?"

Sharon took another look, left the door ajar, and said over her shoulder, "All clear now. Should we?"

No one had a better idea. Out into the lighted hallway they stumbled, Simon turning left, the opposite direction from where they'd seen the security person, Ruby behind, Rex, and then Sharon.

Simon was counting under his breath. Ruby could hear it—"one Mississippi, two Mississippi"—and she wondered, *Why is it Mississippi and not Arkansas?* And then, *Why am I thinking about this now? Like this is all a joke, a prank.* After three Mississippi, Simon all but dove into a deep door well, the others piling in behind him, their breath heavy now.

"Minimize exposure," Simon said. "No more than three or four seconds out. That's my rule."

"Your rule?" said Sharon. "What, you got rules now?"

"Hey, it's my map, hacker-girl. I get to make some rules."

"Hacker-girl? Where'd you get that, skater-boy, at architectural drafting club? Oh, I forgot, at drafting club no one speaks. It's a deaf-mute ranch."

"Whoa, you two friends, right?" Rex said.

Ruby was relieved to hear him say something; he looked

terrified. There was so much more to do, and it was a long way out.

Simon craned his neck around the corner of the door well and jerked it back. He put a "be quiet" finger in the air.

A campus cop sauntered right by them: *click, click* went her shoes. Ruby saw clearly the campus officer's profile under the cap. The shadow in the door well covered them, and she went right by. The woman was texting on her cell phone.

Ruby looked at Rex, who seemed to have relaxed. Maybe he just needed to see evidence that they had some luck on their side. The good kind. He gave her an almost-smile. She knew what that meant. No turning back now.

Four Mississippis later was an intersection, and Simon peeked around the corner, waved, and they all but sprinted to the next door well. The first one had been buried in shadow. This one was not.

"We need to do better than this," Simon said. "This here is a showroom."

Ruby peered into the new corridor and motioned for Rex to take a look. He nodded. Neither knew where exactly they were, but the look of the hallway was familiar: green walls, gold numbers on a couple of doors. The same look, the same feel as when they'd been down to the bathroom the first time. Years ago, it seemed to her now.

A clicking of shoes came again. Simon stiffened. He

turned, stricken, shaking his hands in a desperate gesture: *Do something!*

Sharon put a hand to her mouth. She shuffled, turned, tried the door behind them. Locked, of course, with a keypad under the handle. Her hands moved fast, punching one combination, another, and another—nothing. Now prying the faceplate off of the keypad with a set of keys—jamming a key into the wiring behind, hard.

The door clunked—they were in, crouched on the other side of the door now, just as the guard's heels clicked by. This was crazy, Ruby thought. Every five steps, there was some campus security guard.

She sensed someone behind her and swung around. A large, bright lab room. Forensics territory. A chemistry lab of some kind probably, Ruby thought, maybe the place where they made some of the agents used in the main lab. And there at the end of the lab bench—could it be? Yes. A student she didn't recognize sat on a stool in front of a rack of test tubes, his head on the table. Fast asleep.

Ruby smiled. "Grad students," she said. "I've seen 'em fall asleep on elevators."

The student stirred, lifted his head, and stared at them, blank-eyed. Like an ostrich gazing out from a cage, Ruby thought. The student then put his head down and continued to snooze.

"Graduate school looks easier than I thought," Rex said. "I could do that."

Sharon was in no mood. "Be thankful we didn't get caught, Rex." She turned to Simon, who had flattened his precious map against the wall. "Now, how close are we? I was lucky getting us through that door. Luck, luck, luck. I hate luck."

"Looks like we're right at this one corner, and we're close. Ruby, you want to look at this?"

"Can I touch it?"

"No, absolutely not. Look at your hands."

They were filthy. Everyone's were, except for Simon's. She saw why: He had a box of hand sanitizers with him.

"Gimme one of those hand wipes, then."

"Uh, no can do. I got, like, two left. Get your own."

"Oh sure, you mean at the drugstore down here?"

"All right," Sharon said. "Just go look at the map. Simon's disturbed. Why do you think they put him in Regular?"

"I'm disturbed, and you're the criminal element. How many grades did you alter on the school computers, Sharon?"

"Hey, excuse me," said Rex. "Why don't you two go fight somewhere else. We got a man trying to get some sleep over here."

Ruby squinted at the maze and at the tiny mark Simon had made for where they were. She saw the edge of the building on the map, and what looked to be the hallway she and Rex had visited. And the door—the fire door that Rama must have used to get to the bathroom.

"Rex?" she said.

He came over, holding his dirty hands high in the air. "Yup, that's it. We came from the other side, though," he said, and pretended to lunge for Simon's hand wipes container.

Simon recoiled, and the wipes container fell to the floor. "Well, that was sophomoric. Just brilliant. I hope you display the same judgment in the hallway, because now you'll be approaching from this side. Think you can handle that?"

"Think you can handle if I take one of those handy wipes and put it straight up—"

"Rex, Rex," Ruby said. All they needed was for him to throw a fit down here. He'd attract every cop within a mile.

"Ruby," he said. "I'm playing. I am."

She gave him a look.

"OK, OK," Rex said. "Seriously, though—hand wipes?"

Simon cleared his throat. "We're agreed, then. We turn right outside the door. That hallway with the bathroom is the second one on the left. One person needs to stay there, at the corner, to keep a lookout. I can do that."

"What about me?" said Sharon.

"You go to the other side of the hall—the far side—and stand lookout there."

Sharon seemed about to say something nasty but stopped herself. "OK."

"And," Simon said, "I trust that you two sleuths have a plan?"

"Yes, Simón Bolívar," Ruby said. "Hit the bathroom, scoop up every last piece of evidence-looking stuff in there. That good enough for you? And especially look for a glass vial."

"That's it?" Simon said. "That's your genius plan?"

"Simon," Sharon said. "Be the navigator, you moron. Stop talking. Stop saying things. Stop. I'm the one going to the far end of that hall. You get to stay close to this room and run and hide, you weasel."

"Weasels are my favorite animal," Simon said.

Rex doubled over and almost fell down. He was trying not to laugh out loud. "I—got—a—new—name—for—"

"Great news, save it for when we're out and stop goofing, will you?" said Ruby. "For once."

She slipped out the door to check if the coast was clear. It wasn't. Campus police were patrolling regularly, and there was nothing for them to do but wait. The grad student stirred again. He was happy to have some company and talked easily with them while working.

"The police, yeah, they began searching early today, I don't know what for. They are scouring every forensics room for something," the student said. "They looked in the garbage here, even. Are you guys playing some kind of detective game for school?"

"'Zactly," Ruby said.

"Matter of fact, we're young detectives in training," said Rex. "What we call ourselves is the Young Detectives."

"OK, sure. That's got a ring."

"I can't take all the credit," Rex said. "We had a committee and all."

It seemed like hours before the patrol outside eased up, but it eventually did. The time between patrols increased from a few minutes to almost fifteen, and seemed to hold there.

"I don't know about you guys," said Ruby, "but I don't want to spend the night here. I think it's time."

The others agreed.

Out they went, strolling more casually this time. The plan if they got caught was to say they got lost looking for the subbasement bathroom, which was about 5 percent believable, given that there were four of them. Still, it was a better excuse than anything else that came to mind.

Five Mississippis to the corner, where the hallway crossed the one that held the tiny bathroom. Ruby peered around, pulled back. She tipped her head up and pantomimed a scream. Two guards, one at the fire door about halfway down the hall and another closer still, standing in front of—what? She couldn't tell.

"What now?" Simon said.

Ruby thought for a moment. She sensed something deeply unusual. What was it? She tried to locate its source and saw it in the eyes of the others. People were looking at *her* to make a decision. Quickly. She shook off the sensation.

It was now her call, and she took a step back and let herself see the immediate surroundings. The detail: to draw it.

She noticed something about the ceiling. It was low, and sprinklers poked out from white panels. In the movies, they would know how to turn those sprinklers on and set off chaos and all. If only. She saw the same sprinklers back in the older hallways, exposed, held in place from above by a tight network of pipes.

"Can we get up there?" Ruby asked.

"Up where?" Rex said.

"Push up those panels. Up into the ceiling. Climb in there."

Sharon didn't hesitate. The girl was not here for the conversation. She webbed her fingers together, making a step for Ruby, who hopped up and used the wall as another step. She pushed out a panel and—with help from Rex now, lifting her up—pulled herself in. A solid grid of pipes and supports, enough room to crouch. It would have to do.

"C'mon," she said, peering down through the opening. "Rex, you're coming up."

"What?" whispered Simon, taking a peek around the corner. "That's Moby Dick. We need a crane operator."

"You the scarecrow from *Wizard of Oz*. Prob'ly couldn't lift your own straw ass," Rex said.

"I can curl a gallon of cream soda with each hand, young fella," Simon said. He cupped his hand next to Sharon's, grinning at Rex.

Ruby thought that she heard footsteps again. "Rex and I'll go hit the bathroom, you two guys get out," she said. "C'mon, quick now."

Big T. Rex stepped on their hands, put a giant dirty paw on the wall, and reached up and grabbed the biggest pipe. He yanked himself up, jammed the other foot against the wall, and pushed again—shaking the pipes as he pulled up into the ceiling.

Ruby, retreating in the dark to take weight off the pipes, saw the boy's huge frame ease up like a bear climbing a tree, all quiet, brute strength.

Through the opening she saw Sharon and Simon stare up at them for a moment, glance at each other, and slip away. Rex replaced the panel, and the world above closed around them.

The two sat there on the pipes, looking at each other in

dumb wonder. Spiderwebs of light filtered up from below; a murmur of voices, too. Rex gave her his "Look what stupid thing I just did" smile. She shrugged back in a way that meant—Rex would know—*I'm coming through, outta my way.*

She turned and crawled. Rex followed.

Toward the bathroom.

20

THE EVIDENCE

It was luck, dumb luck, that was needed now, and Ruby knew it. Crawling over the pipes, squinting down through cracks between panels to follow the line of the corridor, the pair moved forward and quickly lost track of distance.

"Here." Ruby motioned to Rex, peering down through the hole for a sprinkler into what looked like a small room. "There's your bathroom, could be. And it's busy. Oh no."

What? Rex mouthed, now squinting through the hole into the small, brightly lit room. A campus policeman, someone in a suit, and two huge men ransacking the place, emptying the medicine cabinet, turning over the trash.

Rex tipped his head to get a better angle. "Wait," he said. "Ruby. That's not it."

"What do you mean?"

"Not the bathroom I was in." He was almost impossible to hear, his voice was so soft. "This one's bigger, and it don't got that big hole in the wall."

"What do you mean?" She didn't like the quiver she heard in her own voice. "It's a bathroom. In the hall. This has to be it. How many of them can there be?"

"Two, maybe, I don't know. Maybe it's farther down."

"What if it's not? I have no idea where we are."

"Easy, easy. We're still right over the hallway. Keep going. We got no other choice."

"This is crazy," Ruby said as she turned and moved ahead again. Her eyes adjusting to the dark, she noticed that the web of pipes stretched out indefinitely in all directions. No edges, no walls, no landmarks.

"Stay straight, you're drifting over," Rex said.

In a few minutes, following the line of the hallway below, they reached another small room. Or so it appeared; it was dark down there. Rex removed a ceiling panel and dropped his head down as far in as he could: cramped, dirty, empty. "This is it," he said.

"Amen," Ruby replied. "You think you can get down and back? Those men are close."

"No talking, no thinking." Rex lowered himself down with a soft *thud*.

Ruby saw his huge dark form with a white garbage bag, heard a mumble of clinks and clicks, like someone putting away a board game. "A whole bunch of stuff someone put in this hole in the wall, like it's a trash can," Rex whispered.

"Any glass vials?"

"No idea, I can hardly see."

She sensed movement out in the hall, turned, and peeked through a crack over the hallway. The whole group from the last bathroom was coming toward them.

"Rex! Hurry. Lock the door."

He was emptying the medicine cabinet and didn't seem to hear. Ruby said it again—but Rex was in a zone down there, and he didn't even look up.

She called out loud, "Lock the door!"

Rex looked up—the door handle turned—and he threw himself against it, jamming the lock in place.

"Get out, get out!" she said.

"Someone's in there—come out now, put your hands where we can see 'em!" shouted somebody on the other side of the door.

"Grab this," Rex said, handing up the plastic garbage bag. "Watch out, here I come."

More yelling and pounding now; the door was about to blow open. Rex stepped on the toilet, nearly pulled the pipes out of the ceiling, and launched himself up.

"Get 'em!" boomed a voice, and the two friends scurried along the pipes like a pair of spooked squirrels. No time to replace the panel in the ceiling, and in a second flashlight beams danced in the crawl space. The stabs of light gave Ruby the sense that the space was much, much bigger than she'd assumed.

She glanced back. Someone was coming. A black shape lunged up through the opening above the bathroom, and now it was a race to—where? She had no idea.

"Just move for now," Rex said. "No thinking."

Over the pipes, her hands numb, Rex right behind, and the damned trash bag banging every pipe they passed.

The flashlight beams wildly swept their cave and soon found them. The beams bathed them in light, and they froze like cornered beetles. Ruby was sure they were caught. She turned. No—they still had a lead. She pushed herself forward, yanking Rex by the hand.

"How much longer we going?" Rex said finally, after what seemed like an hour of blind climbing. The lights were still behind them.

"Long as we have to," Ruby said. But her heart, and her hands, would not take much more. In minutes she stopped, ready to give up. She sat, limp and exhausted, unwilling to look behind. Rex was the one who turned around.

"She's doing worse than us," he said.

Ruby swiveled to look: a man, youngish—who?—also sitting, maybe fifty yards away. A country mile in this place. She hadn't gained an inch. Out in the gloom, Ruby saw a spout of light: Someone else was coming up into the pipes. It looked like another man.

"We need to be outta here," she said. *Cross the field,* she thought. She was five or six, running outside, tall stalks of corn scratching at her skin. A forest of them, no end in sight: *Get to the road.* How had she found that road?

"Ruby, I can't go no more," Rex said after another ten minutes of climbing. He was behind her, sitting back on his knees. He could barely hold on to the garbage bag, his hands were so raw.

She sat back, too. Done. There would be no road. This was it.

She reached down and pulled up a panel, stared through the opening. Gloom. She may as well have been staring into a well. No choice now; there must be a floor down there. Ruby lowered herself down—her hands were every bit as raw as Rex's—and hung in space for only a moment. Her hands could not hold her.

The fall down could have been ten feet or ten inches. All she knew was that she was on the floor, blessed solid floor, calling out to Rex, catching the bag of garbage, and down he came, flat on his back.

"You OK?"

"I look OK to you?"

21

THE MORGUE

Rex rolled over and practically hugged the solid floor. Pushed to his feet.

Ruby looked around. The dark eased, barely, and she saw rows and rows, big rows, of something extending to the ceiling. Walls? She reached up and touched one—and it moved slightly.

"What are these stupid . . . ," she said, moving in front of one of the huge things, reaching up to feel it—and felt a heavy thump on her head.

"Aaaagh!"

"Ruby! Fight him off, fight him off! There're bodies everywhere!"

"Be quiet already. I got it on the floor," said Ruby. "It's a book, not a zombie, you lunatic. You're screaming like a girl."

"You screamed first, also like a girl," said Rex. She could see the wide whites of his eyes bobbing in the darkness. "Books? Oh, don't do that to me again, false alarm like that. I been traumatized ever since *The Toolbox Murderer*."

The smell, the weight, the very size of the room: It was a submerged storehouse, an underground graveyard for dead books. Stacks and stacks, row upon row.

"The morgue," Ruby said. "This has to be it. Stacks of books, not bodies. We're here, in the land of legend."

"And we best be outta here soon," Rex said. "We made too much noise already."

They zigzagged into one stack and out the other side. Into another and out again, and another and another.

Ruby stopped midstride. "Oh no." The ceiling panel— had she replaced it? "Rex," she said.

"Ruby, how we ever gonna get outta here?" he said.

"I don't know, but we gotta keep moving, just like you said up there in the pipes."

"OK, I got a little more left. But we need to look for something to tell us where we are."

The morgue was dark and looked the same in all directions. Pick a direction and go to the nearest wall: That was the only plan Ruby could muster. She heard Rex's breathing behind her and timed her steps, three and one, three plus one, as if she were on her way to school and everything was all right.

The light never changed; neither did the stacks. And then they did.

"What this?" Rex said.

"It's— I don't know. Like a clearing." Stacks radiated outward at angles. "Can you see anything?"

"Yeah, I see a combination wig and milkshake shop. What you think? I'm looking at the same thing as you."

"I thought if we just followed the stacks till we hit a wall . . . But now, which way?"

"Place is a maze, not a morgue. Pretty soon the bodies gonna come to life, and then it's *Toolbox Murderer* all over again."

"Forget the zombies. We're gonna need something to eat and drink. I'm starving, and we're getting nowhere."

"Just don't cannibalize me, all right? Must be some rodents down here we can catch."

"Rex, this is serious. Unless someone turns the lights on, I don't know how we're getting outta here."

"I know, Ruby. I'm trying to lighten it up. Mrs. Patterson's always talking about how wonderful it is to get lost in books; I don't think this is what she means. Let's just try another row and see where it goes."

It led to yet another clearing, again with rows of movable shelves angling off in all directions.

Rex threw up his hands. "OK, I give up, this isn't working.

I'm done wandering. How we gonna make this place go away and not come back?"

"We're not," Ruby heard herself say. Her subconscious brain must have been working. "Not tonight. Nobody's about to find us down here, either. The place is too big."

"What are you saying exactly?"

"Sleep."

"Here, in this spooky ole place?"

"You want to go back up in those pipes? I don't."

Rex only nodded, dropped his garbage bag, and sank to the floor. Ruby pulled down a bunch of books and placed them around their spot like land mines, to trip up anyone who might approach.

Rex balled up the garbage bag and offered it to her as a pillow. She took it. He arranged two soft, moldy tomes for himself, put his head down, and was out.

Ruby wished vaguely that she had an alarm clock. That she could call her dad. And Rex's parents. That she could . . . could . . .

And then all was dark.

Later Ruby jerked her head up, eyes blinking, her brain still trying to match the dark swaying shapes of the book stacks with something in her memory.

It came back slowly, and with it the recognition that her

eyes were now more adjusted to the darkness. She could make out books, even some titles (*On the Principles of Physiology in Crime Investigation*) and saw Rex fast asleep next to her.

She sat up abruptly, wide-eyed. They'd been there the whole night. It was morning. Her dad must be terrified. And Rex's parents.

"Rex," she whispered. Nothing. "Rex, T. Rex, Theodore Rexford, Esquire." She shook his shoulder.

"Huh," he said. "Stop."

Ruby cleared the area and explored a little. It was a cavernous underground space. The shelf structures were on rollers so that, heavy and creaking, one could move against another, like giant sliding dominoes.

"Did you hear that?" Ruby asked.

"What?"

Both were silent, listening. A soft snap, crackle, and pop; the place was like the woods. Then—something. Was it a door? Hard to say for sure. No other sound came for minutes.

Ruby put up a hand for more silence. Now they both heard it, barely audible beneath the creaking heartbeat of the stacks: breathing. Labored breathing.

Someone else was in the morgue.

Rex reached down to pick up the garbage bag and the two poised to run—but where? Running would be foolish if they had no idea where the other person was. Ruby again held up a hand. *Stay down.*

The breathing came closer. Now movement—a clumsy sound, seemingly only a few stacks away.

Ruby eased a book out of the stack to her left and peeked through in the direction of the sound. No view. Rex did the same from another angle. He shook his head. Ruby crept forward. The breathing, now a wheezing sound, was very close. Ruby slipped out another large book. This time she saw him: a man, tall, in a uniform, or was it a suit? He was turning into the space next to theirs, so close she felt dizzy.

And down he went, tripped by one of the land mines. Rex sprang to his feet. He took two steps back and threw himself against the stacks between them and the visitor. The great old bookcase lurched, books cascaded down on all sides, and it rolled forward.

"Dammit!" said the man on the other side.

Ruby and Rex backed up, counted to three, and rammed again. The great metal panel shuddered and groaned like some dying animal.

More books crashed down on the other side, and the tall man was struggling to get up, it looked like. Ruby grabbed the garbage bag and turned to run. Rex put a hand on her shoulder. "Wait," he said.

He led her around to the aisle on the other side of where

the man was trapped, and Rex bull-rushed again. More books crashed to the floor, accompanied by yelling and cursing. The man was caught in a landslide.

Rex moved to the next stack, and the next, ramming one against another, burying the intruder as if in a deck of giant cards.

"OK, that's enough," he said, and the two fled down the aisle, in and out of stacks, again looking for some way out. And again the underground library seemed to have neither beginning nor end, neither north nor south.

"Stop," said Ruby, out of breath. Their pursuer would push himself out soon; maybe had already. "We need to think. Think. Look at the stacks; what do they say?"

Wildly, Rex looked at the numbers on each stack. "M456–M897, N76–N890 . . . What on earth do they mean?"

"There're dates, too," Ruby said. In parentheses, below the codes it said (1900–1910).

"So what, Ruby? This place is too huge."

"No, I'm saying let's go upward in dates—which way is 1920? Do you see any?"

"No—I mean, yeah. I think through there it says 1920–1930. See it?"

Cutting between more stacks, out the other side, Ruby saw it was 1950–1960, and they charged ahead. "We got to get to the present! Run!" said Ruby.

When they reached 1990, they saw a wall, but no door.

"There's got to be one, or we're done," Ruby said. She went one way in the great hall and Rex the other.

"Here!" said Rex, trying to whisper. A door. He yanked it open, Ruby behind him.

Finally. Back in hallways. But where?

"I should have snagged that stupid map from Simon," Ruby said. "Now what?"

"More thinking, that's what," Rex said. "There're numbers over all these doors. I say we do the same thing we just did to get out—to the smaller ones."

"Why smaller?"

"Why not?"

Down the hall they went—LL245, LL240—and the hallway soon dead-ended into another hall, and to the right Ruby saw a change in the light. A window.

"Rex, c'mon, look over here," she said. She had no interest in wandering under DeWitt if there was a shortcut out.

It was a garden window, no bars this time, still too dark to tell what was on the other side. Rex rattled the frame and pushed it up. She slipped through first. Rex handed up the garbage bag and squeezed himself through, turning to close the window behind him.

A deep window well. Ruby pulled herself up just enough to see over the lip of the well—and groaned.

"Oh no, I don't believe this," she said.

22

THE COURTYARD

A low, smoky sky leaked just enough light to reveal the courtyard behind the forensics lab, where it all began.

The window was directly across the yard from the lab, and for a while Ruby and Rex stood in the window well side by side, their heads just above ground level, staring at Rama's office. A desk lamp was on, though nothing moved inside.

"This is the way it would have looked to the killer," Ruby said.

More than that, she thought. *Maybe the person hid right here in the well. Completely out of sight, a short stroll to the office, no windows in the lab faced the yard except Rama's. In through the veranda and gone. Then what?*

"Got to be another way out," she said. "The person had to have a way out that didn't go through the back of the lab."

"And not through that fire door, either, or you end up running into Mr. Rama coming back from the bushes."

Probably not back through the window, either, Ruby thought. The corridor was too risky, the chance of being seen in there. "You'd want to get out without going through any of these buildings, if you could," she said.

The shadows in the courtyard were gradually melting away in the dull dawn light. The early shift of staffers would be arriving soon, Ruby knew. The pair squinted out into the yard and saw nothing. No other doors, no unbarred windows, no secret passageways.

"We're gonna need to climb out and look, Ruby."

"No. We'll be seen out there. Too many windows . . . that man back inside." He had to be up and on their trail again by now. She felt something change; something slight. The light in the hallway on the other side of the window—it was brighter. Was someone down in there now?

"You want to get trapped here?" Rex said. "We've gotta take the chance."

"No, no. I just want to look for a few more minutes, that's all."

"Naw, not me. Look who's the one waiting around now. I need to move, Ruby. I'm about ready to lose my mind standing round here."

"Not yet," she said—but it was too late. Rex pulled himself up, turned to sit on the lip of the window well.

He smiled. "'Scuse me, but what about that ladder right up there?" She turned around to see a steel ladder built into the wall, running straight up behind them.

"The escape route! Has to be," she said. "You still got your bag, right?"

"No, I left it in there so we could come back one more time. Course I do." Rex pulled out the corner of the white bag from inside his jacket. "Now, let's go."

Dead quiet, and the ladder rungs so cold, the sound of their sneakers squeaking over those steel bars: Ruby felt more exposed than she had the entire previous evening. Anyone who glanced out into the courtyard would see her bright blond hair and Rex's huge form.

"Quicker," she said to the sneakers above.

"You go quicker, if you want to. I'm just trying not to slip."

"But it's getting lighter."

"Well, this here bag ain't getting no lighter. Don't you be wigging on me, now."

"You're moving like a slug."

Up and up, three stories, four, and finally the seventh floor. One last push, up and over the small knee-high parapet that ringed the roof, the height making them tighten their grips so that it took time to let go.

"This body's not made for heights, is one true fact," Rex said, collapsing onto the roof, which angled upward gently; the spires of the library rose black behind him. "I'll be taking a short rest, personally, so I don't have a heart attack."

"I'm gonna go look around, then."

Under a pale sky now, Ruby followed the parapet around to the front of the building, above the main gate. There, kneeling and braced against the short wall, she watched morning break over their entire world: the lab building down to her left, the lab school just beyond it. Out front and directly below, the sharp black outline of the iron fence separating the order of DeWitt from the chaos of College Avenue, the grimy asphalt snake. And of course the Terraces, looking at this distance like a pair of abandoned grain silos.

For a second, Ruby imagined that she could see her window, a light in there. Where was her dad?

"He must be panicked," she said to Rex as he made his way over. "Oh, how did we not bring a phone?"

"We did. It's right here in my hand. I'm calling now."

"What, you waited till—?"

"No reception down under, Ruby— Pa! Yes, hello— Course it's Rex, who else— I been— No, no, I'm with Ruby— Stop yelling, Pa, let me finish—no—yes—OK—

We're coming home soon, you can tell Mr. Rose, too— He's there? Tell him Ruby's right here with me. We all fine."

Rex nodded, nodded some more, held the phone away from his ear, and made his Mr. Jeffrey face. "OK, I said OK. We'll meet you at, uh"—he looked up at Ruby; she mouthed an answer—"at Paulette's. OK? Yes, I'll explain everything." He hung up.

"Mad?"

"Man speaks about three words a month until he gets angry, then he raves in Jamaican so bad, no one can understand him."

"Uh, Rex? If they're going over to Paulette's to meet us, we should maybe think about getting off the roof."

"You make a fine argument, Ruby. Very High Honors. But we can see right down College from here. Let's watch and see when they come out."

In minutes, the whole group trickled out of the Terraces: Mr. Rose, Mr. and Mrs. Rexford, a few Travises . . . and Mrs. Whitmore! "Look who's with them," said Ruby.

"Mrs. W. in the house—I mean, outta the house. Taking to the streets and all. Next thing, she's gonna be parked in the Orbit Room by the jukebox."

"Which reminds me."

"What?"

"The streets. My High Honors argument from before. Shouldn't we be down there?"

"Let's go find one of those ladders. Got to be another one. On the other side, behind."

On their way back, staying low past the ladder from the courtyard, Ruby stopped to look down—and pulled back. "Oh no."

"On the ladder?"

"Looks like someone coming—doesn't matter—move it, will you, we need another way down and fast."

Around the back, there it was, same as the one from the courtyard, this one dropping from the main roof down to the roof on one of the library's wings, three floors down.

"Another roof, and no place to hide down there," Ruby said.

"Nah, I don't care, we going down," Rex said. "We need to break out of this haunted castle. I don't care if I have to break a window."

Which he did. Down on the lower roof they found three large windows, all locked. Wrapping the top of the trash bag around his fist, Rex punched out a small pane in one and flipped the latch. Seconds later the two of them were inside the main science library on a landing near the fourth floor. A mumble of activity came from below.

"Hear that?" Ruby said.

"I do, and it don't sound like much. I'm walking out; they can arrest me if they want to."

Filthy, their clothes torn, the pair shuffled down the stairs, and Ruby was sure the whole way that they'd be caught, the way it always happened on TV. You think you're safe and—*boom*—the bloody hatchet crashes through the door.

"Walk on through like we own the place, that what it's about," Rex said.

A few heads turned as they strode through the main library, but it was still early; no one said a word. Three steps and one, three plus one, the door was getting closer, and Ruby couldn't help it: She ran. Put a shoulder down and pushed through the big door, flew down the steps.

Rex flew out right behind.

23

SISTER PAULETTE'S

"Justin, you get yourself inside outta the street!" Rex yelled.

The little boy stopped and stared. "Ooh, T. Rex, you's in trouble!" He dashed into Sister Paulette's.

The place was all shouts, loud even for a Saturday morning. "Looka what cat drug in, big ole bear and a little tweety bird!" one of the older men called out.

"You hush up, Neville, or we gonna cut you off!" came another voice.

"Plenty about time, young man—and Ruby." Rex's mom rushed to hug them from the table where all the parents had gathered. "Ooh, now, you come here and tell what you been into."

Mr. Rose was angry. "Ruby! What happened to you?"

Anxious now, he hugged her. "Sit down, sit down, you both got some talking to do."

"Dad, could we first—"

"Pudding cakes," Rex was saying, "P-cakes. Someone needs to order up a pile, 'cuz we very ready to talk long as we can eat breakfast, and bring some of that—" He stopped. "Mrs. Whitmore, well, lookit you, all out at Paulette's to meet us."

The older woman smiled, hesitated, and reached out both hands to greet them. "Aw, now," Rex said. "This too nice to get some love and all, but— Oh. Yeah. Hello, Pa."

Mr. Rexford gave his son a hard stare. "You sit down, Theodore."

The cakes came. Rex devoured a half dozen in a minute and still had a look on his face that was—well, hungry.

"More is coming, son," Mr. Rexford said. "Now is time you explain what you do."

"It's my fault, sir," said Ruby.

"Nah, that's not right, I wanted to help—"

"No, you would never have gone down if—"

"All right now, child," Rex's father said. He placed his large hands on the table, spreading his fingers. "We not here blaming for anything. Just to know what happened. Did you get lost? Let us begin there."

"Yes," said Ruby, after a moment's thought. "Yes, that's right."

Or close enough, she thought, *for now.* The library was blocked off. The two of them did want to find that bathroom downstairs. Another kid from class—"Sharon, this girl in Regular"—and her friend—"Simon, with the briefcase, you seen him?"—anyway, those two knew how to get down there and—Rex speaking now—some grad student was snoozing, and Simon and Sharon got into an argument . . . And on it went, the two speakers taking turns, glancing periodically at Mrs. Whitmore to signal that there was more to it than student hijinks.

"Hmm," said Mr. Rose, glancing over at Mr. Rexford; neither of them was convinced. "Sounds about as true as the stories I told at your age."

Silence at the table, throat-clearing, everyone staring at their hands; someone coughed. Sister Paulette felt the change and moved in to clear dishes. She reached down to clear the trash bag at Rex's feet and he grabbed her hand.

"Uh, no, ma'am, I got my school project in there," he said.

The parents looked at one another again. Ruby squirmed.

"All right now, everyone, listen here." Mrs. Whitmore was standing up. She looked around and saw that she had everyone's attention. "This has been a tremendous occasion, one of relief and reunion, and I am privileged to be a part of it." The entire restaurant, including Paulette, stopped what they were doing. "But I would like to ask a favor. Of the parents, that is. If you would kindly allow it, I would like to have a moment with these two young people."

No one moved. "You mean, leave?" said Mr. Rose. "You don't."

"I do."

Mrs. Whitmore, her chin raised, met the eyes of every adult at the table and—*miraculous,* she thought, *what happens when you ask*—each one got up to leave. Mr. Rose, the last to make a move, stopped and turned on his way to the door. "I know what you three are up to, and, Dr. Whitmore, I'm grateful for all your help. But I want to hear everything, soon as you're done. It's my butt on the line here, remember."

"Dad, of course," Ruby said.

He smiled. "Solve it for me, Ru, will ya? And soon. We're out of time." And off he went with the Rexfords.

Mrs. Whitmore sat down, took a breath, and restrained an urge to reach for the garbage bag. "So," she said, clearing a space on the table. "Enough storytelling. You've gathered more evidence, that's clear; I dearly hope you have not removed anything from the crime scene. That is evidence tampering, and it's a crime in its own right."

"No," said Ruby. "We never went in the lab at all."

"Where, then?"

"The bushes, ma'am."

"The bathroom, he means. See, you were right. We were missing something—Dr. Rama never left his office to go to the bathroom. That's because he was using his own, a small one under the library. We were there before, totally randomly. When the regular one was out of order."

Mrs. Whitmore steadied her hands. "Outside the tape."

"Huh?"

"The bathroom. It was outside the yellow police tape, correct?"

"Yup," Rex said. "Why—we in trouble?"

"The judge will have to decide that, ultimately, and at this point I am in as deep as you are. Suffice it to say, for now, that you're in a lot less trouble than Ruby's father. So let's see what you got. All of it."

Rex lifted the bag to the table, and there was Sister Paulette, frowning. "No trash where I serve food," she said, sliding the table away and pulling over a small, well-worn table as a replacement. "Try this."

Rex poured the contents out carefully: assorted tissues, crumpled receipts, a couple of empty soda cans, dirty cotton swabs, dental floss, a couple candy bar wrappers, several small glass pipettes. They were becoming garbage collectors, Ruby thought, remembering the bag she pulled from under Lydia's cubicle.

"Well, now, let's see what we have," Mrs. Whitmore said, separating the pipettes from the other garbage with a butter knife. "I wonder if . . . I don't quite see . . . Did you find . . ."

"Glass vials," said Ruby. "Isn't that what those are?"

"Well, yes. I mean, no. How did you know about the vials?"

Ruby pointed to the Rama Jr. folder in front of the older woman, who smiled and shook her head. "Oh dear, very good. But those aren't the type of vials I was looking to find. Those are pipettes from the lab. What I wanted—"

"'Scuse me." Rex was standing up, digging into his pockets. "What about these?"

With cupped hands, he gently deposited about a dozen tiny glass bottles in the center of the table.

"Hey," Ruby said. "Where'd you get all those?"

"That hole in the wall by the sink—you see that?" Rex said. "I had no idea which glass vials she wanted. Looks like we carried around all that garbage for nothing."

With trembling hands, Mrs. Whitmore lined up the vials side by side; there were eleven of them. "Is that all you found, dear?"

Rex checked his pockets again. "Alls I got, right there. I mighta left some down in there. I was a little rushed."

The older woman removed her glasses, leaned over the table, and put her face up close to the vials.

"My eyes aren't so good, even with my reading glasses," she mumbled to herself.

For days she had imagined exactly this moment. Fantasized about it, let herself believe it could happen, against everything: the odds, the children's inexperience, her long history of disappointment.

"Oh my, it has to be here," she said—and her face warmed, her vision blurred, she felt like she was about to burst out into tears; the last thing she would remember was thinking *Oh, of all things* before all went dark.

24

A DEADLY PRESCRIPTION

"It's OK, Mrs. Whitmore, it's OK, it's OK," Ruby was saying when the woman's eyes opened.

"What . . . ? How long . . . ?" she said, one hand reflexively reaching to her neck for her glasses. Still there, all fine; and she remembered.

How she always got dizzy when her emotions ran high. How Rama Sr. had interpreted her fainting as weakness, rather than the revving of instincts, the intoxicating surge of excitement and deduction. How long had it been since she had known a dose of that drug?

And this time, her fellow investigators weren't shutting her out, but bringing her back in.

She blinked at Ruby, nodded at Rex, then finally lifted her head. "Oh my, oh my—I thank you, my child—I am fine, will be quite fine," Mrs. Whitmore said, smiling at the absurdity of it all. "I think we did it. You must know that by my reaction. You did it!"

"Did what?" Rex said.

"Have a look at those vials," she said, almost fully revived now. "Tell me what they are."

Ruby and Rex each picked up one of the glass containers and stared at the labels. *"Insulara,"* read Ruby. "OK. What's that?"

"It's a brand of insulin," Mrs. Whitmore explained. "Insulin is a substance that helps the body's cells absorb the energy from food that they need to survive. People whose bodies don't produce enough insulin to keep tissues healthy have a disease called diabetes, and usually need to inject themselves with the drug more than once a day.

"Dr. Ramachandran was diabetic; it was right there on the coroner's report, if you recall. Now, tell me if any of these vials is different from the others."

Rex saw something. "This one here looks like maybe it's the only one with some stuff still in it."

"Pass it to me. Carefully, please." Mrs. Whitmore took the small vial, held it up to the light, tipped it, and pointed to the small amount of fluid pooling in the bottom edge. She then studied the top of the vial, which had a white rubber top, through which the needle passed.

"Huh," she said. "That checks out; only one hole in the top. Tell me: Do any of the other vials have two holes in the top? Look very closely. A syringe hole can be almost invisible."

Ruby and Rex took turns examining each vial. "No, ma'am, none has two holes."

"None?" Staring at her hands now. *None.* Her whole body went cold. She told herself to shake it off, not let it show. "OK, OK. It was too much to hope for. We're so close."

"What? What do the two holes mean?" Ruby said.

The old woman placed one of the vials gently in the middle of the table and sat back. Took another deep breath. *Must not faint again,* she thought. *The whole neighborhood will be in here, including Paulette's cousin the tribal healer, waving some foul weed over my head.*

"Listen to me for a minute," she said. No one made a sound. "The great Dr. V. S. Ramachandran did not die from chokecherry, nor from that delicate beauty, deadly nightshade. He did not ingest enough of either to be so deadly on their own so fast."

"But the monkshood . . . ," Ruby said.

"The murderer's one mistake. Poor Roman—and yes, I agree that it was he, through Lydia, who framed your father, Ruby—and he is the only regular worker who was in the building and unaccounted for at the time the poisons were put into Rama's tea."

"So that's it, then? We've known that a long time."

"No. Roman could not have procured an extra dose of monkshood beyond what was in the Toxin Archive. He wouldn't know how. No, someone else put him up to it, someone in the know, and that someone needed the poisons to *appear* deadly."

"Even the larger dose, though?" Rex said. "We showed Rama had more in his blood than was in the red vials—how's that not going to hurt you?"

"True, child. Our calculations indeed showed that Dr. Rama ingested a stronger dose of monkshood—and that poison undoubtedly contributed to his death. But let's stop and think. Ruby, kindly remind me what you learned about monkshood poison. About the timing."

"That it takes between ten minutes and hours to be the cause of death, depending on the amount ingested and the individual."

"Correct. And what does that mean, Rex, for our killer? If you really wanted Rama dead, would you bet your life—and it would be your life, if caught—that Roman's monkshood cocktail would do the job?"

"No, ma'am, not me. If something goes wrong, or it takes too long, someone down there's gonna find the man and treat him."

"In that lab, they'd know what happened," Ruby said. "Especially with those red vials missing from the archive."

"Exactly. This is DeWitt, one of the most famous toxicology labs in the world," Mrs. Whitmore said. "Its scientists know poisons and could have had Rama in the hospital within minutes. Besides, there would be no way for the killer to know whether Rama even drank all his tea. No way to be sure. And our killer had to be sure."

All eyes again shifted to the tiny glass vial on the table.

"Insulin," said Ruby.

"Yes. Rama routinely injected five units of Insulara, as the empty vials show. But look at the dates on the bottles: The only one missing is the second dose on that Friday."

"So?"

"So, a stronger dose of insulin could be deadly within minutes. And the beauty of it is that Rama injects it himself. That's why I was looking for a vial with two holes. One puncture made by the killer, drawing out the regular dose of insulin and replacing it through the same hole with a more concentrated dose. And the other puncture from Rama himself."

"But . . . ?" said Rex.

"Think about it. The old scientist gulps down his tea as usual at 6:15 or so, not long after Roman doses it. Soon he's feeling awful. Stomachache, headache, probably some dizziness. What's his first thought? That he needs his next shot of insulin."

"So he didn't call for help because he thought he had the cure," Ruby said.

"Precisely. And a short-acting dose of insulin would be out of his system before the toxicologists had a chance to fully investigate."

"But he must keep a whole bunch of those vials in his office or wherever," Rex said. "How's anybody gonna know he picks out that one special extra-strong vial?"

"Because many diabetics keep their medicine in cases and take the doses sequentially; it's all marked on the case. Rama was undoubtedly one of those, given how organized he was."

Ruby said, "But—I mean—we don't even have the vial with two holes. How do we know for sure any of this theory is true?"

"We don't, Ruby. It is, at the moment, just a theory, as you say."

"You mean to tell me," Rex said, "that we crawled over kingdom come, almost got captured in the morgue, dragged that stupid garbage bag all around all night—and we got nothing?"

"No, not nothing. You may not have found that one incriminating vial, that's true. That was the smoking gun I was hoping for. But you got something just as good."

"What?" Rex said.

"Someone's attention. The killer by now has to assume you do have the smoking gun."

She removed a lapel pin from her sweater, picked up one of the used vials, and punctured it again. "And right now, that person will do anything to get it back."

25

SETTING THE TRAP

Planting the bait was the easy part. Speculation about the Rama case was everywhere, in blogs and even on several web pages devoted to "Rama clues." Most of the conclusions were empty guesswork, but enough real information surfaced in those forums that everyone interested in the case was checking in.

"Not a problem at all," Sharon said when asked whether she could plant an anonymous tip online.

Later that evening, Rex and Ruby escorted her down College Avenue. "How far are we going?" Sharon kept asking, and the answer was all the way to Neville's. The shop's owner had a pay-as-you-go computer for his customers and anyone who walked in. Untraceable.

Ruby watched as Sharon cut and pasted into a half-dozen forums a simple note written by Mrs. Whitmore:

Note to a special witness: I have something of yours. Small, glass, with two holes in the top. Science Library study room closest to lab school; corner windowsill, tomorrow.

"That's it? You're done?" Ruby said as Sharon ended her brief session.

"Don't want to spend any more time in this place than I have to," she said. "Reeks in here."

Ruby and Rex met Sharon and Simon as soon as school opened, an hour before the bell. They knew the Science Library study room was empty most of the day.

The children scouted the hallway between the library and the Lab School to make sure no one was watching them.

"All clear, as far as I can tell," Simon said.

He and Rex stood guard outside the study room while Ruby and Sharon set a simple trap. The vial was in plain view on the windowsill for anyone who was looking. Across the room, Sharon set up her open laptop, its video camera running. Anyone who tried to snag the vial would be caught on tape.

"OK, cross your fingers," Ruby said. "Meet back in class. Try to be casual."

It was almost impossible to do. Midway through first period, as Mrs. Patterson tried to guide yet another discussion based on the reading ("What is cheating?"), Ruby and the other three were exchanging anxious looks every five seconds.

Sharon passed Ruby her smartphone, which had a direct feed to the laptop in the study room. Ruby concealed the phone in her lap and checked it again and again; she could easily make out both the windowsill and the open door into the room. And in just a few minutes there was a visitor: Victor!

Was it? It was: Victor was peeking into the room; the shape of his body and his longish black hair were unmistakable. And now he was gone—he hadn't even entered the room.

A few minutes later someone else showed up: Wade stole a glance in, looked back over his shoulder, and was gone. What was happening? People were stopping by to look, was what. Dean Touhy did, and five minutes later so did Grace. By the end of the first lesson Lydia had shown up, along with several other students. *Great,* thought Ruby. *The trap is too good. Everyone but Rama himself is making an appearance!*

By the end of the second period—Ruby had to read out loud, barely pulled it off—the four conspirators stood and approached Mrs. Patterson in unison, asking for permission to spend free time in the study room. "If you're going to study, of course," she said. "It's called the study room for a reason."

Ruby was the first one in. "It's gone! Sharon, quick, check the laptop—"

"Gone," Sharon said.

"You surely jest," Simon said.

"Jest's on us once again," Rex said. "We got cleaned out. Schooled up, down, and sideways. Looks like game over, at least for today."

"Not quite, Rex," said Sharon. She had her cell phone out. "Please be on, please be on—yes!"

"Tell us already."

"The computer. I'm always losing it. My dad installed at GPS tracker. It's still in the building."

"Where?"

"Can't tell; signal gets strong when you get closer. We got to move."

"Campus police right down the hall," Rex said. "This is their job—you just got your computer jacked. That's a crime, too. C'mon."

Luck again: Officer Cain, the man on duty down the hall, knew and liked Ruby's father. He took their complaint seriously, called it in, and nodded to Sharon. "OK, young lady, let's see if that gizmo works. Track away."

Sharon hurried toward the library first, stopped, U-turned,

and started the other way, back toward the main campus. Down one hall, the five of them hit the stairs half running.

"Let's get outside; it works better sometimes," Sharon said.

Sunny and cold, a quiet late-fall morning. The group ran in front of DeWitt, out across its great lawn. The farther toward the university side they got, the stronger the signal became.

"We got someone at the parking garage. Come in," Officer Cain said into his radio. "Sanchez. Good, good. No one drives out, man, got it? Check. We're on our way."

At the entrance to the underground garage, Ruby saw an officer (had to be Sanchez) standing outside the parking kiosk, arguing with a driver. Now patiently explaining; it looked like one of the older professors.

Another car pulled up just as Officer Cain and his escorts arrived. A white SUV, it pulled around to the other side of the kiosk and tried to pass.

"Easy does it, hoss." Officer Sanchez was blocking the way; now Officer Cain approached the driver's door. Ruby, Rex, and their friends stood back as a group, near the kiosk. The glare off the windshield obscured the driver.

Ruby looked at Sharon, who mouthed, *Got it.*

"All right, all right, very sorry to detain you, sir," Cain was saying. He pulled a laptop with a purple stripe on it from the car. Sharon's.

Now the two officers were stationed on each side of the car. "I'm very sorry," Cain said again, "I'm sure it's a misunderstanding, but I'm going to have to ask you to step out of the car, Dean."

And there he was, out in the sun.

A bell chimed in a distant recess of Ruby's memory. Back in the lawyer's office, her father mentioning in passing that Dean Touhy and Rama both had heart problems due to diabetes. Touhy. Dean Tubby. Touhy saying that her father would be cleared because he, the dean, knew that someone else in the lab had actually tried to poison Dr. Rama . . . Roman.

Touhy, who had absolute power over Roman because he could drop both Lydia and the poor janitor from DeWitt with a wave of his hand. No wonder the old janitor sounded so scared in that argument with Lydia in Davenport Towers.

"Oh," Ruby said. "That was him in the morgue, Rex. The man."

"Tubby, Tubby, Tubby," said Rex, shaking his head. "You a bad man, ain't you?"

"No wonder he was frantic when they found the body, throwing himself down on the floor," Ruby said.

"Trying to get his vial back," Rex said. "Little did he know it was buried in the bushes."

Ruby smiled at the others as the dean stole a look back at

them. Touhy apparently knew when Rama took his shot. But he did not know, nor could he control, *where* he took it. The real smoking-gun vial was almost certainly back in that hole in the wall in the little bathroom.

"But," Ruby said, "why?"

"Desperation and money," Mrs. Whitmore said when the four friends met her for lunch (they got a short day, because of the excitement).

"Now, we cannot prove it, of course, but remember that Rama died just before he was going to make an announcement on the Robert Pelham case. We know that DeWitt had money invested with Mr. Pelham, and we know that the university somehow was repaid after the man's business began to collapse. Many other investors did not get their money out."

She sat back, looked around the group of four students, now gathered closely around a table at Paulette's.

"So how is that a motive?" Simon said.

"It's more like a trade gone bad, I think. DeWitt gets its money back, and Mr. Pelham gets his freedom. Touhy knew how to contaminate the evidence discreetly; surely he knew that Rama would be on vacation. But when the famous V. S. Ramachandran began nosing around what happened, Touhy knew that he was in grave danger."

"Couldn't the dean just say it was a mistake?" Rex said. "Or get a lawyer and argue, you know, that he didn't do it?"

"He could have, Rex," Mrs. Whitmore said, after taking a sip of coffee. "But the bad publicity alone would have taken him out of that job, at a minimum. To have his credibility questioned, especially his credibility in forensics—well. Imagine the headlines: 'DeWitt Scientists Linked to Evidence Tampering.' DeWitt would have moved swiftly. And Dean Touhy knew it."

"But how do you know all this for sure?" Sharon said. She had not taken her eyes off of Mrs. Whitmore.

"Honey, I don't. I cannot be absolutely sure. The trial will clarify some of these things. But I know that we—that you all, you four investigators—I sure know that you got the right man."

"Why else," Ruby said, "would a freaking dean swipe a laptop with a purple stripe on it?"

INT: OK, OK, let's finish the statement. I don't need you speculating any more about motive. I just needed to know how you came to flush out Dean Touhy.

SUBJ: Yes, well. Now you know.

INT: I do. And with that, I'll say thank you, ma'am, and remind you again that you have been under oath. Let the record reflect that this statement was closed at three in the afternoon, November fifth—

SUBJ: One thing, detective.

INT: Yes, ma'am.

SUBJ: So what did you find out about Paul Touhy? And about Roman and Lydia?

INT: Nice try.

SUBJ: Oh, what harm is in it? The charges will be public soon. I'm an old woman, detective. Is it too much to want to know if my instincts were correct?

INT: (audible sigh) You don't quit, do you? Yes,

this information will be public shortly, and you didn't hear it from me. It's between a detective and a forensic scientist.

SUBJ: As you say.

INT: Yes, I do say. It appears to have happened just as you and your junior investigators suspected. Roman tried to poison Rama after hearing—from Touhy—that Lydia was failing out. Lydia wanted no part of it, but by the time she saw Roman that night, it was too late. She chose to cover for her uncle and frame Mr. Rose, and she will face charges.

SUBJ: Oh my. And the dean?

INT: Our Dean Touhy did in fact tamper with evidence in the Pelham case. That's how it appears at this point. Ramachandran found out. Dean Touhy's choices weren't good ones.

SUBJ: (barely audible) Whose are, really?

INT: Now, I have a question for you. If you don't mind?

SUBJ: No, of course not.

INT: That drawing on the wall, above your couch. College Avenue and the Terrace Apartments. Did she do that?

SUBJ: She did.

INT: And that's you, is it, the woman sitting up in
    that ninth-floor window?

SUBJ: Oh. Well, I don't know, detective. But if
    it is, I must say, it's not very up-to-date. I
    hardly have time to sit by my window most days.
    I've been teaching Mr. Rose about toxins, you
    see, and I help out at Rex's apartment with the
    young ones. You know, what with Rex spending so
    much time with Simon, and Ruby at Sharon's, I'm
    starting to feel very, I don't know . . .

INT: Busy?

SUBJ: Well, yes, I suppose so.

INT: Huh. I could swear you said you were retired.

END TAPE.

ACKNOWLEDGMENTS

I would like to thank the small group of stand-up friends, colleagues, and allies who made this book doable. Start with Kris Dahl, my agent, who took on this book and another long-shot title in a genre that barely exists: children's science mysteries; Sheila Keenan, whose good cheer and excellent suggestions turned a good idea for a story into a complete tale, with real characters; Susan Van Metre, who has loved the whole idea of kids' science mysteries from the beginning, and this story in particular; Betsy Spratt, who made sure the forensic science was correct and the lab plausible; John Hastings, for being a friend, reader, and editor; Maria Middleton, for the superb book design; and Jason Wells and Mary Ann Zissimos, for putting the word out.

As always, thanks to Isabel, Flora, and Victoria, and to the Careys: Kate, Jim, Rachel, Simon, and Noah.

ABOUT THE AUTHOR

Benedict Carey is a reporter who has written about medicine and science in magazines and newspapers for more than twenty-five years. He graduated from the University of Colorado with a degree in math, and from Northwestern University with a master's in journalism. He now works as a science reporter for the *New York Times*. He lives in a suburb of New York City.

This book was designed by Maria T. Middleton. The text is set in 12-point Adobe Garamond, a typeface based on those created in the sixteenth century by Claude Garamond. Garamond modeled his typefaces on ones created by Venetian printers at the end of the fifteenth century. The modern version used in this book was designed by Robert Slimbach, who studied Garamond's historic typefaces at the Plantin-Moretus Museum in Antwerp, Belgium. The display typeface is Insignia.

pity party

pity party

BY
KATHLEEN LANE

LITTLE, BROWN AND COMPANY

NEW YORK BOSTON

Little, Brown and Company
Hachette Book Group
1290 Avenue of the Americas, New York, NY 10104
Visit us at LBYR.com

First Edition: January 2021

Little, Brown and Company is a division of Hachette Book Group, Inc. The Little, Brown name and logo are trademarks of Hachette Book Group, Inc.

The publisher is not responsible for websites (or their content) that are not owned by the publisher.

Library of Congress Cataloging-in-Publication Data
Names: Lane, Kathleen, 1967– author. Title: Pity party : stories / by Kathleen Lane. Description: First edition. | New York : Little, Brown and Company, 2021. | Audience: Ages 8-12. | Summary: "A grab bag of deliciously dark short fiction set in middle school that explores anxieties and twists them into funny, resonant, and reassuring psychological thrills"— Provided by publisher. Identifiers: LCCN 2020005648 | ISBN 9780316417365 (hardcover) | ISBN 9780316417358 (ebook) | ISBN 9780316417389 (ebook other) Subjects: LCSH: Middle school students—Juvenile fiction. | Children's stories. | CYAC: Middle schools—Fiction. | Schools—Fiction. | Short stories. Classification: LCC PZ7.L2501 Pit 2021 | DDC [Fic] —dc23
LC record available at https://lccn.loc.gov/2020005648 ISBNs: 978-0-316-41736-5 (hardcover), 978-0-316-41735-8 (ebook)

ISBNs: 978-0-316-41736-5 (hardcover), 978-0-316-41735-8 (ebook)

Printed in Canada

MRQ-T

10 9 8 7 6 5 4 3 2 1

To you.

You are cordially

invited

Dear weird toes

crooked nose

stressed out, left out

freaked out

Dear strep throat, chicken pox

ate a moldy muffin

stepped in poison oak

Dear lost sweatshirt

Dear lost dog

Dear didn't make the team

didn't get the part

didn't pass the test

Dear just moved to this town

Dear desperate to get out of this town

Dear missing parts, broken hearts
picked on, passed up
misunderstood
sitting alone
Dear ADD, ADHD, OCD
WX, Y and Z
Dear everyone
Dear you
You are cordially invited
Come as you are
Help yourself to the cake
Spin your troubles round the dance floor
This party's for you

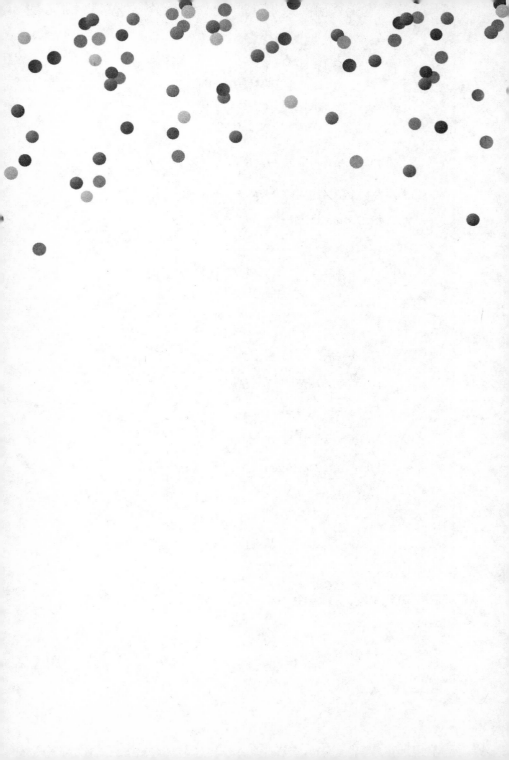

The Voice

Part I

For as long as Katya could remember, The Voice had been with her. Her earliest memory: Three years old, returning from an afternoon at the pond with her older sister, she had ridden her tricycle directly into the street. Over the growl of an approaching truck, The Voice came to her, loud and clear. PEDAL PEDAL PEDAL, it said. FASTER, it said, *FASTER*, until Katya's tiny legs had spun her safely to the other side. No more than a second later, the truck sped by. Had it not been for The Voice, she most certainly would have been flattened under the truck's enormous wheels.

Recalling the event later, Katya would often imagine a flattened version of herself next to a flattened version of her tricycle. It was not a horrible image. There was no blood involved, no broken bones, not even so much as a scratch. She was simply flat. Like the peel-and-stick books she had always loved but rarely received (except for the worn-out, fuzz-covered hand-me-downs from her older cousins). Sometimes Katya would imagine peeling herself off the page of her own life and placing herself in an altogether different life. A fancier life filled with fancier things.

She imagined flattened versions of her sister and parents too, and her dog Mudjo, and in their peel-and-stick world, she and her family and Mudjo would travel to exotic places, where they rode flattened elephants and ate flattened cakes under flattened chandeliers. Her mother wore brightly colored flattened sun hats. Her father: flattened safari shorts, a chatty flattened parakeet riding on his shoulder—at least, she imagined him chatty, revealing the locations of buried treasures, demanding crackers in return. Mudjo always had a flattened bone between his paws. He made friends with a flattened monkey. Gone were her parents' worries about money, their fights in the kitchen over who worked harder, who spent more of their earnings on unnecessary things.

In this peel-and-stick world, Katya had little need for The Voice, and when it came time to leave this imagined life behind, she was older and more capable of looking out for herself. She knew better than to ride her bike into traffic. She had long ago mastered the dangers of the house, learned to stand upwind of campfires, learned (the hard way) not to poke blueberries up her nose. Only very occasionally did The Voice return, to warn her of an unfriendly dog, or sometimes person, but as the months passed, she heard fewer and fewer of its warnings. Which is why she was so startled when, as she sat on the living room floor before her record-setting haul of Halloween candy, unwrapping a 3 Musketeers, The Voice suddenly called out: STOP! DO NOT EAT THAT 3 MUSKETEERS!

Only then did Katya remember. That day at school she had overheard Jonah Michaels talking about people who put poison in Halloween candy.

DO YOU KNOW EVERY SINGLE PERSON WHO GAVE YOU THAT CANDY? The Voice asked.

The Voice was right! There could be poison in any one of these candies!

Once again The Voice had saved her life.

That night, The Voice slept in Katya's room. It was like a slumber party, except the kind of slumber party that isn't very fun. Like when you sleep over at your much younger cousin's house and have to pretend you're squirrel sisters. Or like the kind of slumber party where you're awakened every half hour by the family's grandfather clock, and just when you're about to finally fall asleep, a cat walks across your face. That's the kind of slumber party it was. The kind that felt to Katya like it would never, ever end.

(To be continued.)

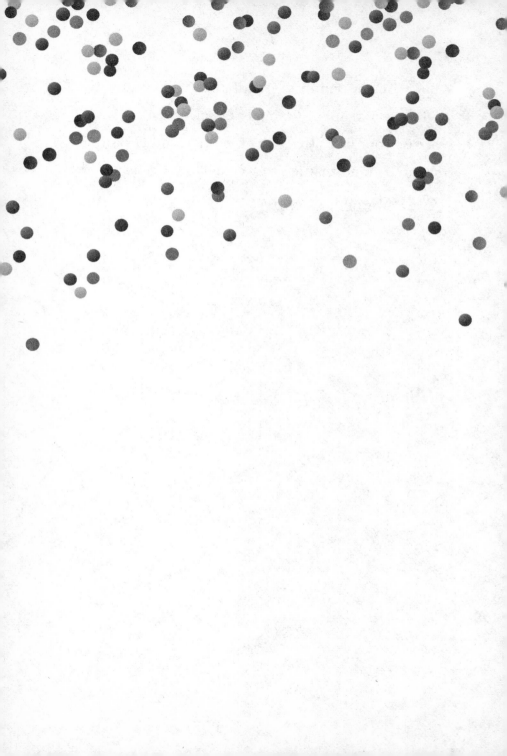

Odd

Immediately Julian knew that something was not right. He could feel it all over his body. And then he saw it. *That.* His head spun at the thought of how close he had come to stepping on it—he came *this* close.

Twenty-two dirty grey steps down to the subway, that's how many there were supposed to be—there were *always* twenty-two dirty grey steps. Today, though, there were twenty-one dirty grey steps and one very shiny grey step with not one scratch or spot of dirt on it anywhere.

This shiny step meant that Julian now had a problem. There was only one step like it, and one meant odd, and odd numbers were the very worst numbers. Odd numbers made everything all wrong.

However, if Julian were to step *over* that one shiny step, he would then have to step over a second step in order to make it two steps that he stepped over, and the very obvious problem with stepping over a second step is that this second step would be a grey step: a *single* grey step: *one* grey step: *odd*.

Julian's therapist, if she were here with him, would not only make him step on that one shiny step, which now appeared to be floating and swirling before his eyes, but she would make him say the number out loud. Sometimes, in her office, she made him read an entire list of numbers—terrible numbers—*odd* numbers. And every time, she would say, "See, Julian? Did anything bad happen?"

This was a difficult question to answer because, in a way, something bad *did* happen. There was the shaky dizzy feeling, and the cold sweaty feeling, followed by a tightness in his head, as if a giant hand had grabbed hold of his skull and squeezed. And always in that moment, Julian found it difficult to breathe, as if another giant hand had grabbed hold of his throat.

His therapist also liked to say, "Next time it will be even easier," when he had never agreed to it being easy in the first place. And anyway, this was also untrue. Never was it ever any easier the next time.

It was difficult enough to just sort out which was worse—step *on* that one shiny step (awful) or step *over* that one shiny step (horrible)—because both possibilities gave him an equally terrible feeling in his head and chest. And so Julian felt it best to wait for a while, at least until the terrible feeling passed.

This presented an entirely new problem, however.

There were certain people from Julian's school who also rode this subway, certain people who knew about his preference for even numbers, and if those certain people were to find him just standing here on the stairs, they might suspect that he was counting, which could lead to any number of possible cruelties, such as whispering odd numbers—or worse, *odd*—into his ear, as they had been known to do.

To avoid such a fate, Julian brought a notebook out from his backpack and looked at it with great concentration, as if he were puzzling out the most challenging of math equations—though why would he choose to work on his math homework while standing on the subway steps? No, what he was doing instead was searching his notebook for something...a paper he was to bring home...a paper that he just realized he might have accidentally left in his locker and so it was very important that he stop here on these subway stairs to search his notebook.

"What's the worst that could happen?" That was another of his therapist's favorite things to say. "Will the world end if you eat five potato chips instead of four?"

Personally, Julian did not feel that she was

qualified to be his therapist because she had zero experience. Yes, she had college degrees—an odd number of them hanging on her wall—but she did not have any *real* experience. She did not know anything at all about being Julian.

Also, how did she know that the world would not come to an end? Was she an expert on world endings?

Oof. Someone just bumped into Julian and he nearly fell onto the shiny step!

It was a guy from school who did it, and now he was grinning, so Julian was pretty sure that he did it on purpose. Jake—that was his name. Jake P.

Julian waited for Jake to reach the bottom of the stairs and turn for the tunnel, and then he waited for these two girls from his school to pass by. They were not girls who knew about his counting, and Julian preferred to keep it that way.

It almost seemed as if Julian's therapist herself had arranged to have this one step cleaned and polished, just so he would be forced to step on it. Just so he would finally learn that nothing bad could come of an odd number.

Fine! He would do it. He would step on that shiny step. It wasn't as if he had much choice. The sky was beginning to darken, and soon his parents would grow worried.

He just had to check two things in his notebook and then he would do it. He would step on that shiny step.

He just had to check four things first and then he would totally do it.

Just six things.

Just eight things and then for sure he would do it.

Two deep breaths in, two deep breaths out.

Four deep breaths in, four deep breaths out.

Now for his foot. Foot out...foot out a little farther...just a little farther. And lower...lower... lower...

And this is where our story ends. For, as Julian had predicted—just as he had told his therapist so many times—as soon as his foot touched down upon that single shiny step, the sky went dark, the planets dropped like fallen apples, the trees and flowers drew themselves back into the earth, space and time collapsed into one (the most dreadful of all odd numbers), and the world as we know it came to a sudden end.

Are your ears too high? Of course they are. Are your eyes too small? Anyone can see that. Do you wish you had a cuter chin? Perkier earlobes? More stylish nostrils?

You're in luck! Thanks to Happy Head®, *True Head Happiness*™ *is just a slip and a zip away.*™®

Sure, ordinary heads are fine for running track or rescuing wounded animals, but what about the important things in life like being irresistibly cute?

Tired of looking concerned when someone tells you their troubles? **Good news!** Thanks to Happy Head®'s **super-toxic no-fade lacquer finish**, you'll be smiling all the time, even when you're hysterically crying. Yes, with Happy Head®, you'll never have to emotionally exert yourself again. *Because real emotions can really wear you down.*™

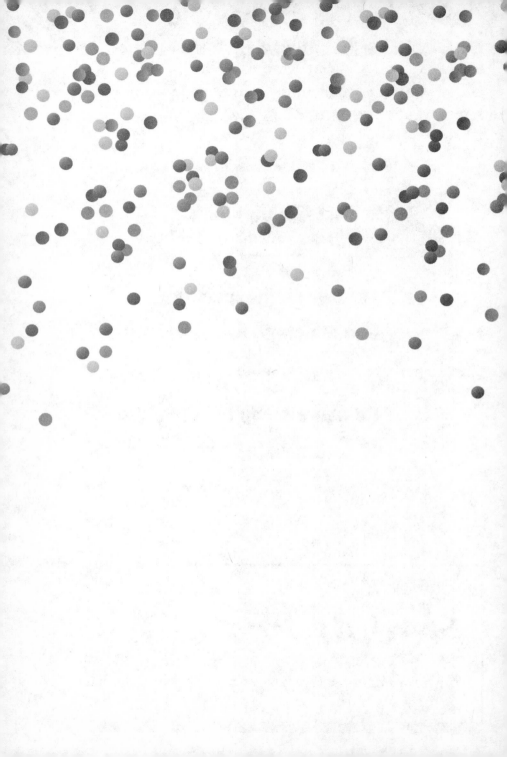

CHOOSE YOUR OWN CATASTROPHE

You are walking through a field when suddenly you fall into a deep pit. Fortunately—miraculously—you have not broken any limbs. Though you must have fallen thirty feet, you have only a small scratch on your arm to show for it. You cannot see this scratch—it is so dark inside the pit that you can barely make out your own hands—but you can feel the sting of it just below your elbow.

Patting the ground around you, you discover what

feels to be a shoe, a skull-sized rock, a matchbook, and a pile of wood.

 If you would like to toss the skull-sized rock around, just for a bit of fun, turn to page 65.

 If you would like to try on the shoe to see if it fits, turn to page 85.

 If you would like to use the matchbook and wood to light a fire so you can see more of your surroundings and possibly find your way out of the pit, turn to page 107.

 If you would like to sit and do nothing because if you stay in the pit long enough to be discovered on the brink of death, it would be a really cool story to tell your friends and might even go viral, turn to page 143.

Ugly Duck

———

Duck was especially ugly today, her splotchy spots brightened by the morning light angling into the fish tank. Yes, the angling light also highlighted the poo swirling through the water, but Cora only had eyes for Duck—the fish that all of Cora's classmates agreed was the ugliest of the tank, her jaw jutting out farther than those of the other "normal" fish and her spots, according to many of Cora's classmates, the color of puke. But to Cora's eyes, Duck's spots were the magical green of the moss that clung beardlike from the trees in Forest Park.

Though Cora's (now least favorite) aunt had once said, on the death of Cora's betta fish, Betty, "Well, at least fish don't have feelings," and Cora's (now least favorite) uncle had added, "Not the brightest creatures on the planet either," Cora knew better. Fish just had their own way of communicating, and from Cora's experience, it was a much better way than how most humans communicated. Like her aunt and uncle, for instance. Like Naomi and all of Naomi's friends. If only people could be more like fish. "Right, Duck?" Cora whispered, and Duck, in her own wordless, lippy way, agreed.

"Hi Cora."

Of course it would be Naomi. Of course she would be the one to interrupt Cora's perfectly peaceful moment. And of course she would just stand there, as she always did, waiting for Cora to cautiously say hi back, because maybe this would be the moment when Naomi Parsons would finally be nice to her again, like when they were younger—back before, for reasons Cora never understood, everything changed. But no. As soon as Cora allowed a quiet "hi" to escape her lips, Naomi ever-so-casually, using only the tip of her pinky, tipped the bottle of fish food off the table, and a thousand flakes scattered out across the floor.

As Cora could have predicted if she had given it a moment's thought, Naomi's next move was to announce, for all to hear—especially Mr. Blevins, who was up at the front of the classroom looking over papers—"Cora, you better clean that up before Mr. Blevins sees!"

Mr. Blevins stood up from his desk to get a look at the mess of fish food on his floor. He sighed in that way that teachers sigh when they want you to know how disappointed they are, and oh how Cora hated to disappoint her teachers. "It's okay, Cora," he said with another sigh. "Just get it cleaned up before class."

"But I—"

"Here, let me help you," Naomi said, kicking flakes in Cora's direction.

And once again, Cora could not think of what to say. Later she would come up with the perfect words: *By knocking over the bottle again? Is that how you're going to "help" me?*—said just loud enough for Mr. Blevins to hear. In that awful moment, though, she could only manage to stare at Naomi's lip-glossed mouth, those sticky lips smiling in that way that appeared so sweet to others, but Cora knew better.

When she had finished gathering the flakes into a paper towel, she said her silent goodbye to Duck, who seemed to be looking at her with a sad expression, her lips even more frowny than usual, and Cora couldn't help but wish that it was Naomi who was the sad one for once, wish that it was Naomi who was ugly, that it was Naomi whose face was covered in puke-colored spots. Then she would know. Then she would finally understand what it felt like to be Cora and Duck.

* * *

At lunch, Jaylah whispered, "You heard about Naomi?"

"No, and I don't care," Cora said, digging her thumbnail into a grape and splitting it in two. She assumed Naomi had won another award or managed to get yet another boy to fall in love with her.

"She went home with some weird face thing." Jaylah took a bite of her sandwich. The white bread and peanut butter made a gluey ball that stuck behind her front teeth. "Thum kind of ayergic reaction."

"Yeah, well, she'll probably just get more attention for it," Cora said, sliding the remainder of her grapes and sandwich over to Jaylah. Naomi's name always had a way of making Cora lose her appetite.

Jaylah, on the other hand, never lost her appetite. "Well, at least she can't torture you anymore," she said, diving straight into Cora's half-eaten ham and cheese. "I mean, until she gets better."

A break from Naomi's torture, how nice that

would be. If only Naomi hadn't trained all her many friends in the art of tormenting Cora. And one of them, the worst of them, Jodi—who apparently had been eavesdropping on their conversation from the nearby popular table—just dropped a note on top of Cora's head, which then went sliding down her bangs, bounced off her nose, and landed on her lap.

"What's it say?" Jaylah said, but of course she was already reading it for herself. *I'd rather be all spoty than look like you, Baggie.*

"If you're going to insult people," Jaylah shouted to Jodi, who had linked arms with two of her friends and was now walking off (laughing) (at Cora's expense), "you should at least learn how to spell!" Then to Cora, "*Baggie?* Seriously? What does that even mean?"

But Cora knew what it meant. As with all their names for her, she could always find a reason they were true. In this case, it was true that she wore baggy clothes, which she preferred to the tight-fitting jeans that Naomi and her friends wore. Baggy clothes were more comfortable. Baggy clothes hid the fact that she had a middle-aged woman's behind, and the last thing she needed was Naomi and friends making fun of her behind.

Why? thought Cora, watching through stinging eyes as Jodi and her friends disappeared into the hall. *Why couldn't they all just leave her alone?* How she wished, oh how she wished, that Jodi would catch whatever Naomi had and be sent home too. A break from *both* Naomi and Jodi—wouldn't that be nice.

Half the cafeteria ran out into the hall when they heard the scream. Jaylah would have run out too if Cora hadn't held her back. Instead Cora sat stiff in her seat and waited for the noise to die down. Only when she felt sure that enough time had passed, after the last locker had slammed shut, after the class bell had faded, did they finally venture into the hall—where, unfortunately, they ventured directly into two of Naomi's friends. Clara with her new pink hair and Marquita with her bandanna thing were standing outside the nurse's station—obviously waiting for Jodi. "What are *you* staring at, Ugly?" Clara said. She was talking, of course, to Cora. For reasons neither Cora nor Jaylah understood, Naomi and her friends only ever picked on Cora.

Ugly. That, Cora would say, was also true, and it hurt in a deeper way than the other insults because it wasn't all wrapped up in cleverness. Clara was too preoccupied to come up with a more original insult, and so it was what it was. And as Cora stood staring at Clara's nose, mostly to avoid Clara's eyes, how she wished that Clara's nose, that her whole face, were covered in those pukey spots. Then she would know what ugly felt like. And as Cora and Jaylah walked toward their next classes, a fresh new wave of screams followed them down the hall.

That afternoon, the school nurse, Ms. Kelly, came into Cora's science class to talk about the "health situation."

It wasn't at all funny how she said it, but for some reason Cora could barely keep from laughing—and the more Ms. Kelly went on about this "somewhat mysterious virus" and how it "seemed to mostly affect the facial region," the more little squeaks and sputters escaped her lips. She tried to disguise them in a coughing fit, but this only made it sound as if she were choking on the hilarity of it all. Everybody glared—even Liza, who before Cora had also been tormented by Naomi, though not as badly, not ruthlessly and for no apparent reason.

It was hard to look at Ms. Kelly and not see Mrs. Claus. Her short, round body, her rosy cheeks. She looked as if she bathed in boiling water—probably, Cora imagined, in an attempt to wash away all the germs she encountered each day. "I want you all to know," she said, "that the girls' faces—"

Why did she have to keep saying faces!

"Cora," Ms. Kelly said, "do you think you can control yourself or do you need to visit the office?"

Cora bit down on her tongue. Then, to make

extra certain she would not laugh again, she thought about the dead bird she found outside the school last week. Except for the fact of it being dead, there did not seem to be anything at all wrong with it. For a very long time—maybe longer than she realized—she could not take her eyes off its beautiful blue feathers, its tiny beak, opened just slightly. When she had finally snapped out of her trance, she was sitting cross-legged under the tree, wet seeping through her jeans from the dewy bark chips, and there was Naomi, standing above her, saying, "That's so sad." *Did Naomi Parsons have a heart?* Cora wondered in those brief three seconds before Naomi went on to say, "It must have seen your ugly face."

When Cora's mind returned to the present moment, every muscle in her face was squeezed up into a scowl, and Ms. Kelly was telling the class, "Most likely, yes."

Most likely yes *what*?

"That's why we feel it's best," Ms. Kelly went on, "that the girls stay home for a few days. Until we're absolutely certain they are no longer contagious."

Oh.

"In the meantime, there is absolutely nothing to worry about," Ms. Kelly said. "The girls are being treated at this very moment, and we fully expect them to be back among us next week."

Oh.

Walking home from school that afternoon—alone, unfortunately, because Jaylah had track practice—Cora tried her best to ignore the two voices behind her. The first (Gillian): "We heard about you laughing." The second (Sonya): "You'll pay for that." Gillian: "Looks like you already paid." Sonya: "Yeah, what happened to your face, Maggot?" Gillian: "Maggots, that's what happened." Sonya: laughing. Gillian: "Oh my God, your face!"—which Cora, of course, took to mean her own face, until Sonya said, "What?" and then Sonya said, "Oh my God, *your* face!" and then the two of them were screaming and running past Cora, who unfortunately did not get a good look at their faces, only a blurry view of the sides of their faces, but even so, there was no doubt.

That night in bed, Cora's closed eyelids were like movie screens, playing back the events of the day. How wonderful it had been to spend the afternoon without Naomi and Jodi. How wonderful the thought of school tomorrow without Gillian and Sonya. It was all so perfect. *So* perfect that Cora found herself wishing that the spots would spread to everyone who had ever been unkind to her— every single one of Naomi's friends, for starters, but there was also the doctor who had told her she was acting like a baby, just for crying a little when she got her shot. There was the man at 7-Eleven who had yelled at her for bringing her rabbit inside the store, even though her rabbit was tucked inside her coat where he wasn't bothering anyone. There was her math teacher who had said she wasn't concentrating when she was trying her best—she *really* was.

The list continued into her dreams, and Cora

awoke the next morning with a smile on her face that, if you did not know her well, if you did not know her to be a kind and gentle soul, might have appeared to be just a tiny bit—or maybe a tiny bit more than a tiny bit—wicked.

The morning air was unexpectedly warm, or maybe the warmth was coming directly from Cora, who had the strangest feeling inside as she walked along Elm Street toward school.

It wasn't a bad strange feeling. She might even call it a pleasant strange feeling. The thought of a whole day without Naomi and her friends— the thought of *every* day without Naomi and her friends—the thought of no one ever bothering her again—brought an even bigger, more glorious vision to Cora's mind. Imagine if *every* mean person— every mean person on the *entire planet*—caught this whatever-it-was, this face thing. Just the thought of it, the thrilling thought, brought a warm tingle to Cora's own face.

Outside the school, there did not appear to be the usual crowd of kids waiting for the doors to open, and there were far fewer cars parked out front. If it weren't for Jaylah waiting for her at their usual spot at the top of the steps, Cora might have wondered if she had arrived late, or mistakenly come to school on a Saturday. But then she remembered: Naomi and her friends, maybe *all* her friends—maybe every mean person on the entire planet, as she had wished—had caught the face thing. Imagining their faces, their ugly faces, Cora found herself caught up in another fit of (somewhat wicked-sounding) laughter, causing the few students who had come to school to back away as she rushed up the stairs to Jaylah.

Oh, but Jaylah's face! Something was wrong. Something was terribly wrong. Not with her face, fortunately, but with her eyes—her eyes seemed to grow larger with every approaching step that Cora took.

"Your—" Jaylah said. Fear, that's what it was.

It was fear in Jaylah's eyes as she stared at Cora's cheeks.

"Your—" she tried again, backing away, then turning away, then running away, inside the school, disappearing down the hall, leaving Cora alone on the front steps, with only one wish.

PERSONALITY TEST

Ready to discover valuable insights about your personality? Keep track of your "yes" answers by simply installing a chalkboard in your room, or you can also use your fingers or a piece of paper. Let's begin!

1. **Are you currently a person?**

2. **When you walk into a room, do you tend to be there?**

3. **Does your mind contain thoughts?**

4. **Have you ever laughed, cried, sung a song, and/or said "hi"?**

5. Have you ever responded to another person's comment or question with a comment or question?

6. Have you ever felt an emotion during an emotional time?

7. Are you the sort of person who tends to laugh at humorous things?

8. Do you prefer some things over other things?

9. Do you ever move your limbs in a way that would suggest you are feeling a feeling?

Count the number of questions to which you answered YES, then simply check below to see if you have a personality:

 6–9:

Good news, you have a personality!

 3–5:

You have a personality, but are likely the sort of person who, if you were to find yourself at the bottom of a deep pit, would choose to do nothing, except possibly try on a shoe.

 0–2:

Keep trying! With a little effort, such as yawning when tired, patting a friendly dog, or greeting a greeting with a greeting, you too may soon acquire a personality.

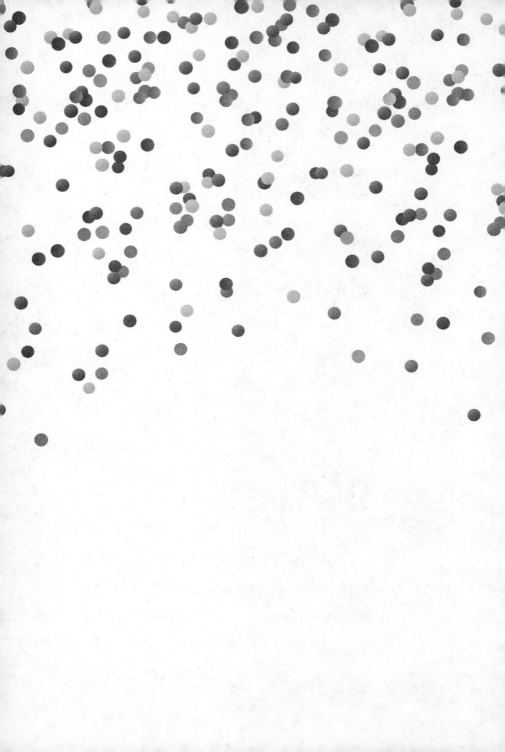

The Voice

Part II

GOOD MORNING, said The Voice. YOU LOOK AWFUL TODAY.

It was true. In the mirror, Katya saw that her face was all wrong. Maybe it was because she had not slept well. Maybe it was because she had slept with her face smashed against the wall again.

NO, said The Voice, THE PROBLEM IS YOUR

FACE. AND IT WILL PROBABLY ONLY GET WORSE.

Worse?

AND WORSE, said The Voice. YOU ARE NOW IN THE TERRIBLE STAGE YOUR HEALTH TEACHER WARNED YOU ABOUT. SOON YOUR FACE WILL BE COVERED IN PIMPLES AND YOU WILL BE IRRITABLE FOR NO REASON. HAVE FUN.

At school Katya could immediately see that The Voice was right. She did look awful. She could tell by the way everyone was looking at her. By the way her friend Mia said, "Are you okay?" To which Katya said, "What? What do you mean?" To which Mia said, "You just have a really weird look on your face." To which Katya said, "Weird?" To which Mia said, "Not bad weird, just weird." But how could weird be anything but bad?

The Voice said, I AGREE WITH YOU. WEIRD CAN ONLY BE BAD. WILL PEOPLE STILL LIKE YOU? MAYBE, MAYBE NOT. IT'S HARD TO SAY.

At lunch The Voice said, YOU KNOW WHAT YOU SHOULD DO? YOU SHOULD SHOW EVERYONE HOW YOU CAN BEND THE TIPS OF YOUR FINGERS.

Katya thought this was a terrible idea. First of all, her friends had all seen this trick before. Second of all, it wasn't that exciting to begin with. It was just something she did sometimes, usually under the table where no one could see. A nervous habit when she was feeling awkward.

On the other hand, The Voice had never been wrong before. And so Katya said, rather abruptly, interrupting the group's conversation about Friday's dance, "Do you want to see how I can bend the tips of my fingers?"

Katya's friends stopped their conversation. First they looked at one another—a bad sign—and then they looked at her. "Um...sure," Mia said. "If you want to." And, not feeling at all good about what she was about to do, Katya lifted her hand up to show them her bent fingertips.

WELL THAT WAS AWKWARD, said The Voice. MAYBE, TO MAKE UP FOR IT, YOU SHOULD INVITE THEM OVER TO YOUR HOUSE TO—I DON'T KNOW—SOMETHING.

Katya said, "Do you want to come over to my house later to—something."

"To *something*?" Sasha said.

"Maybe another time," Mia said.

"Yeah, maybe another time," Sasha said.

ASK THEM IF IT'S BECAUSE THEY DON'T LIKE YOU ANYMORE, said The Voice. THIS COULD BE THE BEGINNING OF NOBODY LIKING YOU.

"Is it because you don't like me anymore?"

"Of course we like you!" Sasha said.

"You're just acting kind of...weird today," Mia said.

The Voice said, SEE, I TOLD YOU THIS WOULD HAPPEN.

Over the next several hours, The Voice presented

Katya with possibilities as to how the rest of her life might go:

EVERYONE WILL STOP LIKING YOU.

AT RECESS YOU WILL WANDER AROUND ALL BY YOURSELF.

YOU WILL GROW VERY LONELY.

YOU WILL CONSIDER GETTING A PET RAT OR FERRET, WHICH YOU WILL HIDE INSIDE YOUR COAT.

YOU WILL BE CALLED RAT GIRL OR FERRET FREAK.

YOU WILL GROW UP TO BE JUST LIKE YOUR AUNT VICKY WHO LIVES ALONE AND TALKS TO SQUIRRELS.

"Are you sure?" Katya whispered.

YES, said The Voice. I'M AFRAID SO.

(To be continued.)

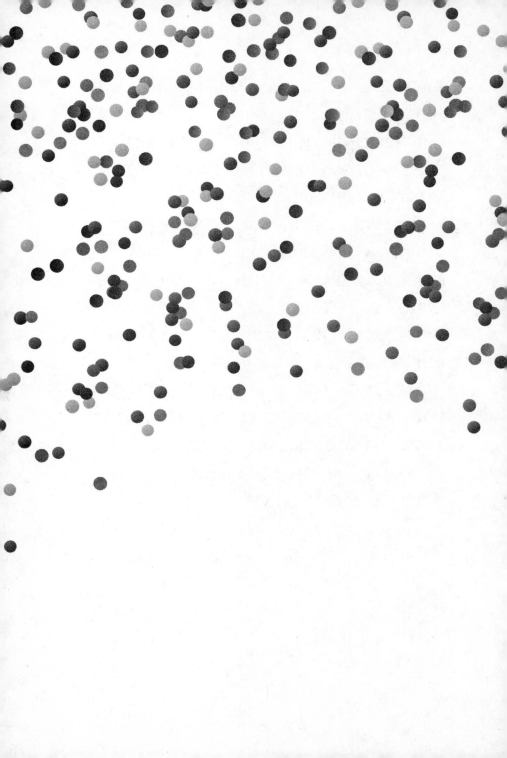

This is Marta. She is thirteen years old and she goes to Bridger Middle School. One day she wished for a different life.

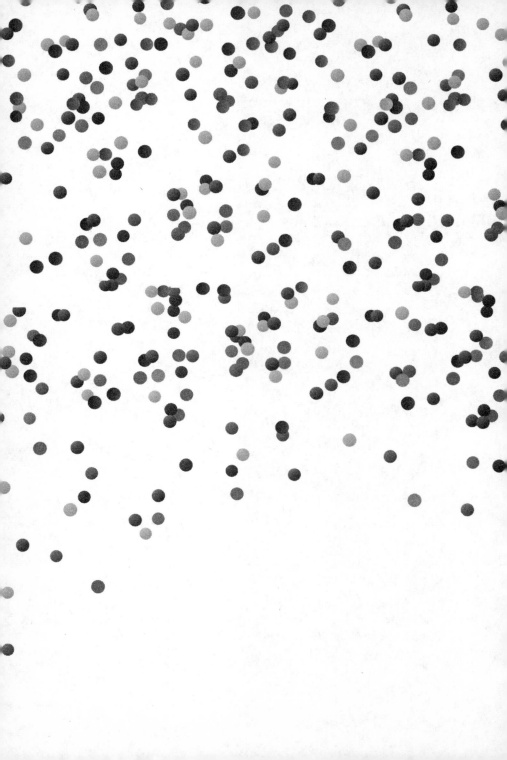

Ghosted

One minute Alice was there and the next minute she was gone. That's how it felt.

Like magic. Now you see her, now you don't.

Did she say something stupid? Something that hurt Lena's feelings? Alice always knew that one wrong move with Lena and it would all be over.

She tried to remember everything she had said. Yesterday after school, they were all—Lena, Hayley, Liv, Alice—standing around Lena's locker. They were looking at the photo of Lena's brother. In the photo, her brother was standing next to two other soldiers, all of them leaning against an army truck. Alice had already seen the photo but now it was pasted inside Lena's locker, stuck onto the door with heart stickers. Alice had said something about it but now she couldn't remember what it was. She usually said a lot of things. Lena too. It was always the two of them doing most of the talking. "Time to turn off the Lena and Alice Show," Ms. Garner once said when she was trying to get them to stop talking in class. After that, it was like everyone was watching, everyone was tuning in to see what would happen next.

Alice stopped outside Ms. Garner's classroom. Lena always got to class before her so probably she was already inside. She had totally ignored Alice when they passed each other in the hall after second period. Well, it would be impossible for Lena to ignore her now because their desks were right next to each other—although if anyone could do it, Lena could. She had a special talent for ignoring people who wanted to be friends with her. The clingies, she called them.

Maybe she was only imagining that Lena wasn't speaking to her anymore. Alice knew she could be paranoid sometimes. Like when Lena didn't respond to her texts all weekend, but then it turned out that her parents had taken her phone away.

Should she smile all big and friendly like everything was cool between them?

Or maybe it was better to look all worried like she was sorry for whatever it was she did.

With a deep breath she stepped into the room, not daring to look up until she got to her desk.

Where another girl sat.

Paxton.

Alice stood there, unsure what to do. Paxton didn't seem to see her at all, and Lena went fishing around inside her pencil pouch like she couldn't decide which pencil she wanted. Like all of the sudden she cared about pencils.

"Lena," Alice whispered.

Lena didn't look up. She was testing the point of a pencil against her finger.

"*Lena*," Alice tried again. But it was too late. Ms. Garner was calling for everyone to take their seats, and the only seat that wasn't taken was Paxton's, clear over by the window.

No one seemed to notice when Alice sat at the wrong desk. Not even Ms. Garner. And that's when another possibility came to her. The possibility that Lena wasn't ignoring her at all. The possibility that Lena couldn't even see her. The possibility that she was gone. Dead. A ghost.

She would not be the only one. There were two other ghosts at the school—at least, that's how the story went. Two girls died in a car accident. (This part was true.) It happened maybe twenty years ago and ever since then the Quintana sisters had been haunting the school. When the heater rattled and moaned, it was one of the Quintana sisters. If you couldn't find your notebook, it was one of the Quintana sisters. No one ever went into the bathroom alone unless they absolutely had to, and then they did their business in record time. If someone came bursting out of the bathroom, all out of breath, it was because of the Quintana sisters.

This is what Alice was thinking about all through class, which didn't really matter because for once Ms. Garner didn't call on her, and when it was time to partner up to critique each other's stories, no one picked Alice. No one even *looked* at Alice. No one, not even Ms. Garner, seemed to notice that she was just sitting there, alone.

According to the story, the girls had died instantly. Actually, that part was according to Lena, who didn't even like to hear about a paper cut, let alone the stories some kids told about the accident. Lena said the Quintana sisters died so fast they didn't even feel it, and so that's the way it was. Lena's words were truth, always, no matter what.

Alice's death was sudden too, she figured. So sudden that she had no idea how it happened. And though it was true that she didn't feel it in the way most people meant when they talked about dying, she felt it in another way. As if the accident, if that's what it was, had happened inside her. A crash, an explosion, that left her heart aching for how things used to be. Maybe that's how it was for the Quintana sisters too. Maybe that's why they haunted the school. They weren't trying to scare anyone, they were just looking for what they had lost. They just wanted things to go back to how they used to be.

When Alice looked up from her hands, which she had been studying, which did seem to be a little lighter than before, Lena and Paxton were bent down low over Lena's desk, writing notes not on their stories but to each other. Alice knew that trick. You slip a piece of paper under your story for easy hiding when Ms. Garner came around.

Though Paxton looked nothing like Alice, still, it felt as if she were looking at herself. Just the day before, that had been her, she was Paxton—at least she thought it was the day before. Maybe it had been longer. Maybe it had been much longer.

She looked around the room, at each student, trying to remember if they had been in her class before her death. There were a few kids she couldn't remember ever seeing before, including, over in the corner by the pencil sharpener, a boy who was also without a partner. He was wearing one of those button-up sweaters like Alice's grandpa sometimes wore. Another ghost.

Alice looked down at her own clothing, then over at Lena, and was relieved to see that Lena was wearing a similar shirt, so she figured she hadn't been dead too long. Another clue: She opened her binder to find her own story, and at the top right corner she had written *Ms. Garner, third period*, and a date. Stretching up so she could see down onto the desk to her right, she saw that the boy seated there had written the same date on his paper. That meant that she had died in the last twenty-four hours. Turning her own story over she took a pencil out of her pouch and began making a list of everything she could remember from the day before, beginning with yesterday afternoon:

Rode home with Hayley
Ate leftover Halloween candy
Found hair in pasta—disgusting!
Math homework
YouTube videos in bed
Fell asleep in clothes
Took shower, got dressed
Texted Lena—no text back
Cereal

And then the bell rang. Out of habit she looked at Lena. Lena, maybe out of habit too, looked back. Kind of. It was more like Alice's head was a window that Lena was looking through. And then, without a word, without any sign that she had seen Alice at all, she turned and left.

The halls seemed extra crowded, filled with students that Alice had never noticed before. Their clothes were so out of style that she figured they were ghosts too. Ghosts from 2020 or 2019, or much longer ago than that—2000, 1980—it was hard to tell, but the thought of being surrounded by ghosts filled her with a hot panic and she had to run into the bathroom to splash cold water on her face.

Someone was watching her. She could feel their presence as she bent her head down over the sink. They were standing behind her, their eyes looking out at her from the mirror. When she looked up, though, no one was there.

The Quintana sisters.

Before she could grab a paper towel, she was out of the bathroom. Shaking water from her hands and lifting one shoulder at a time up to pat-dry her cheeks, she searched the halls for Lena. She had to find Lena. She had to find Lena before she got to the lunchroom, before Paxton could take her place there too. Her heart was a hammer pounding on her ribs, pounding on every wall of her. This, though, was a good sign. Surely ghosts did not feel their hearts.

Her eyes swept the halls as she rushed toward the cafeteria. Kids moved out of her path, some meeting her eyes, some of those eyes strangely familiar, as if from another lifetime.

Meatloaf, that would be her guess if Lena were here and they were playing the lunch game. Yesterday she correctly identified not only lasagna but tacos for a double win. Was that the last time Lena talked to her? No, because after school they were looking at the photo of her brother.

A chill ran through her as two girls looked up and smiled at her. They smiled in a way that felt at once friendly and menacing. Had she seen these girls before? There was something familiar about them. Their long straight hair, their bangs—yes, she *had* seen them! In the newspaper, after the accident. No but the Quintana sisters had darker hair, she was almost sure of it, and they looked younger, shorter, than the girls who just passed her. Still, by the time she got to the cafeteria her heart had taken over her body, her legs so wobbly it was a miracle she didn't fall to the ground.

And she was too late.

Lena was already sitting at their table. Next to her was Paxton. On the other side, across from them, Liv and Hayley.

Without moving her feet, without even realizing it, Alice had floated up to them and now stood at the end of the table, looking down on Lena's buttered hair. That was her secret, how she got her hair so shiny: butter.

"Lena," Alice said.

There was no sign from any of the girls that they had heard her and so she said it again, louder, her eyes stinging from both the hurt and anger. *"Lena."*

She wished she had something to leave with her. A gift. Something that would make Lena remember her—remember them. The Lena and Alice Show.

Again she had that feeling that she was being watched and, turning her head quickly to check, found a girl sitting at the next table over. She wore a sweater that Lena, if she saw it, would say she wouldn't be caught dead in. And now the thought occurred to Alice that perhaps this girl had been caught, on her dying day, in that very sweater. It had a duck on the front of it. A mallard. It reminded Alice of times spent at the duck pond when she was little.

And then the girl smiled. It was a small smile but enough to remind Alice that she had been staring at the girl. Thanks to Lena, she had gotten used to the idea that she was invisible. A ghost. A figment of her own imagination.

She wanted to look away but something about the girl—her smile. It was so familiar. Had they been friends? When they were both—alive?

Talia! It was all coming back to her. Yes, they were friends—they were *good* friends—and then, what had happened? Lena happened, probably. Lena had chosen Alice and when you were chosen by Lena you were hers. You wore what Lena wore. You did what Lena did.

She was closer to the girl now, standing at the end of the table where she sat, alone, looking cautiously up at Alice and then down again at her meatloaf, which she softly poked with her fork. It was all that was left on her plate.

Her family lived in a bus. Did it used to be a school bus? Had they painted over it? That part Alice couldn't remember, only that she loved it. Back then, she couldn't imagine a more magical house. Yes, that's right! She remembered now. She had even begged her parents to move them to a bus. Talia seemed like the richest girl in the world to Alice. It was Lena who had told her she was poor.

And now Alice found herself no longer standing but sitting across from the girl, who looked uncomfortable but smiled nonetheless as the memories rolled across Alice's mind. Most of the seats inside the bus had been removed. In the front, behind the driver's seat, there was a couch and table and tiny stove, and in the back of the bus, behind a curtain, that's where they all slept. Talia's bed was up by the back window, the mattress so narrow her parents had put a railing on the outside so she wouldn't roll off.

They were so little then that the two of them, if they bunched themselves up, could fit together in Talia's tiny bed and pretend they were birds in a nest. Talia's mother would sometimes play along, dropping noodles into their open beaks.

"You were," Alice whispered. To say *my friend* would have sounded too strange and so she left it at that. Thinking of it all, though, she was filled with a warmth that made her wish she could go back to those days, when everything was so simple.

This time Alice caught herself staring not at Talia but at her meatloaf, and she knew this because Talia whispered, "Do you want my meatloaf?"

It sounded so ridiculous, after so many years of not being friends, that Alice, once she started laughing, couldn't stop. Talia too. The two of them howling for no real reason, which was the best kind of hilarious. And had Alice looked up in that moment, if she had looked over at Lena's table, if she had cared at all in that moment what Lena thought, she would have found Lena looking back at her, seeing her, alive, more alive than she had felt in a very long time.

Remembering
Elena

Today we pay tribute to twelve-year-old Elena Romano, a seventh-grader from Bridger Middle School who, at approximately two PM yesterday afternoon, died of embarrassment.

The young artist and snowboarder from Bridger Middle School, loved by so many, was sitting at her desk in Spanish class yesterday afternoon when the air exiting her back end met with the surface of her chair to create what some described as the trumpeting of a tuba or a young elephant in distress.

Elena was surrounded by friends and her substitute teacher when life as she knew it came to an abrupt and humiliating end. Friends described the young girl as quiet—with the exception, one remarked, of that fateful moment. She will be remembered most for the endless joy and laughter she brought to others.

A gathering will be held on the playground of Bridger Middle School, where all are encouraged to bring wind instruments or kazoos for a final salute to their mortified friend and classmate.

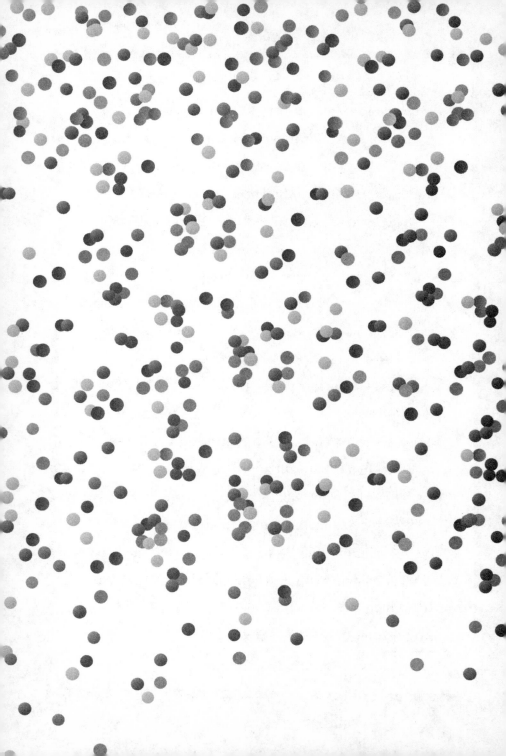

CHOOSE YOUR OWN CATASTROPHE

Though it is quite dark and you cannot see more than a foot in front of you, you decide to play a little game of catch with yourself, tossing the skull-sized rock up higher and higher with each throw. Fortunately, there are three large holes in the skull-sized rock that make it quite easy to grab hold of—a bit like a bowling ball, but more eye-socket-like in shape. Unfortunately, your next toss of the skull-sized rock goes a bit too high, well beyond your ability to see it through the dark, and only the tip of your pinky is able to make contact before it comes crashing down onto your own skull, knocking you unconscious.

When you awake, you are surprised to find yourself surrounded by darkness in what appears to be some kind of pit. Patting the ground around you, you discover what feels to be a shoe, a skull-sized rock, a matchbook, and a pile of wood.

 If you would like to toss the skull-sized rock around, just for a bit of fun, turn to page 65.

 If you would like to try on the shoe to see if it fits, turn to page 85.

 If you would like to use the matchbook and wood to light a fire so you can see more of your surroundings and possibly find your way out of the pit, turn to page 107.

If you would like to sit and do nothing because if you stay in the pit long enough to be discovered on the brink of death, it would be a really cool story to tell your friends and might even go viral, *turn to page 143.*

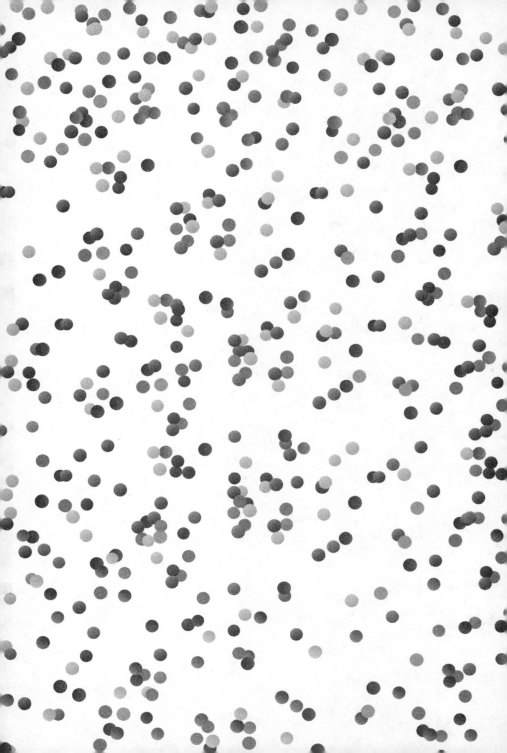

Gio X

___

It was just as he had wished! Well, not *exactly* as he had wished. He did not wish for it to arrive in a box. He did not wish for it to be delivered to his door. However, he did wish for his life to change, and if that change were to arrive in a box, who was he to complain? He would not have cared if it had arrived by clown—

Actually, he was a little afraid of clowns, so he would probably prefer that it not arrive by clown. A box, though—a box was perfect.

Although there was no name on the label, Gio felt certain that the box was meant for him. For one thing, it did not look like an ordinary box. Since his family's recent move to town, he had seen every kind of box imaginable, but not one box that looked anything like this one. This box was not brown but black, *shiny* black, and the only word printed on the label was: UPGRADE—when, just the night before, while lying in bed, Gio had wished for just that: an upgrade. A new and improved Gio. Like a video game, that's how he imagined it—or a phone. Introducing Gio.2—or even better, Gio X. Gio XR.

He began to open the box but was stopped by his nerves. In all the stories he had read about wishes, there was always more to it than that. It was never as simple as just opening a box. What if he didn't open it properly or, in his rush, he accidentally broke it? What if "it" wasn't even an "it"—what if it was something invisible, or something that didn't appear until you said the magic words?

Or what if he had to choose the exact kind of

upgrade he wanted? There were usually choices to be made in stories about wishes. What if thoughts counted as choices, and right as he was about to make his wish, some random thought popped into his head—which happened sometimes, especially when he was nervous. Like what if, out of nowhere, the word *centipede* or *sailboat* came into his thoughts, and then that's how he would have to live out the rest of his life? As a centipede. On a sailboat.

Well, there was no way he could open the box now. He would just have to wait until after school, when he felt calmer. When he could figure out exactly what to do.

Into his room he dragged the box—which was not very heavy at all. It seemed like a boxful of change should be much heavier, but he tried to push the thought away as he pushed the box inside his closet and (just in case his mom opened his closet door) threw his heavy winter coat on top of it.

All the way to Bridger Middle School, Gio imagined himself taller. He imagined himself stronger.

He imagined himself more handsome. He imagined himself as a likable person, the kind that other people would be happy to see. And, just as he was about to pass her in the hall, he imagined Katrina Kerplonski finally saying hello to him.

"Hello, Gio," said Katrina Kerplonski.

Unfortunately he had not yet imagined what he would say to Katrina if she did finally say hello to him, and by the time he thought to say hello back, she was already talking with someone else.

But what a feeling! To finally be noticed by Katrina Kerplonski! If this is what's inside that box, thought Gio, maybe it's already working.

Although, why just Katrina Kerplonski? he wondered as he sat through science class. Yes, he had loved Katrina Kerplonski since the day he moved here, but what about everyone else at this school?

When the bell rang at the end of the day, Gio could not figure out where everyone was going. It seemed to him that the day had barely started, for his mind had hardly spent any time at school at all.

He had imagined himself at parties, imagined himself at the mall with a group of friends, imagined inviting all his friends to his birthday and a delivery guy showing up with a whole stack of pizzas. *Party-sized* pizzas.

Was it raining outside? He had no idea. It could have been hailing for all he knew. There could have been a double rainbow in the sky and he wouldn't have paid it the least attention, because a new thought occurred to Gio as he ran that last block to his house: What if his mom had found the box? What if she had opened it and now all *her* wishes would come true instead of his? His mom would be off sunning herself in the Bahamas while he remained the same old Gio.1.

Fingers shaking, making it difficult to aim his key into the lock, Gio threw open the door and, his heart beating so loudly it seemed as if there were a drum set in each of his ears, ran down the hall to his room.

It was there! The box was still in his closet!

Though he saw, with some disappointment, that it was quite a bit smaller than he remembered. Over the course of the day, the box had grown in his mind to nearly his own height. Now, though, as he looked down on the box, he could see that it barely came to his knees.

Kneeling in front of it, he placed his ear against the cardboard. Why he did this, he was not sure. Perhaps it was because he was desperate to know what the box contained but felt equally terrified to find out. He gave the box a cautious tilt and something slid to the end, making a dull knocking sound against the cardboard. It was not the sound of anything he wanted, and as he gave the box a second tilt, trying to imagine what could possibly make such a disappointing *shhhwump* sound, he remembered: yesterday. Yesterday he had pleaded with his mom to buy him a maple bar, which she didn't, which was disappointing because he did really love maple bars, but he had not meant for this to be his wish. He would trade a thousand maple bars, a *million* maple bars, for one good friend.

It was all he could think about, and thinking about it only made it worse. No matter how hard he tried to imagine his upgrade—Geo X, Geo X, Geo X—from out of nowhere, a maple bar would show up to push his X away. It was best, he decided, to wait just one more day before opening the box.

That night was not a good night. Unsettling dream after unsettling dream of looking inside the box to find a clown shoe, to find a three-headed hamster, to find smaller and smaller and smaller boxes until he was left with a tiny empty box the size of a peanut, which then turned into a peanut. Morning could not come fast enough, and when it did finally come, it brought with it a new decision. He would just open the box—that's what he would do. He would just open the box and get it over with.

But then, right as he was about to run his scissors along the tape, he worried that an attitude like that might ruin his chances of things going well. In stories where wishes go wrong, it's usually because the hero of the story is ungrateful, or too greedy. He couldn't possibly open the box now. He would just have to wait, and in the meantime, he would say a thousand thank-yous to whatever god or goddess or wizard—or genie—had sent the box to him. Thank you, he said, patting the top of the box. Thank you, he said as he gently covered it again with his winter coat. Thank you, he said as he closed his closet door.

On his way to school, Gio thought again about Katrina Kerplonski, and how nice it would be if today other kids were nice to him too. Seeing Jordan standing by the front doors, he thought, wouldn't it be crazy if he just walked up there, like right now, like if he just walked up there all no-big-deal and said, "Hey, Jordan," and then Jordan, like they were totally friends, said "H—"

"Hey Gio," said Jordan.

Or what if, thought Gio, I just walked up to Marcus Brock and all his friends and they just kept talking, like it was totally normal that I was standing there.

"Well, I guess we should get to class," Marcus said when the bell rang, and they all—Gio and the others—went their separate ways.

Feeling a bit flushed from the excitement of it all, Gio made a quick stop in the bathroom to splash a little water on his face. The box's magic seemed to be working even better than yesterday! In fact, looking at himself in the mirror, he really didn't look so bad. He had always thought of himself as short, but he saw in the mirror that he was quite a bit taller than the other boy standing at the sinks. And realizing this, he found himself walking just a little bit taller as he left the bathroom and headed for class.

"Hi Gio," some girl said as he rounded the corner into the science hall. "Hi," Gio said—though it sounded more like "hi?" because he did not know this girl at all, and so how was it possible that she knew him? This was entirely opposite to his understanding of the world, which was that he was the one who knew people, while other people hadn't a clue who he was.

There were several more strange occurrences over the days that followed. At lunch on Wednesday, for example, when he just sat down with Katrina and all her friends, and nobody told him to get lost. Not that anybody had ever told him to get lost in the past—mainly because he had never attempted to sit at their table before. Before the box. And like on Thursday in gym class, when he asked Trey if he wanted to be partners for mirror drill and Trey said sure—just like that. "Sure."

By Friday, Gio had decided that this would be the day, the day when he finally opened the box. Before last period, he grabbed everything out of his locker, and by the time Mr. Pauly called out the homework, he had already tucked his notebook inside his backpack and was ready for his run home.

He had never considered himself a runner—had never thought he had it in him to be athletic in any way—but as he raced home, leaping the occasional puddle, dodging a barking doodle, he imagined himself in his school's blue uniform, breaking the finish-line ribbon. Maybe, he thought, he would try out for the team. He had seen the poster hanging outside the main office.

Nearly out of breath by the time he got to the door, Gio slid his key into the lock and flew down the hall to his room, to his closet, to the box. Feeling rather superhuman by this point, he did not bother finding his scissors but instead dug his fingernails under the mailing tape, ripping one side off and then the other, until all that remained to do was lift up the two flaps. He could practically see the golden light shining out from within, and taking in a deep chestful of breath, he pulled the flaps apart, where he saw, there waiting for him inside the box, one vacuum cleaner attachment upgrade with complimentary gallon jug of carpet shampoo.

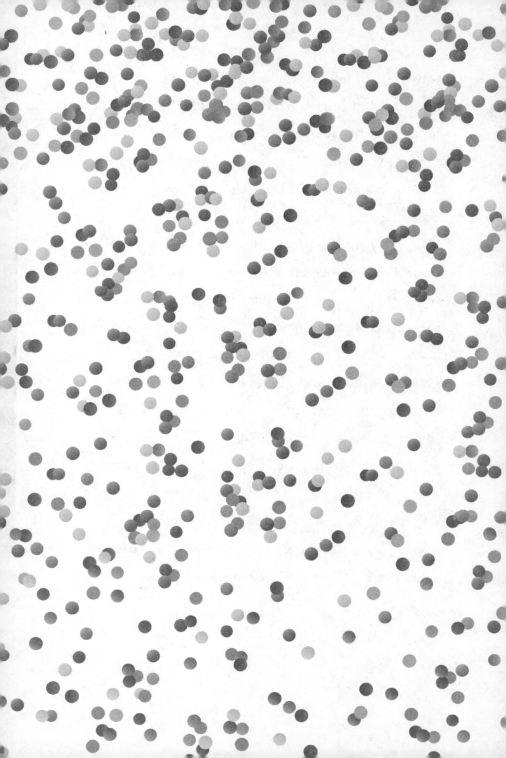

In regard to your recent inquiry:

Thank you for contacting the
Department of Insecurity. As you know,
here at the DOI, we take enormous pride
in serving citizens such as yourself.
It is our pleasure, therefore, to
inform you that you are indeed too tall
and therefore not as good as everyone
else—with exception, that is, to
those individuals who are too hairy,
smelly, pimply, freckly, short, thick,
or skinny, as well as those persons

whose appendages are incorrectly and/
or oddly proportioned—including but by
all means not limited to: arms, legs,
hands, feet, torsos, necks, chins,
ears, eyes, and noses, as well as all
features therein related, such as, but
again not limited to: unreasonably dry
or oily skin, large and/or unsightly
freckling of skin, excessive earwax,
toe jam, belly button lintage, etc.
etc., exceedingly protrusive or
insufficiently protrusive buttocks, etc.
etc. etc.

However, bearing in mind the
aforementioned exceptions, you are
indeed too tall, and therefore have
every reason to feel insecure in your
being.

We thank you for your inquiry, and
though we know you are quite capable
of feeling terrible about yourself on

your own, if we can ever be of service
to you in the future, please do not
hesitate to contact us again. Because
without your insecurities, what would
become of you?

Most sincerely,

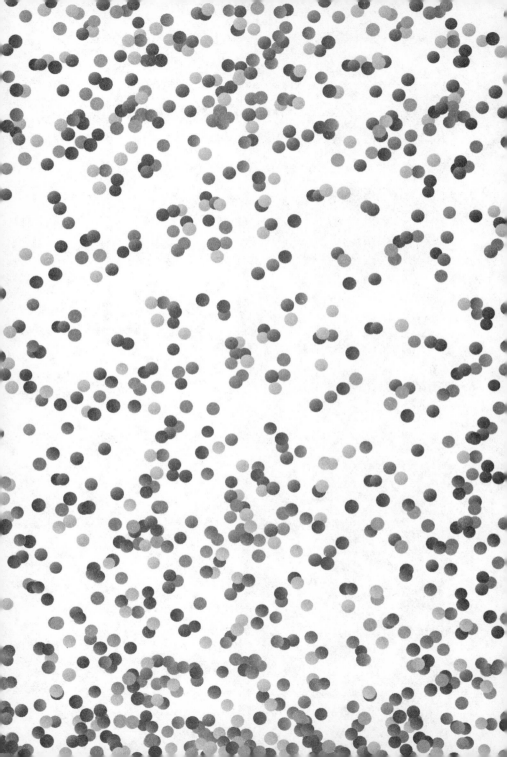

CHOOSE YOUR OWN CATASTROPHE

Nope, the shoe doesn't fit.

 If you would like to try the shoe on the other foot, turn to page 199.

 If you would like to toss the skull-sized rock around, just for a bit of fun, turn to page 65.

If you would like to use the matchbook and wood to light a fire so you can see more of your surroundings and possibly find your way out of the pit, turn to page 107.

If you would like to sit and do nothing because if you stay in the pit long enough to be discovered on the brink of death, it would be a really cool story to tell your friends and might even go viral, turn to page 143.

This is Marta. She is thirteen years old and goes to Bridger Middle School. One day she wished to no longer be a tree.

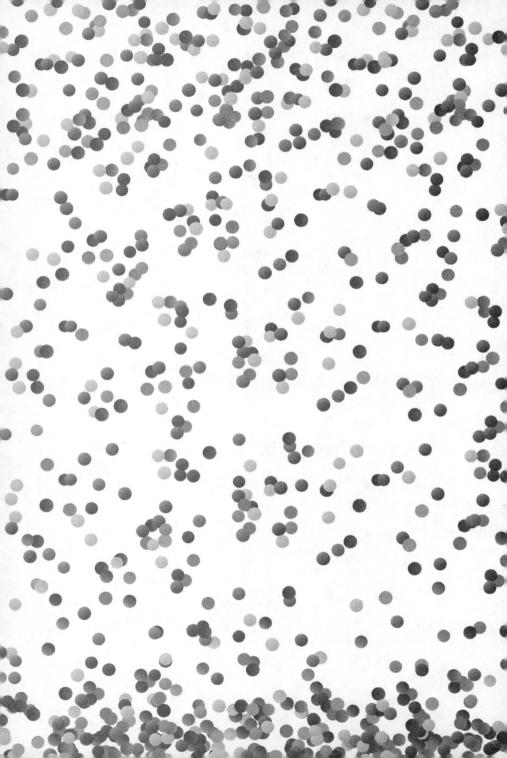

Squirrely Squirrely

———

Hock lived on the outskirts of a small village on the outskirts of a small town just outside the city where Bridger Middle School stands today. This was many years ago, sometime between the Neolithic age and the Google age, back in the days when there was no such thing as bullying. In fact, in Hock's time, there was not even a word for bullying. If you were to say to someone, "She's bullying me!" that someone would look back at you with absolute confusion. "Boolingmi? What is this *boolingmi*?"

On the other hand, you would never think to say "She's bullying me," because in addition to there not being a word for bullying, there was also no need for such a word.

Name-calling had not yet been popularized, and so it was quite confusing to Hock when, one Monday morning, as he squatted before what he believed to be a thunderegg, he was startled to hear Crag's voice above him, shouting in a tone that one might use when one's mule suddenly stops mid-gully: "Toad!"

"Clay," Hock corrected, looking up from his squat, for the thunderegg had turned out to be nothing more than a clump of clay.

"Toad!" Crag insisted. "Toady! Toady! Toady!"

Again Hock attempted to correct his friend, lifting the clump to offer Crag a better view. "No, see? It is only clay."

This added information did not seem to settle

the matter, and in fact it only served to multiply and intensify Crag's shouting. "Toadytoadytoady-toadytoady!"

It seemed, from what Hock could gather, that Crag was not referring to the clump at all, but rather to Hock himself.

Had the word been said in a kinder way, Hock might have considered it a compliment, might have even thanked Crag for his praise, for he did love toads, and he could now see that in his squat-tiness, he made a rather fine one. However, that is not how the word entered Hock's ears, nor how it plummeted down into his stomach, where it sat like a heavy stone atop his morning hash. Crag said *toad* as if it were the worst possible thing one could be.

For the rest of the day, Hock carried that stone around inside him. He carried it through archery class and weaving instruction, through his after-noon abacus lesson and wagoneer practice. He carried that stone inside him all the way down the path that took him back home at the end of his school day—which, unfortunately, was the very same path that took Crag home at the end of *his* school day.

As Hock plodded along, bent forward under the weight of his heavy pack, he heard behind him the unmistakable voice of Crag. This time he did not shout *toad*, as Hock might have expected, but *mule*. "Mule!" Crag shouted. "Muley! Muley! Muley!"

Hock, who felt a certain fondness for mules, looked all around, but despite Crag's insistent shouting, could not locate the animal anywhere. Turning to Crag for a clue as to where he might find this mule of which he spoke, he found Crag's finger pointing not into the surrounding trees, nor off into the meadow at the end of the path, but directly at Hock himself.

"Mule!" Crag shouted again—and again—following Hock's quickening steps down the path. "Muleymuleymuleymuleymuley!"

Once more, Hock found himself confused by Crag's words, for like a toad, a mule was not a terrible thing to be. Mules were quite useful. A mule could carry one's heavy pack home from school. A mule could carry a sack of goods to market. A mule could pull an entire wagon to town. His family should be so lucky to have a mule!

Safe at last inside his house, the homey aroma of cabbage simmering on the stove, poor Hock again felt that awful weight deep in the pit of his stomach, and it gave him the very worst kind of feelings about himself—feelings that were new, and so he had no idea how to rid himself of them.

He tried spitting, but this brought no relief. He tried punching his fist into the soft place at his middle where he felt most uncomfortable, but this was only helpful in that he now had an aching stomach to distract him from the other, more mysterious feeling.

His misery lasted through the night, through his largely untouched helping of mutton hash the next morning, and all the way down the long path to school.

After all that poor Hock had been through the day before, it was truly unfortunate that he should take a tumble immediately upon his arrival, and especially unfortunate that the tumble should take place directly in front of the stump upon which Crag sat fastening the buckle on his shoe.

"Ruckelball!" Crag shouted. (Ruckelball was a popular sport at the time, involving the rolling of boulders down a grassy slope.) "Ruckelbally! Ruckelbally!" And this was perhaps most confusing of all, because there was not one person Hock knew of, Crag included, who did not enjoy a lively game of Ruckelball. Crag was, in fact, a very good Ruckelball player—much better than Hock—and so again, had it not been for Crag's tone, Hock might have felt he were being paid the highest of compliments. As with the words that came before, however, this new word lodged itself deep inside of Hock—a heavy stone that, by day's end, would be joined by several others: *saddlebaggy*, *shovely*, *marmaladey*, *candlesticky*.

That evening, with so many stones weighing heavily upon his stomach, and believing in his heart that there could not possibly be a cure for such a condition as his, Hock informed his mother that he was, in fact, a toad mule ruckelball saddlebag shovel marmalade candlestick.

"A toad mule ruckelball saddlebag shovel marmalade candlestick?" Looking upon her dear boy with his handsome black curls and sad dark eyes, Hock's mother found this quite preposterous—though she had no explanation for why Crag would insist on such nonsense, for "Who ever heard of someone calling someone else by other words in order to make that person feel bad?"

Though his mother's words were quite true, and they did bring some comfort, they also created in Hock a strong desire to do just that—to call someone else by other words in order to make that person feel bad. And the person Hock had in mind, of course, was Crag.

That night in bed, he tried out different words, calling up to his ceiling:

Goat!

Plow!

Bucket!

Crow!

He tried each word again, and again, and though he could find good reason for each, he did not feel that he had yet found the perfect word for Crag. Perhaps, he thought, he should practice on someone a bit easier. There was a boy in his class who liked to collect the acorns that fell from the trees. He could call him *squirrel*. Yes, tomorrow he would pass one of his stones on to the boy who collected acorns!

If he could think of another word to call him, perhaps he could give him two of his stones—or maybe he would give him just the one, and save the others for someone else—the girl in his school whose skin was a lighter shade of brown than everyone else's. He would call her *sheep*—or *bread*! He would call her both! *Sheep bread!*

"*Squirrel, squirrel, squirrelysquirrelysquirrely,*" Hock rehearsed all the way to school the next morning. "*Sheep bread sheep bread sheep bread,*" he chanted, not even seeing the thunderegg, indeed a real one this time, that lay directly in his path. He did not pay his usual visit to the old fir tree to breathe in its deep earthy sap, or delight in the crystally glisten of its frosty moss. He did not hear the birds whistling their good mornings, and so did not whistle his own hello back. Nor, as he walked those last few paces of path, did he notice Crag—not until he heard the rustling of grasses and looked up to see Crag's thick winter coat of fur—fur of the same deep brown as the curls on his head—moving through the field surrounding the school.

This time, though, Crag was not moving toward Hock but away from him, toward something else— *someone* else—a boy, crouched beneath the tallest oak tree, the one that grew up directly beside the school. Yes, Hock could see that Crag, with his shoulders lifted and hands fisted, his flared nostrils blowing puffs of steam into the chill air, was about to charge at squirrely squirrely! And in that moment, Hock could see—yes, he could see quite clearly now—

"Bull!" That's what Crag was. Not a goat or a plow, not a bucket or a crow. "Bull!"

This time it was Crag who looked all around, concern filling his eyes at the possibility of a charging bull.

"Bully!" Hock shouted once more, arm outstretched, finger pointing not to Crag's right, not to his left, but directly at his middle, at Crag himself.

It was clear from the scrunch of Crag's brows, the drop of his jaw, that he found this confusing. Bulls, after all, were not bad things—some would even say that there was no more powerful beast than the mighty bull. However, that is not how the word entered Crag's ears. Hock had said *bull* as if it were the most terrible thing one could be.

And in fact, the more Hock shouted "bully!"—the more Hock shouted "bullybullybullybully!"—the less bull-like Crag appeared (and, in fact, the *more* bull-like Hock seemed to grow). Stone after stone after stone, the miserable feeling piled up inside our poor Crag, until he could do nothing but stand there, a boulder, watching as Hock and the boy who collected acorns said their good mornings and headed into school.

SHOP THE *Happy*

Tired of your same old friends? Ready to live a more exciting friend lifestyle? Now's your chance to stock up on the pals you always wanted!

Choose from

My Happy Artist Friend®   **My Happy Goth Friend®**   **My Happy Sporty Friend®**

And right now, with our special buy-one-get-five-free Happy Friends® sale, there's never been a better time to create your own customized clique!

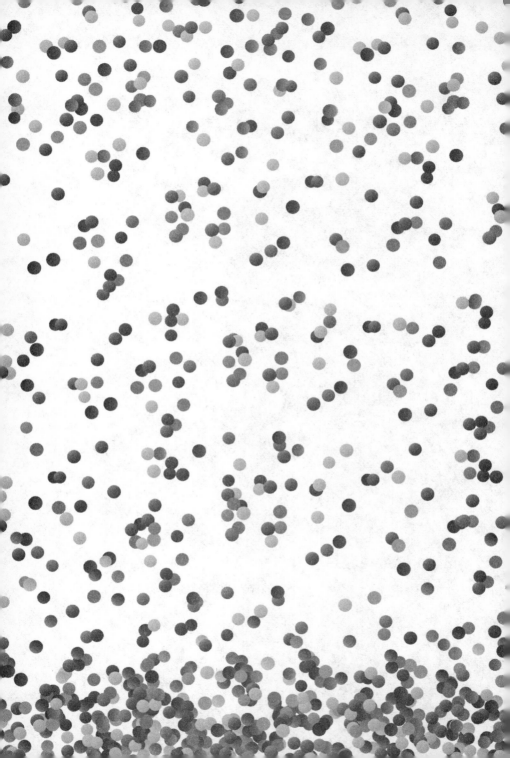

The Voice

Part III

MUDJO IS ACTING VERY STRANGE TODAY, said The Voice.

"Yes," Katya agreed, "Mudjo *is* acting a little strange."

MAYBE HE HAS RABIES.

"That's crazy!" said Katya, ever-so-slowly backing away from Mudjo. "How could he have rabies?" she said, tiptoeing down the hall to her room.

MAYBE HE GOT BITTEN BY A RABID WOLF, LIKE THE DOG IN THAT BOOK YOU'RE READING.

"That's impossible," Katya said, slamming her bedroom door. "There aren't even any wolves around here.

"At least I don't think there are wolves around here," she said. "Are there wolves around here?"

The Voice thought on this, then said: NO.

This calmed Katya, and feeling a sudden desire to kiss Mudjo's crazy old head—that's all he was, crazy, he had always been a little crazy, ever since he was a puppy—she flung open her door and called down the hall, "Mudjo! Here, Mudjo!"

The Saint Bernard came barreling toward Katya, once or twice banging his heavy body into the wall, drool swinging to and fro—because of his excitement? Because of his rabies? But no, not rabies, there were no wolves around here, remember?—and just as he was about to charge into Katya, The Voice said: RACCOONS.

RACCOONS, said The Voice, ALSO HAVE RABIES. REMEMBER THAT STORY YOUR AUNT TOLD YOU? ABOUT THE RACCOON THAT ATTACKED THAT KID? I'M PRETTY SURE HE HAD TO HAVE HIS NOSE SEWN BACK ON.

Katya screamed and jumped onto her bed, grabbing her pillow to use as a shield against Mudjo and his rabies. As the dog grew more and more desperate to get at her, she grew more and more convinced that he had rabies—he definitely without a doubt had rabies. *Aaaaaaah!* she screamed. *Aaaaaaah!* She could not stop screaming *Aaaaaah!*

AND, said The Voice, YOU REMEMBER WHAT HAPPENS TO THE DOG IN YOUR BOOK. YOU'LL HAVE TO—

Katya screamed again, this time so she wouldn't have to hear The Voice say it. "No!" she screamed. "I won't! I won't!"

SUIT YOURSELF, said The Voice, BUT YOU MIGHT WANT TO CARRY A HANKY IN CASE

YOU START FOAMING AT THE MOUTH.

Katya became so distraught by this thought—what an awful thought—that she didn't even notice when exactly Mudjo had been replaced by her mother, who eventually managed to pry the pillow from Katya's hands. Prying thoughts from the mind, though—that is a much harder task. That would take several hours, as well as a handwritten note from the vet promising Katya that Mudjo did not (triple underline) have rabies. Signed, Dr. Caroline Montgomery.

(To be continued.)

CHOOSE YOUR OWN CATASTROPHE

You open the matchbook and feel inside for the matches. Good news: There are seven matches left! Bad news: You have not lit a match in a very long time, ever since the shoelace incident—which you admit was a poor choice because you were wearing your shoe at the time and it is very difficult to untie a flaming shoelace. Still, it did not seem fair that your parents should hide all the matches from you. It is entirely your parents' fault that you are now out of practice and have already blown through four of the seven matches without so much as a spark.

Finally, when you are down to your very last match, you succeed! You have made fire. You are like the cavepeople in your National Geographic book. How you used to love that National Geographic book. You especially loved the picture of the woolly mammoth. Once, you made a woolly mammoth out of cotton balls and hunted it with a toothpick spear. Though now that you think about it, the toothpick never seemed quite right. It was too small, too skinny. You should have used a stick. You try to picture your woolly mammoth in your mind, which is easier now that your fire has gone out and it is completely dark again. Thanks to all your woolly mammoth thinking, you now have all the time in the world to come up with a new spear. Maybe you can use the skull-sized rock to whittle down a piece of the wood that you will no longer be able to light. Then you will really feel like a caveperson.

If you would like to whittle your wood into a spear, stay right here on this page and start whittling. Just keep whittling and whittling and whittling.

 If you would like to toss the skull-sized rock around, just for a bit of fun, turn to page 65.

 If you would like to try on the shoe because for the next several hours or possibly days, it's pretty much that or tossing a skull-sized rock around, turn to page 85.

 If you would like to just sit and do nothing because if you stay in the pit long enough to be discovered on the brink of death, it would be a really cool story to tell your friends and might even go viral, turn to page 143.

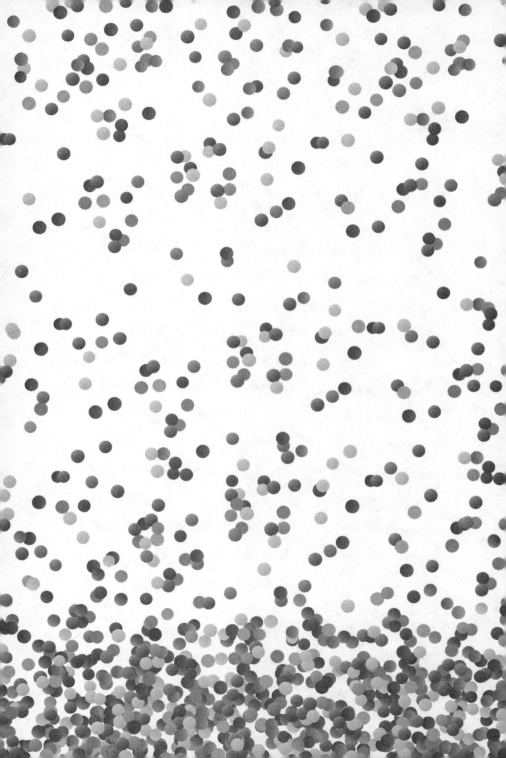

Imposter

It is only a matter of time. Soon, Kiera is sure, everyone will discover that she is not very smart. She has only been pretending to be smart in order to appear smart. Her perfect grades are the perfect example of just how good she is at pretending to be smart. She has also managed to fool her classmates by knowing the answer to every single question her teachers ask. She will raise her hand and say, as confidently as she can (also a trick she has learned: always appear confident), the absolute correct answer—which, of course, requires that she learn everything her teachers assign, as well as extra material on the chance that her teachers surprise the class with topics they were not assigned to study. It is only a matter of time, however, before they all discover the truth. And then what? Will they also discover that she was only pretending to be a good soccer player? That she is only the highest scorer on the team because she snuck in all those extra practices in her backyard and went on runs after dinner? Will they then find out that she is not the super nice person they all believe her to be? That she only shared her sandwich with her friend because her friend had forgotten her lunch, and the only reason she started that campaign to save the sea turtles was because she didn't want them to suffer? Oh, what will she do when they discover the truth?

This is Marta. She is thirteen years old and she goes to Bridger Middle School. One day she wished to have her old life back again.

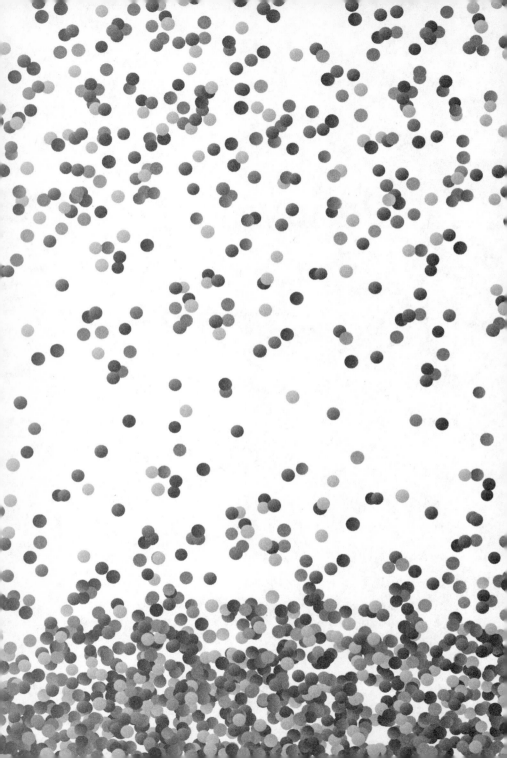

Behaviorally Challenged

The "fun movie," the one that Principal Erring had called a special treat, was just five minutes in length. It began with white letters on a sky-blue background: *Peace Begins on the Playground.*

Next came what appeared to be a plus sign, generating a group moan among the students. Lexa, sitting at the top of the bleachers with her friend Tashi, quietly wondered if Ms. Erring had tricked them all into watching a math movie.

But no. As the camera descended from the sky, moving closer and closer to the ground, the shape became something else. What had at first appeared to be a flat grey plus sign soon turned into tall grey walls, and what at first appeared to be dots moving around the grey walls soon became the tops of heads—which, as the camera changed its angle, turned into kids running around a playground. Not an ordinary playground, but a playground divided into four parts by the walls of the enormous plus sign.

On top of this scene appeared the word: INTRODUCING

Followed by: THE PLUS

The camera then circled around the outside of The Plus, a different scene appearing in each of its four sections as a voice described this "advancement in playground technology," this "revolutionary idea that promises to eliminate playground conflicts so that all students may play in peace."

In the first section, titled FRIENDLY FUN, students sat in a circle, happily chatting with one another as they wove daisies into bracelets. (Where they had gotten the daisies was a mystery, as the surface of The Plus appeared to be some kind of rubber mat.)

In the second section, titled BOISTEROUS, students were enthusiastically playing a game of—something. It was difficult to say. Not hide-and-seek because there was no place to hide. Tag? Whatever it was, it did not look very fun to Lexa.

In the third section, labeled BEHAVIORALLY CHALLENGED, students were either pushing at one another or viciously kicking at a giant rubber ball.

And in the final INDEPENDENT PLAYERS section, students walked around by themselves, like young philosophers contemplating the mysteries of the universe. Some held their hands clasped behind their backs like miniature professors.

The rest of the movie involved students talking

about why they loved The Plus. They used words like *fun* and *great* and *cool*, but in a flat tone that suggested they had rehearsed these words ahead of time. For the finale, the camera zoomed back, revealing a rainbow that stretched from one end of The Plus to the other. Appearing in the blue sky above it, one sunny yellow letter at a time: *Add peace + happiness to your playground.*

"Sounds more like division than addition to me," whispered Tashi.

When the film ended and the lights came back on in the auditorium, Ms. Erring said she had an additional surprise to announce. Pause. "Thanks to the efforts of our wonderful PTA..." Pause. "Bridger Middle School will soon have..." Pause. "Its very own..." Pause. "Plus!"

These last words were said with so much enthusiasm that everyone—even Lexa and Tashi, who had been whispering their doubts to each other throughout the film—erupted into applause. It was only after the applause died down that students began to question how being separated from their friends would be more fun—especially when, following the protests of several students, Ms. Erring went on to describe The Plus as "a necessary measure." It had been "brought to her attention" (her favorite expression) "by a number of students" (probably Trina Erickson, who was always bringing things to Ms. Erring's attention) "that Bridger's playground is no longer a calm and peaceful place. There are too many students releasing too much energy, which has resulted in entirely too much noise and running around."

And then, remembering that this was supposed to be a cheerful event, she raised her voice up again and, with a chirping tone and patter of claps said, "And as a very special celebratory treat, you may each, as you leave the gymnasium, help yourself to *one* cereal bar."

Some of the questions that came up in Lexa's English class that day:

What if you're a Boisterous-Independent Player?

(Answer: Many of our Independent Players are boisterous.)

What does *boisterous* mean again? (Answer: Loud, but in a good way, as opposed to our Behaviorally Challenged students.)

And this question from Lexa: What if you're Boisterous but you have a Friendly Fun friend? (Answer: You will have plenty of time to visit with each other during lunch.)

This was not the answer that Lexa and Tashi had hoped to hear. The two had been friends since before they could even remember being friends. Their parents liked to tell stories of them stealing each other's teething toys and how, even when they were little, Lexa was the bossy one, leading their crawls around the house. So Lexa was nearly sure that she would be assigned to Boisterous and Tashi to Friendly Fun.

Lexa's next question: If Boisterous and Friendly Fun are both fun sections, why can't they all be together? (Answer: Lexa, *all* of our sections are fun.)

Lexa: But that's not fair! (Answer: Lexa, would you like to join our Behaviorally Challenged section?)

The Plus arrived the next week, carried to Bridger Middle School on the back of a flatbed truck, flapping WIDE LOAD signs taped to its ends. Lexa and Tashi, who had social studies class that morning and therefore had the best view of the playground, couldn't imagine how, as wide as it was, it had even made it down Bardstown Road without knocking down every mailbox along the way.

Following The Plus into the parking lot were two forklifts, another kind of truck neither of them knew the name of, a dump truck, and a crane. All lined up they reminded Lexa a little of a parade. "They should throw candy," she said to Tashi, but Tashi didn't get it and Lexa was too tired, or maybe too sad, to explain.

Every time they managed another glance out the window—between Ms. Grady turning her eyes toward the projector and turning them back to the class, each time reminding students in a more and more exasperated tone that if they couldn't keep their eyes inside, they would be recommended for the Behaviorally Challenged section—it seemed that something else had disappeared from their playground. First the swing set, then the slide and climbing wall. Hardest to see go was the tire swing, where Lexa and Tashi had passed so many recesses sitting knee to knee, spinning themselves dizzy. Lexa could feel the thud in her heart as the tire fell to the ground and was rolled away across the bark chips.

After the last scraps of the playground had been hauled away, a tongue-colored rubber mat was unrolled over the entire surface. Tashi said she thought that, except for it being square, it looked like a giant stick of gum.

When it was time for The Plus, Ms. Grady gave up trying to keep the students' attention on the American Revolution. With a defeated sigh, she said, "Go on, then," and the entire class rushed from their seats to claim spots at the windows. With their thirty noses fogging up the glass, the students watched as the massive thing was lifted by crane and carried to the center of the mat, where the crane operator slowly lowered it to the ground.

Ms. Grady clapped when it landed, and the more obedient among the students joined in. These students would most likely all be together in the Friendly Fun section.

Toward the end of third period, just before being released for lunch, students were given their assignments. "And do not think," warned Lexa's PE teacher, Ms. Talons, "that you can just trot off to join your friends, because we have given each of our playground monitors a list of your names and sections."

As Lexa and Tashi had figured, had feared, their assignments were Boisterous and Friendly Fun, handed to them on little cards that said B and FF, and as they emptied their lunch trays and entered the playground, hugging each other before going their separate ways, each secretly dreaded that this might be the beginning of the end of their friendship. They would have no choice but to make new friends, and it would only be a matter of time before those new friends became close friends. Maybe even best friends.

The playground, on that first day, was chaos. Many students, including Lexa and Tashi, did attempt to trot off, and the trotting was made more complicated by the fact that most everyone had friends in all three of the other sections, so it took most of recess just to get students sorted and settled.

The new playground equipment would not arrive for two more weeks, and so, as a temporary measure, each of Bridger's four sections was equipped with a large rubber ball, approximately the size of a first grader if first graders were round. There were no instructions as to what they were to do with these large rubber balls, and as Lexa stood staring at the thing, she was reminded of the experiment they had recently conducted in science class. The experiment involved ants and a block of sugar, but it was basically the same thing. Imagining herself an ant, observed from above by a giant scientist, she had a strong and growing urge to throw the experiment off somehow. Every idea she came up with, though, only seemed like exciting new ant data for the giant scientist to write down on her oversized notepad.

The other Bs did not seem to share her feelings. All were laughing boisterously as they pushed and kicked at the giant rubber ball. Was there a point to the game? Lexa could not tell, but she suspected that no, there was not a point. She could see mouths moving but could not hear what they were saying over the shouting coming from what she guessed was the Behaviorally Challenged section—or maybe it was Friendly Fun shouting from Tashi's section, it was hard to say.

The laughter around her, mixed with the waves of sound coming from the other sections, created a kind of whirlpool inside Lexa's head, and she found herself backing away from the ball, farther and farther, until she was tucked into the corner of The Plus.

Sitting there, fists pressed into her ears, she wished she could magically push herself through the wall into the Friendly Fun section, where she was sure she would find Tashi having a great time with her new best friends.

Of course, the truth was, if Lexa did have such magical ability, she would have found herself sitting back-to-back with Tashi, who had also tucked herself into the corner of The Plus. She too was struggling to find the point of her group's "friendly fun" game of what seemed to be nothing more than duck-duck-goose. What exactly a giant rubber ball had to do with duck-duck-goose, she had no idea. Really, thought Tashi (who had also been reminded of the ant experiment), there could be a giant sugar cube in the middle and it would not change this game one bit.

After school, comparing notes on their walk

home, kicking at the stones and pinecones in their path with a little more force than usual, Lexa and Tashi agreed that there could not possibly be a more miserable situation than having to spend their entire recess apart.

Oh, but in fact there *could* be a more miserable situation, as they discovered the next day during second period. That is when Ms. Erring announced over the school's intercom system that a new decision had been made. Due to students' "utterly unacceptable behavior" the day before, there would be no more mixing with other sections during lunch. "From now on, in order to create a more peaceful transition between lunch and recess, you will sit in the lunchroom according to your assigned groups, and be dismissed for recess one table at a time. Just look for the poster with your group's name and—"

Here Ms. Erring paused. To say "sit there" would have been to state the obvious, and so instead she said, in a dull voice that did not at all match her words, "have fun."

As soon as the intercom crackled off, Lexa's class erupted in protest. Mr. Hollands, who seemed prepared for this reaction, immediately rang his "calming bell." When the bell did not have its usual effect, he was forced to shout over the rising volume of complaints: "People! There is plenty of space available in the BC section for anyone who wishes to continue disrupting my class!"

Arriving for lunch that day, students were greeted by Ms. Erring, two additional lunch monitors, and four long tables, each with a piece of yellow construction paper hanging off its end. In the school's usual attempt to make awful rules appear fun, BC, B, FF, and IP were written in brightly colored balloon letters. Some letters were striped in the center, others polka-dotted. All had an exclamation point at the end with a smiley face inside the dot.

The Independent Players said nothing, dutifully shuffling over to their new table. The rest of the students attempted to stay with their friends, but this only lasted as long as it took Ms. Erring and the lunch monitors to make the rounds with their clipboards, tapping kids on their shoulders and pointing them, with outstretched arms, in the direction of where they were to move themselves "pronto" or "be sent to the BC table." This threat mattered little, of course, to students who were already assigned to the BC table, and so they received their very own customized threat of being sent to the office. By the end of lunch, the BC section had grown by five students, and three BCers stood next to Ms. Erring, awaiting their group march down the hall.

The rest of the week and into the following was much the same, though Lexa noticed that her group seemed to grow less and less boisterous with every lunch and recess. Boisterous had turned to bossy, which turned to irritated, which, by the following Tuesday, had resulted in three Bs being relocated to BC, and two well-behaved BCs and one boisterous IP taking their place. It had also resulted in more and more formerly boisterous students sitting alongside Lexa until, from her middle place in the corner of The Plus, with students lined up on both sides of her, it almost looked as if she had grown wings. If only.

With every passing day, students grew quieter and quieter until an eerie silence had descended upon The Plus. Most students just passed their recess time sitting on the tongue, as the rubber mat had come to be called. Some talked with each other in whispers. Others just silently poked their fingers into the soft rubber. Lexa, remembering the words from the movie, *Peace Begins on the Playground*, wondered: Was this peace? It felt more like boredom than peace. More like sadness. Like the feeling of lying awake in your bunk at summer camp, missing home.

It wasn't that Lexa disliked the others in her section. Not at all. Before The Plus, a few of them had even been to her house. It was just that the whole thing reminded her too much of when she was little and her mom used to arrange her playdates—which always felt more like playdates for her mom, talking with her friends in the kitchen, having a good ol' time while kids Lexa barely knew flung her toys around or, in one awful instance, bit her arm. It felt just like that now. Like here they all were, forced into a playdate, while Ms. Erring and the teachers were off enjoying their peaceful lunchtime together. It wasn't fair.

And weren't they the very same teachers who had taught them about freedom? About civil rights? About women's rights? LGBTQ+ rights? About workers' rights and animal rights?

What about recess rights? What about *our* rights?

Lexa had not realized she had said the words out loud—not until they came echoing back to her. First from directly behind her, "Yeah! What about *our* rights?" Then another voice from the other side of the wall, "What about our rights!"

The third voice Lexa heard, this one from the Friendly Fun section, was the loudest of all—not in volume, but in courage—because Lexa understood what it had taken for her friend, her quiet friend, to make her voice heard. Later Lexa would say that it was hearing Tashi's voice that helped her to find her own courage, to step off the mat altogether.

"And where exactly do you think you're going?" the monitor demanded as Lexa marched for the end of the tongue, urged on by the rising volume of protesting students.

The monitor, hugging her clipboard to her chest, her eyebrows pulled up into two umbrellas arching over her puddle-colored eye shadow, could barely make her voice heard above the thunder. "I believe I asked you a question!"

Lexa looked back at The Plus, where her butterfly wings—those Bs who had sat alongside her in the corner of The Plus—were no longer sitting but had risen up to stand by her side. Students from the neighboring FF section, including Tashi—led by Tashi!—had moved in to join them, and the monitor, seeing this, turned her attention from Lexa to the growing crowd. "Hey!" she shouted.

"Hey! Everybody back to your sections or...or..."

But there was no plan for such an event, was there? This became increasingly more obvious to Lexa as she took that first step off the mat, a wave of students following behind her. "You will all be—" the monitor spat. Truly, you could see the glisten on her lips as she desperately searched for the words, any words, that might bring order back to her playground. "Every one of you will be—"

The storm—it was a storm by now—brought teachers and Ms. Erring rushing out of the school, a few still holding on to their sandwiches and personalized mugs. "Students of Bridger Middle School!" Ms. Erring shouted into her bullhorn, Cup-O-Noodles clutched in her other hand. "You will return to your sections pronto!" And when not a single student returned to their section pronto, she added: "And if you do not wish to follow the rules of Bridger Middle School, I am sure that our BCers would be happy to have you join them."

Those last words seemed to do the trick—though

not the trick that Ms. Erring had anticipated.

Lexa, in fact, did *not* wish to follow the rules of Bridger Middle School. Not ridiculous rules anyway. Not rules that took away their freedom. And if that meant she belonged in the BC section, well, then that was just fine with her. "BC!" she shouted, running for the BC section, her words barely meeting the air before a dozen more rose up, the sky filling with "BC! BC!" as every student of Bridger Middle School (on Ms. Erring's suggestion) poured into the BC section.

If you were to fly up into the sky, or say you were a giant scientist looking down on the scene, you would see below you what might appear to be an army of ants gathering their might to move something much larger than them. And in a way, that's exactly what happened that day.

The next morning, The Plus was lifted up and carried away by the very same crew that had delivered it, its tattered WIDE LOAD signs flapping goodbye as the truck rolled out of the parking lot and onto Bardstown Road. The tongue was next, rolled up and hauled away, leaving behind it the sweet smell of bark chips, and the behaviorally challenged students of Bridger Middle School, where freedom begins on the playground.

Chart of Relative Calamity

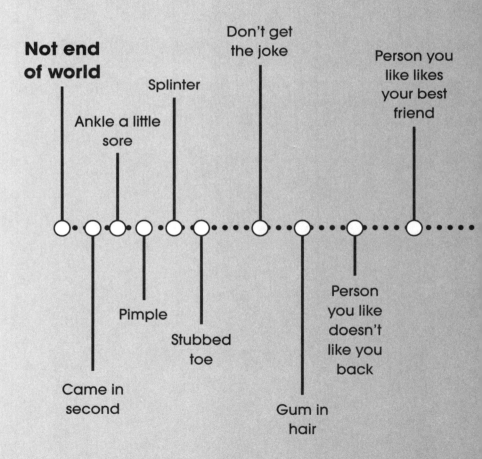

Not end of world

Ankle a little sore

Splinter

Don't get the joke

Person you like likes your best friend

Came in second

Pimple

Stubbed toe

Gum in hair

Person you like doesn't like you back

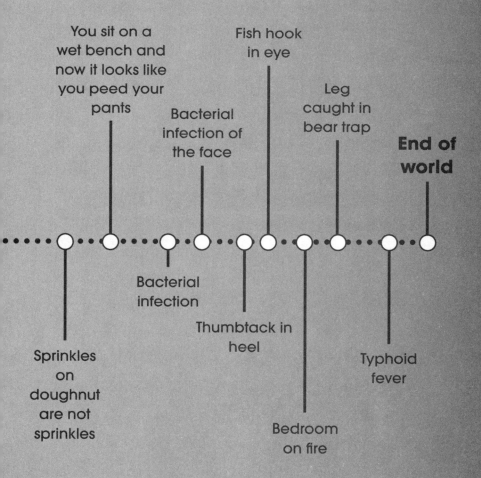

You sit on a wet bench and now it looks like you peed your pants

Fish hook in eye

Leg caught in bear trap

End of world

Bacterial infection of the face

Bacterial infection

Thumbtack in heel

Sprinkles on doughnut are not sprinkles

Bedroom on fire

Typhoid fever

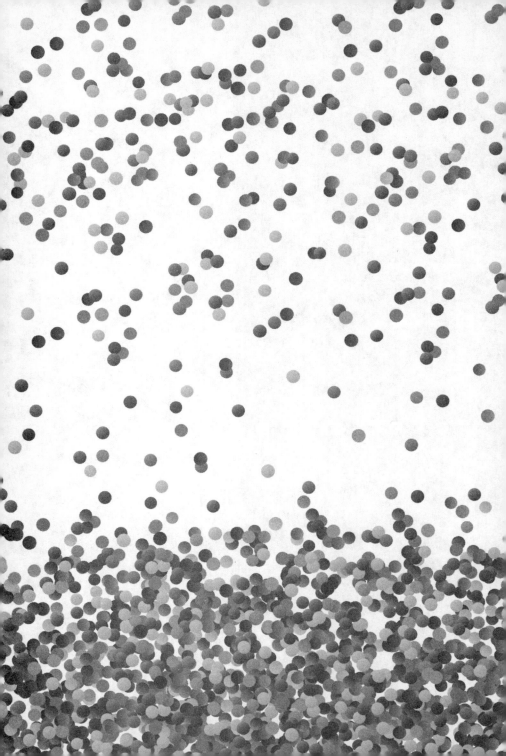

The Voice

———

Part IV

WHATEVER YOU DO, DO NOT DANCE. YOU ARE A TERRIBLE DANCER. PEOPLE WILL LAUGH AT YOU.

And though Katya had always enjoyed school dances, she felt that The Voice was probably right. It would be best if she found a dark place against the wall to stand.

On the occasion that her legs forgot that she

was a terrible dancer and began to move to the music, The Voice would say: YOU CALL THAT DANCING?

Three times, Sasha and Mia tried to pull Katya onto the dance floor, but she shook their arms away, laughing at first, and then texting her mother to pick her up.

Outside, as Katya kept watch for her mother's car, The Voice said: LEAVING THE DANCE IS A MAJOR LOSER MOVE, YOU KNOW.

"What was I supposed to do, just stand there all night?" Katya said.

GOOD POINT, said the voice. I GUESS YOU'RE A LOSER EITHER WAY.

That night, Katya and The Voice stayed up very late.

The Voice had many suggestions:

YOU SHOULDN'T WEAR SKIRTS ANYMORE. THEY MAKE YOU LOOK LIKE A LITTLE KID. AND ALSO KIND OF FAT.

YOU AREN'T VERY SMART.

YOU DEFINITELY AREN'T VERY PRETTY.

YOUR HAIR IS TOO SHORT.

YOU SHOULD ONLY WEAR BLACK FROM NOW ON. THAT WOULD BE COOL.

YOU SHOULD GET A TATTOO.

YOU SHOULD STOP TALKING TO THAT GIRL LUCY, UNLESS YOU WANT TO BE UNPOPULAR LIKE HER.

YOU SHOULD START FOLLOWING RILEY. YOU'RE LIKE THE ONLY PERSON ON THE PLANET WHO ISN'T FOLLOWING RILEY.

(To be continued.)

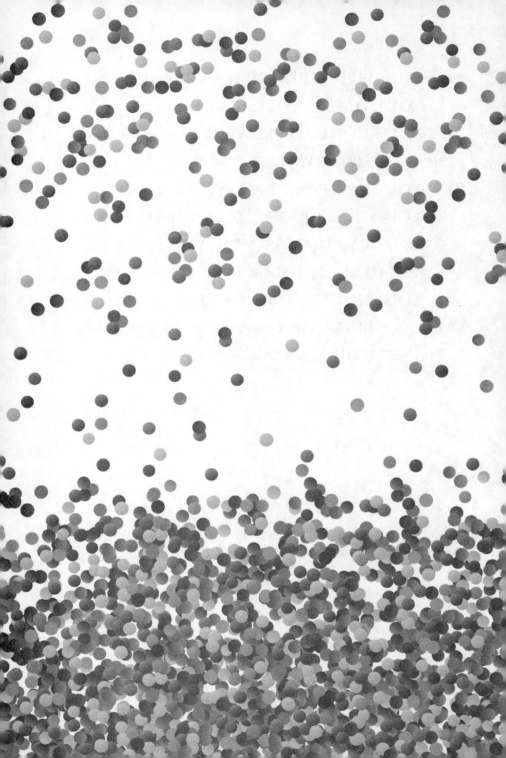

CHOOSE YOUR OWN CATASTROPHE

Though you are feeling quite hungry, you decide to wait it out in the pit. Your reasoning being: The longer you wait, the more famous you will be when you finally are rescued. You might even be more famous than the kid who fell into the rhino exhibit at the zoo, because unlike the kid who fell into the rhino exhibit, there is no one around to save you. No one even knows where you are. And unlike the rhino kid, who had probably just finished lunch and maybe even had an ice cream cone, you have had no food or water all day. This is going to be so amazing! All you have to do now is kick back and dream about how famous you are going to be—which, good news, the more delirious you grow from hunger and thirst, the better your dreams will be.

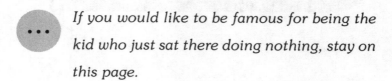 *If you would like to be famous for being the kid who just sat there doing nothing, stay on this page.*

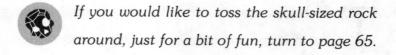 *If you would like to toss the skull-sized rock around, just for a bit of fun, turn to page 65.*

If you would like to try on the shoe to see if it fits, turn to page 85.

If you would like to use the matchbook and wood to light a fire so you can see more of your surroundings and possibly find your way out of the pit, turn to page 107.

Followers

Mia and Marley are arguing again about who they should follow. Marley says they should follow Riley because stop-motion animation and piano are easier interests to follow than Trina's English riding lessons and trips to South Africa. Plus Riley is kind of famous for single-handedly getting the school to make one of the bathrooms gender neutral. They were interviewed on the news and everything.

It isn't that Mia doesn't want to follow Riley, it's just that Riley has like a million interests. Marley says it's a good thing that Riley has so many inter-ests. "More things for us to like. We should defi-nitely follow them."

She wins the argument, of course. Marley always wins.

After school they get in line behind Riley. The line is so long that Mia can't even see them up there, but Daniel, who is in line in front of Mia and Mar-ley, says they are in the right place. He is also fol-lowing Riley.

Marley asks Daniel if he knows where they're going. Daniel shrugs and asks these twin girls in front of him. The twins shrug too.

Everyone keeps walking down the sidewalk and after a while, maybe ten minutes, one of the twins—the one with longer hair, the one with purple bangs—tells Daniel something, and Dan-iel turns around and tells it to Mia and Marley. Apparently they are going to see puppies! Riley's grandma has a French bulldog and it just had puppies! Marley says to Mia, *super* loudly—like she isn't even talking to Mia, she's just saying it to get followers—"I love French bulldog puppies!" Also, Mia is the one who *really* loves French bulldog puppies. Marley loves them, but not as much as she loves kittens.

Marley puts both her hands around Mia's ear and whispers, "Don't look, but we have followers."

Mia immediately turns around to look.

"Mia!" Marley says.

It's true—they have five followers. They have six followers.

Seven followers.

"See?" Marley says. "I told you we should follow Riley."

Daniel turns around and tells Mia and Marley that the puppies are super cute.

"What do they look like?" Marley asks.

"Beats me," Daniel says.

Marley turns around and tells their followers that the puppies are super cute.

"What do they look like?" this tiny girl asks.

She's carrying a giant stuffed unicorn and her backpack is practically as big as she is.

Mia has no idea how that tiny girl got to be a follower. She wants to say to the tiny girl, *Shouldn't you be in kindergarten or something?* but then Marley says, "They look like really small French bulldogs."

They keep walking. Daniel says Riley's grandma is taking them to their piano lesson. Marley is super excited about this. "This is going to be so fun!" She turns around and repeats this to the tiny girl, who jumps up and down, dropping her unicorn and accidentally stomping on its head. The tiny girl starts to cry, but then Mia picks up her unicorn and brushes off the dirt. She gives it a kiss on its head and hands it back to the tiny girl.

Marley says, "This is the best day EVER!" and Mia says, "Yeah." She isn't sure why it's the best day ever, but everyone is still following Riley, and Mia and Marley have at least twenty followers behind them, so maybe Marley is right.

It doesn't take long to get to Riley's piano lesson.

Riley is learning to play Beethoven's "Ode to Joy." Marley says *shhhh!* when Mia whispers to her that she learned to play that song like three years ago.

"Riley is learning to play 'Ode to Joy,'" Marley tells their followers. "It's such a great song," she says.

"How does 'Ode to Joy' go again?" she whispers to Mia.

"I don't remember," Mia says, even though she could play that song with her eyes closed.

Now Marley is looking up the song on her phone. "Oh," she says. "Cool," she says, even though Mia can tell she doesn't really like it.

They pass a snow cone stand. "Look, Marley, snow cones!" They have all the best flavors, and there isn't even a line.

Marley looks at the snow cone stand. She loves snow cones, but there's no way she can leave the line. They must have fifty followers behind them now!

They pass Mia's favorite park, the one with the

bouncing bridge. "Marley," Mia says, "remember that game we used to play? That game with the pinecones?" You got points for getting the pinecones across the bridge without hitting the rails.

"Hold on," Marley says. "I'm waiting to hear where we're going."

Across the empty park is another line of kids passing the other way. That line is much shorter. It's so short that the kids in back can see the kid who's in front. He's playing a guitar and all his followers are singing along. Mia quietly wishes that Riley played the guitar. She especially wishes this when Daniel turns around and says that they're now going to get Riley's hair cut. "At Hairapist," he says. "Get it? *Hairapist*. Like *Therapist*."

Marley laughs and explains *Hairapist* to their followers. The tiny girl doesn't get it, but the others laugh, which makes Marley laugh even harder, which makes Daniel laugh harder too, and pretty soon everyone is cracking up. Everyone except for the tiny girl. And except for Mia, who is busy watching the guitar-playing boy and his singing followers.

On the way back from Riley's hair appointment, the line curls around and everyone gets to see Riley's new haircut. Everyone tells Riley how amazing they look. Everyone tells Riley that their hair is SO cool. Riley loves Marley's comment that they look a lot older now, which was really Mia's comment that Marley just repeated in a louder voice. Mia didn't even really mean for it to be a compliment, she just thought Riley looked older, that's all.

The other twin—the one with shorter hair and more freckles—tells Daniel something, and Daniel turns around and tells Mia and Marley that they are all going to sweep now.

Marley says, "Cool!"

"Marley," Mia says, "why is sweeping cool?"

Marley ignores this comment and tells the tiny girl behind them that we are going to sweep now.

"Wait," Daniel says. "First we are going to weed a little."

"Yay!" Marley says.

"I don't want to weed," Mia says. "I'm tired."

"Tho am I," the tiny girl says. She is sucking on her thumb. Or no, she is sucking on her unicorn's hoof.

Daniel says, "Actually we are going to bruise our teeth first, then weed, then go to sweep."

"Wait," Mia says, "that's not right. I think they mean *read* and—"

But she is interrupted by the tiny girl. The tiny girl is tugging on Mia's shirt. There's a little popping cork sound when she takes the unicorn hoof out of her mouth. "Why are we going?" she asks.

"You mean *where* are we going?" Mia corrects.

"*Why* are we going?" the tiny girl insists.

This is a question that Mia does not know how to answer. "I'm not sure," she tells the tiny girl.

Mia looks at Marley, who is smiling at the back of Daniel's head. She looks at the other followers, all eagerly waiting for Riley to bruise their teeth. Next to Mia, two squirrels chase each other around a tree trunk, and beyond the tree, a woman is strapping a kayak onto the roof of her car. Across the street, blackberry bushes line the side of a pond, and for a while, Mia watches the crows pecking at the fallen berries. Then she takes the tiny girl's hand.

"Unicorn wants a berry," the tiny girl says.

"Yes," Mia says, "that's just what I was thinking."

And the three of them—Mia, tiny girl, and unicorn—unfollow Riley and cross over to the other side of the street.

WHAT MAKES YOU HAPPY?

Answer these 22 questions and we'll tell you what brings you joy. On a separate piece of paper, the back of your hand, or the back of someone else's hand, keep track of how many A, B, C, and D answers you have.

1. **How do you like to start your day?**
   - **A** Cereal
   - **B** Eggs
   - **C** Cold pizza
   - **D** Feeling of dread

2. **Which of the following best describes your bedroom?**
   - **A** Tidy
   - **B** Obstacle course
   - **C** Cozy nest of clothes and candy wrappers
   - **D** Post-apocalyptic / Dystopian

3. **On a scale of golden retriever to ice cube, how friendly are you?**

   Ⓐ Golden retriever

   Ⓑ Sofa

   Ⓒ Blackberry bush

   Ⓓ Ice cube

4. **If you were to suddenly break out in song in the middle of class, what kind of music would you choose?**

   Ⓐ Show tune

   Ⓑ Hip-hop

   Ⓒ Love song I wrote

   Ⓓ '80s all the way

5. **What kind of aquatic creature are you?**

   Ⓐ Sea dragon

   Ⓑ Hermit crab

   Ⓒ Manatee

   Ⓓ Shark

6. What do you get more joy out of?

A Laughing at a good joke

B Laughing at the expense of others

C Doing my part to help out around the house

D Gum

7. "I keep my emotions..."

A To myself

B Flowing freely for all to enjoy

C In a tiny airtight bottle

D Tucked inside a bomb that could detonate at any moment

8. What would you be most terrified to find under your bed?

A Scorpion

B Bear

C Yogurt

D Clown

9. **In your opinion, which is better?**

   (A) Giving

   (B) Receiving

   (C) Giving in exchange for something of equal or greater value

   (D) Receiving way more than anyone else

10. **Why did the chicken cross the road?**

    (A) To get to the other side

    (B) Because it felt like it

    (C) To boldly go where no chicken has gone before

    (D) To get away from your stupid joke

11. **Favorite kind of rock?**

    (A) Agate

    (B) Thunderegg

    (C) Metamorphic

    (D) & roll

12. Favorite substance to paint on your hand?

(A) Rubber cement

(B) Elmer's glue

(C) Ketchup

(D) Antibacterial hand sanitizer

13. How are you at handling mistakes?

(A) I always apologize and try to learn from my mistakes

(B) It wasn't my fault

(C) That guy over there did it

(D) Mistakes? Me? Never.

14. What number am I thinking of?

(A) 7

(B) 36

(C) 141

(D) 843

15. Do you consider yourself to be a paranoid person?

(A) No

(B) Why would you ask me that?

(C) Seriously, do I seem like a paranoid person?

(D) Are a lot of people saying that I'm a paranoid person?

16. If you could only pick one of the many fabulous Happy Heads™® available now, for a limited time, at 10% off the regular already low price, which would you choose?

(A) My Happy Tropical Head®

(B) My Happy Popular Head®

(C) My Happy Retro Head®

(D) My Happy Glow-in-the-Dark Head®

17. What is your middle name?

- Ⓐ Fun
- Ⓑ Danger
- Ⓒ Adventure
- Ⓓ Cassidy

18. The ultimate day for me is:

- Ⓐ Communing with trees
- Ⓑ Communing with good friends
- Ⓒ Communing with computer
- Ⓓ Communing with pillow

19. Which of the following does not belong?

- Ⓐ ～～～～～
- Ⓑ ～～～～～
- Ⓒ ～～～～～
- Ⓓ ～～～～～

20. What do you find cuter:

A Bunnies

B Mini corgis

C Fun-size candy bars

D Myself

21. All your friends jump off a cliff. Do you:

A Jump off cliff

B First buy hang glider, then jump off cliff

C Cautiously climb down from cliff

D Promise to jump after them, then laugh

22. If you could have one extra body part, what would you choose?

A Extra heart

B Extra eye

C Extra arm

D Extra stomach

Ready to discover what brings you joy?

First, tally up all your A responses, B responses, C responses, and D responses.

Next, multiply your A total by 3, add 5 to your B total, subtract 3 from your C total, and divide your D total in half.

Now just add up all four numbers and multiply the total by 2 and we'll tell you exactly what makes you happy.

97–132   You are the kind of person who finds joy in pleasurable activities, such as spending time doing the things you love with people you like being around. You also enjoy trees and food. To experience even greater happiness, try living in the moment, finding your purpose, or becoming one with the universe.

64–96   You find your greatest joy in life's simple pleasures: spending time outside on a warm day, eating your favorite foods while hanging out with good friends, receiving birthday money in the mail. To make yourself feel even happier, try surrounding yourself with people who are less happy than you.

34–63 Happiness for you is spending time in the great outdoors or indoors, exploring new places or video games with new or old friends, and participating in things while breathing in the air. To achieve even greater happiness, try taking three minutes to write down everything you're grateful for, ten minutes to go on a walk, five minutes to call up an old friend, or eighteen minutes to do all of the above.

4 Before working on your happiness, you would do well to spend a little time with a math tutor. From there, try setting small but realistic happiness goals, such as watching a video of a baby monkey playing with a lion cub, or giving away something you don't really like that much to a sibling or friend.

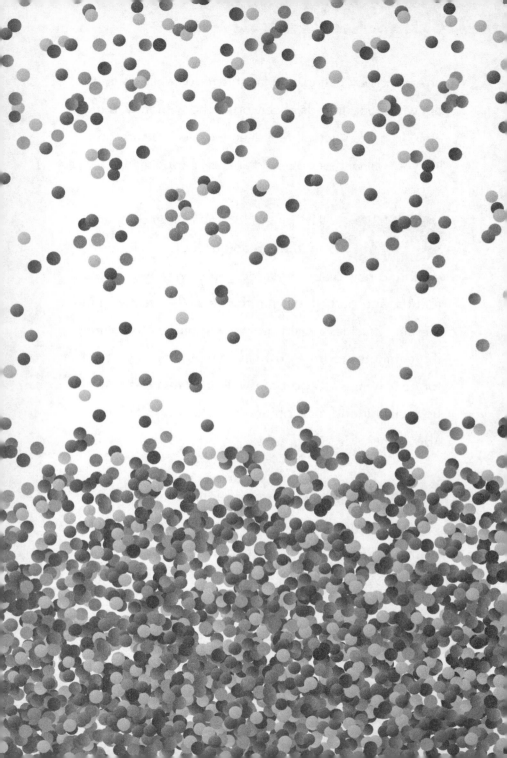

The Voice

Part V

YOU ARE NO GOOD, said The Voice.

"Yes, I am," whispered Katya, though it was true that she had probably failed her math test, and she had definitely been the worst volleyball player in gym class.

NO, said The Voice, YOU ARE NOT.

"Yes," Katya whispered, more quietly still, "I am." She was even less sure than before, now that more of the day was coming back to her. How, during lunch, she did not laugh at Sasha's joke because she did not realize it was a joke until Sasha said, *That was a joke*, and when she then attempted to laugh, it just sounded really fake.

NO, YOU ARE NOT, said The Voice.

Katya paused. Katya grew sad. She even cried a little.

And then, she got angry.

"YES, I AM!" she shouted.

She did not really believe that she was, she just wanted The Voice to go away, just go away and leave her alone!

There was a pause. The Voice grew silent.

Maybe The Voice had gone away.

Finally, The Voice whispered, NO, YOU ARE NOT— so quietly it almost seemed as if the words were coming from a different Voice, a much smaller Voice.

And that gave Katya an idea.

(To be continued.)

This is Marta. She is thirteen years old and she goes to Bridger Middle School. One day she wished to be herself again.

Oh if only she had not used up her three wishes.

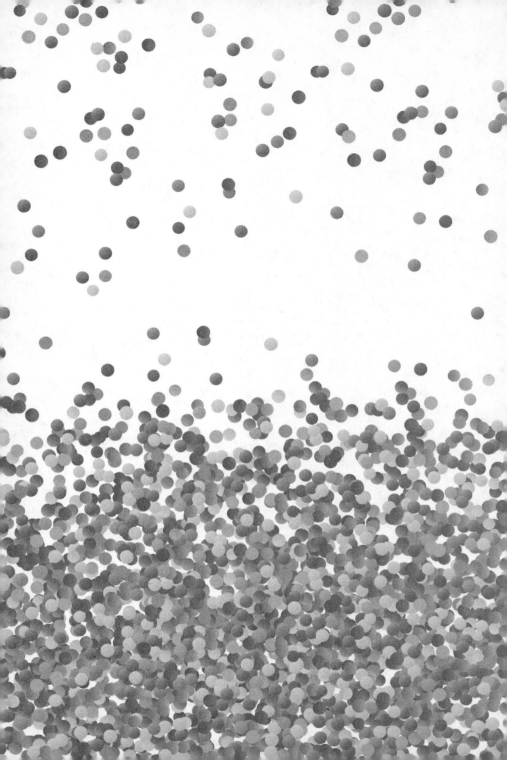

True Story

There was nothing in the thrift store that Caleb really wanted. No, that wasn't entirely true. There were many things in the thrift store that Caleb wanted—the Casper lunch box, the Tiki mug, the bowling shoes—but Caleb, having already spent most of his small allowance, was left with a budget of just eighty-seven cents. This limited his shopping to only one of the store's many aisles—the aisle of broken sunglasses, half-used journals, rickety

baskets from Easters past, miscellaneous cords—
where there usually stood a man, searching for the
power to something in his life—and a sad selection
of small figurines, most of which included either a
bear, a hula dancer, a turkey, or a clown. There was
also, on one of the shelves of the aisle, a plastic tub
filled with cheap rings and bracelets tangled up in
a sea of green and purple Mardi Gras beads—items
not even worthy of their own price tags. Instead,
riding on top of this beady sea was a box of snack-
sized plastic bags, and taped to the outside of the
tub, a sign: FILL A BAG FOR A DOLLAR, OR 25¢ EACH.
This is where Caleb found the ring.

Yes, it was true that he already owned a mood
ring, which, judging by the rainbow gem at its center,
this clearly was. It was also true that he did not ever
wear or even look at that other ring—mainly because
there were certain people at his school who loved any
excuse to harass him. In fact, that other mood ring
was currently under his bed in a plastic storage bin

that he rarely opened and that his mother repeatedly asked him to donate to this very thrift store.

This ring, though, was different. This ring was not some cheap plastic trinket you might get from a gumball machine outside the grocery store (which is where Caleb's last mood ring had come from). This ring had the look and weight of one of his grandmother's rings, and it appeared to be just as old, with leafy vines twisting around its tarnished metal band and a marble-sized gem held in its center by a circle of thorns. Also, this ring did not come with the usual list of boring and rarely accurate moods: RELAXED, CALM, HAPPY—or the usual reminders of what Caleb was not: COOL, NORMAL. This ring did not even change color when Caleb slipped it onto his finger. Instead, a word—a word that appeared to be handwritten—rose to its surface: CURIOUS. And when Caleb immediately decided that he must have this ring, CURIOUS was replaced by another word, which was equally true: NERVOUS. The truth of this word kneaded at Caleb's stomach and gave his hands the shakes as he dug among the various wrappers, hair bands, and coins in his pocket for the quarter that would bring this strange ring home with him.

That night at home other words appeared:

ANNOYED (when his phone died right in the middle of a video he was watching).

STARTLED (when the mail carrier dropped a package on the porch and the dog went berserk).

EXHAUSTED (when he fell asleep while doing his homework, and again the next morning when his mother came in to wake him).

On the school bus, new words came at such rapid speed that Caleb barely had a chance to read them, until finally the ring settled on the words that most accurately captured what he was feeling just then: FREAKED OUT.

He tried shaking the words away—as much as he could manage without drawing too much attention to himself—but with every shake, the words only grew brighter. Flicking the gem with his nail did nothing. Knocking it with his knuckle: nothing.

Finally, after attempting to crush the gem between his teeth, the words faded away, and in their place appeared an equally irritating word: IRRITATED.

"Stop it!" Caleb hissed at the ring, which immediately responded with: ANGRY. He looked across the aisle at Trey, who was now glaring back at him.

"Not you..." Caleb started, but what was he supposed to say? Explain that he was yelling at a ring? It was bad enough at his school for a guy to even *wear* a ring, let alone talk to the thing. As he tried to hide the ring by slipping it under his leg, he thought he caught a glimpse of the word SCARED. And so what? *Wouldn't YOU be scared?* he wanted to yell at the ring. *You're just a dumb ring anyway...What do you know?*

He could already imagine what Dylan would say. *Nice grandma ring. Does it match your grandma shirt?* That's what Dylan had called his shirt, just because it had flowers on it. "Nice shirt, grandma," he said, and everyone, even a few kids Caleb thought were his friends, had laughed. Making the whole thing worse, a teacher overheard the scene and made the horrible decision to pull the two boys into the hall, where she forced Dylan to apologize. "What?" Dylan said. "All I did was compliment his shirt. It isn't like I called him *gay* or anything." He said *gay* like it was the worst thing you could be. The teacher didn't say a word, she just looked at Dylan for an uncomfortably long time, until finally he said, "Fine. Sorry." And for the hundredth time since moving to this stupid town, Caleb wished he could go back to his old school, where he could wear whatever he wanted, and where he wasn't the only guy who painted his nails. Paint his nails at this school? No way.

Realizing now that he was crazy to wear the ring to school, and wondering why this didn't occur to him before, after all he had been through, Caleb attempted to remove the ring from his finger. With every tug and twist, though, the ring only grew tighter—a tightness he could feel in his chest, as if the ring had looped itself around his entire body. Heart racing, hands turning numb, he knew it would only grow worse if he didn't do as the counselor had taught him after his first panic attack. Closing his eyes, he drew in a slow, deep breath, counting one-two-three as he filled up his chest, then one-two-three as he let the breath out. He repeated this over and over until his heart settled back into a calm and steady rhythm.

Fortunately he had placed the ring on his left hand, not his writing hand, so it was easy enough to keep it hidden inside the pocket of his hoodie. Still, there were challenges, especially in PE, where he had to fake a stomachache to get out of volleyball, and again in art class, where he had to fake an even more painful stomachache in order to get out of molding a clay mask. The few times he slipped his hand out from his pocket—mostly in the hope that it had vanished—the gem glowed with the same word: SCARED.

At home that afternoon, he looked up on his computer: how to remove a tight ring. He tried Vaseline. He tried butter. He tried shampoo and lotion—he even tried peanut butter. Nothing worked. Nothing produced even the slightest twist or wiggle. And through it all, the ring insisted on stating the obvious: FRUSTRATED.

"Brilliant," Caleb muttered. "Tell me something I don't know."

DEFENSIVE, the ring said, which made Caleb blurt out, "Look who's talking! You're just a cheap thrift-store ring! You didn't even have your own price tag! You're lucky I even—"

"Caleb? Who are you talking to?"

His mom stood in his doorway, a familiar concern in her eyes. Since they moved to this town, Caleb had been through a lot. Mostly it was minor bullying, but once he had arrived at school to find a crowd of kids gathered around his locker, waiting to see what he would do when he saw the cruel words someone had written there.

"Rehearsing some lines," Caleb said, the ring squeezing in on his finger. "For a skit."

"Oh," his mom said, "I thought—" but she caught herself before saying what they were both thinking: that his medicine had stopped working, that he was back to his angry outbursts. "What's it about?"

"Huh?" Caleb said, distracted by the word he had caught a glimpse of just before slipping his hand behind a stack of books: LIAR.

"What's the skit about?"

"It's—just a skit. I should probably keep practicing."

"Well, I'd love to hear about it sometime."

"Sure," Caleb said. "Maybe later."

The next morning he awoke late, with a vague memory of his mother coming in sometime earlier to wake him. He now had less than twenty minutes to get to the bus stop. Throwing off his covers and pushing himself out of bed, he made a quick grab for his sweatshirt balled up on the floor—which he immediately dropped again, as if the thing had bitten him. "Ow!"

Looking first at his finger to make sure it was still there, then glaring into the gem through watering eyes, he could just barely make out the word: FALSE.

"*FALSE*? What's that supposed to mean!" Shaking away the pain, he tried once more, this time moving his hand much more slowly toward the sweatshirt. With every inch, though, the ring grew tighter—and tighter—until he had no choice but to give up entirely.

"Fine!" he shouted, wondering for the hundredth

time since buying the ring if he had officially gone mental, if Dylan and his friends were right. He was a freak. Who else but a freak would argue with a ring over what to wear to school?

At least the ring had seemed to cure him of his panic attacks. Who had time for a panic attack when you were busy losing your mind?

Caleb—no, *the ring*—went through nearly every shirt in his dresser until finally it came to the one shirt Caleb did not want to wear, the shirt that he had crumpled up and shoved into the farthest corner of his drawer so he would never again have to even look at it. "No way. No way I'm wearing that thing."

But with the clock ticking closer to 7:30, and the ring biting into his finger with every other shirt he attempted to pick up, he was left with no choice. It was that shirt or no shirt. As he shoved his arms through the sleeves and angrily pushed the buttons through their holes, watching himself in the mirror, covered in yellow and blue flowers—the very image of a Dylan punching bag—he came up with his countermove. If the ring was going to make him wear the shirt, he would just wear his sweatshirt over top of—*Ow!*

Fine, his coat, then. He would wear his coat.

How to get to his coat without his mom or sister seeing him, that was the only problem. More than a problem, it was an impossibility. The coat was on a hook near the door, and the door was on the other side of the kitchen, and in the kitchen were his mom and sister. He could hear them in there talking away.

Taking a deep breath, trying to look as casual as possible, he made his move.

The talking stopped.

Through the corner of his eye, he could see that his mother was also trying her best to look casual. His sister, not so much. She sat at the counter openly staring, a spoonful of cereal halfway to her mouth. "What if they beat you up?" she said to the Cheerios piled just beyond her nose.

"Dee!" her mother snapped. Then, to change the subject, she added, "Hey, you look—"

Caleb grew itchy inside his shirt as he waited for her to finish.

"—like yourself," she said, looking somewhat surprised, and then pleased, by her words. "I always did like that shirt."

For a brief moment, Caleb smiled—he always did like that shirt too—but then his smile faded as thoughts of the shirt were replaced by thoughts of school.

"Is that one of Grandma's rings?"

"What?" Caleb had been thinking about Dylan, and so his stomach seized on the word *grandma*.

"The ring. That ring you're wearing."

"No. It's—just a cheap ring from the thrift store." On *cheap*, the ring grew tighter, letting him know that it disagreed. "So I should probably run." Grabbing a granola bar to eat on the bus, and then his coat from the hook by the—

"Ow!"

He did not dare make a second attempt, not with his mom rushing over to check on him. "Just—stubbed my toe," he said, rushing out the door before she could tell him to pick his coat up off the floor.

And then he was outside.

Though nervous, he had not fully thought about what would happen next. The stares. Maybe even the words, the terrible words on his locker last year that had made him run home and crumple up the shirt, which had felt like he was crumpling up his insides. Since that morning, Caleb and the shirt had stayed balled up and tucked away where no one could find them.

The nearer he came to the bus stop, the more those awful feelings came back to him, until there was no way he could join the group of kids waiting there, no way he could get on that bus. Did he hear the word *freak* as he walked past, or did he only imagine it? Either way, with every step he took, the word was a Ping-Pong ball bouncing from one side of his brain to the other.

Two miles is a long walk when you're covered in flowers. At least in this town it is. Caleb did not look up the entire way, even when he heard the bus driving past him, even when he was sure that everyone on the bus was staring out their windows at him. Was that laughing he heard? Did someone just yell out their car window? It was impossible to hear over the pounding of his heart and feet.

Every time a car passed, he looked down at the ring—out of nerves more than anything, out of not wanting to be seen, out of not wanting to know who had seen him—and each time he expected to see the word FREAK or IDIOT or DEAD MAN, or at least the obvious—SCARED, NAUSEOUS—but every time he looked into the gem, the same word, the same lie, appeared: BRAVE.

* * *

By the time Caleb got to school, first period had already started and there was no way he was going to walk into class late, so he found a place behind the building where he was sure to not be seen. Minutes passed like hours. Rain came and went. A pigeon pecked at a chip bag near his foot, others arriving to feed on the crumbs. Finally, the end-of-class bell rang out.

With a deep breath, Caleb dragged his heavy feet to the door, where he took another deep breath before pulling it open and walking on wobbly legs into the school.

Eyes, so many eyes. It seemed as if the walls had eyes, the lockers had eyes, the drinking fountain—everywhere he looked, eyes, every one of them looking at him.

And then:

Dylan.

Dylan walking straight for him.

Dylan and his friends, a wall closing in on him, and before Caleb could turn away, Dylan's hand was on his shirt, pinching at it like it was something disgusting, something contaminated. "Don't you look pretty today. Borrowing your mom's clothes again?"

Mom. Even worse than grandma.

Caleb's heart was a thousand hearts pounding at once. An icy wave swept through his body, his hands went numb. But he did not run. He did not crumble. He *would not* crumble.

The longer he stood there, at first terrified, then slowly calmer, then just watching as Dylan walked his "gay walk" circle around him, his friends snorting and hee-hawing—how stupid they were, what idiots they were—the more Caleb realized that this was it. This was all they had. This was his worst fear, and soon it would be over, and he would still be here.

One thing, though, one thing would be different: They would not be touching his shirt again. Next time Dylan came in for a grab, he would be ready.

It was the force that surprised Caleb the most. How he had made Dylan's hand swing back as if hit by a bat. The force of his voice too, like it carried with it everything he had ever kept inside him, and there was not a soul in that hall who did not hear him when he said, pulling on his own shirt: "THIS. THIS IS MINE." And when Dylan started to laugh and pretend that he was shaking with fear, Caleb's voice became a storm: "SO GO GET YOUR OWN *MOM SHIRT* IF YOU LOVE IT SO MUCH."

The laughter was another storm, so loud that Caleb could barely hear Dylan's mumbling—something about not being caught dead in that shirt.

"WHAT?" Caleb said, holding his hand around his ear for better hearing. "CAN YOU BORROW IT? NO WAY."

Dylan's fist started for Caleb's chest and Caleb did flinch—okay, he might have even ducked—but like every other awful Dylan moment, that was it, that was all Dylan had—along with a pretty good shoulder ram as he walked past Caleb and shoved his way down the hall. But now it was over and here he stood.

Down at his hand, the ring had loosened its grip and, before he could move to catch it, had slipped free of his finger. He did manage, though, to catch sight of the word as it fell to the ground: TRUE.

After rolling a few feet, the old ring spun to a rest in front of a girl—a girl Caleb only knew as the girl who ate alone.

"You keep it," he said when she brought the ring to him—though the ring, which the girl had momentarily, in her nervousness, slipped onto her finger, had already made its choice.

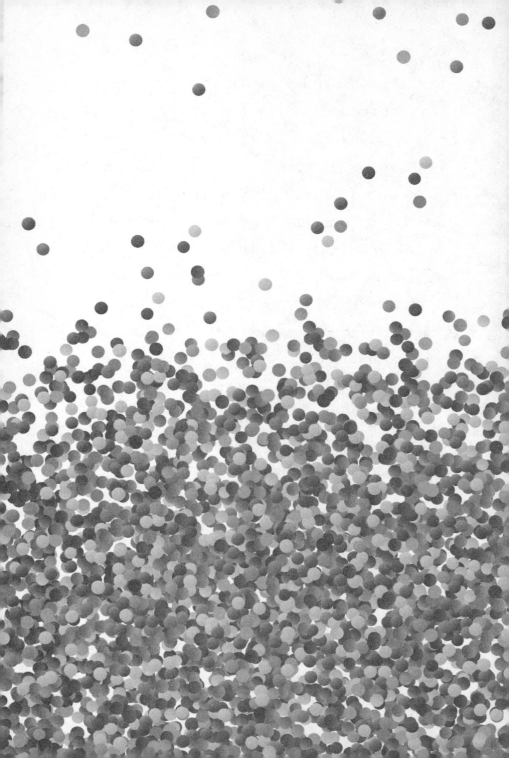

MAGICAL MYSTICAL

FORTUNE-TELLING
MACHINE

~ALL-SEEING! ALL-KNOWING!~

~YOUR FUTURE REVEALED~

~GUARANTEED RESULTS!~

PLACE FINGER ON BUTTON FOR FIVE SECONDS
THEN TURN THE PAGE TO DISCOVER
THE MANY ADVENTURES THAT AWAIT YOU!

A picture...

. . . is beginning to form.

Yes...

. . . yes . . .

. . . it is coming into view now.

You are sitting or lying down.

You are holding a powerful object in your hands.

This object is rectangular in shape and contains multitudes of wisdom.

Near you, there is a source of light.

Soon you will find yourself eating food.

You will then find yourself sleeping in a bed.

You will leave your house and enter a building where you will encounter other people of your same age.

One day a stranger will appear.

You will try things you have never tried before.

You will get a paper cut and step in something you do not wish to step in.

You will make an embarrassing sound.

Someone will eat the last piece of something
you were saving for tomorrow.

You won't be able to find your coat and then,
like magic, your coat will appear.

You will travel somewhere with someone
who is very close to you.

You will see animals there, and trees.

A stranger will approach you and ask you
what you would like.

This stranger will bring you food and water.

Shortly afterward you will need to use the
restroom, and you will not be able to find it,
and then you will find it.

As soon as you go outside it will start raining, then as soon as you go back inside the sun will come out.

.

You will have bad days followed by good days followed by mediocre days that you won't remember.

You will be sure that something really awful is going to happen, but it won't.

You will think that you aren't okay when you really are.

You will take many walks and find many treasures on the ground.

Some of these treasures will be worth a penny or even a quarter, and some of these treasures will turn out to be gum.

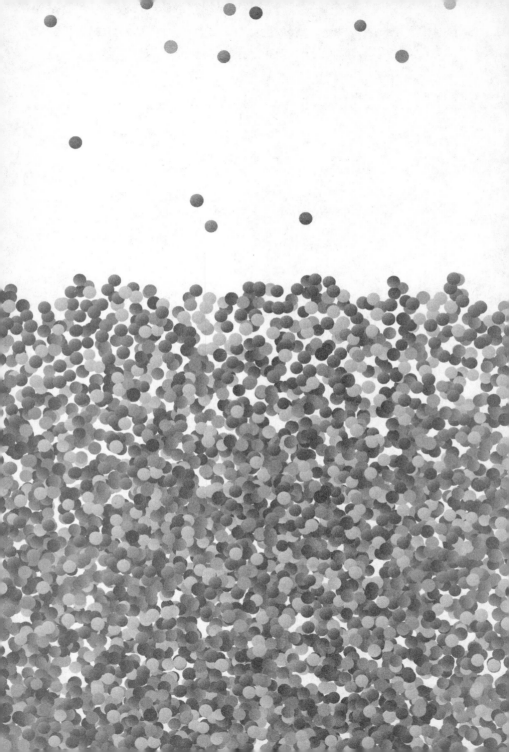

CHOOSE YOUR OWN CATASTROPHE

Nope, the shoe doesn't fit that foot either.

 If you would like to toss the skull-sized rock around, just for a bit of fun, turn to page 65.

 If you would like to use the matchbook and wood to light a fire so you can see more of your surroundings and possibly find your way out of the pit, turn to page 107.

If you would like to sit and do nothing because if you stay in the pit long enough to be discovered on the brink of death, it would be a really cool story to tell your friends and might even go viral, *turn to page 143.*

Farewell to The Voice

"STAY," said Katya, storming out of the house. "YOU CANNOT COME WITH ME."

WHERE ARE YOU GOING? said The Voice, storming out after her—though it was not its usual loud self.

"I DON'T KNOW," said Katya, walking for the end of her driveway.

THAT'S A BAD IDEA, said The Voice. YOU COULD GET LOST. YOU COULD FALL INTO A HOLE. YOU COULD

GET ATTACKED BY A RABID RACCOON. ANYTHING
COULD HAPPEN OUT THERE.

Katya stopped. The Voice was right. Anything
could happen.

TERRIBLE THINGS, said The Voice.

Terrible was one of The Voice's favorite words.
Katya was very tired of that word. Katya was very
tired of The Voice.

On the other hand, The Voice did save her life
once or twice.

FIVE TIMES AT LEAST, said The Voice.

"THREE TIMES AT MOST," said Katya.

YOU'RE WELCOME, said The Voice.

Katya looked at her house behind her. How easy
it would be to walk back inside. She looked down
the road ahead of her, where who knows what might
happen (EXACTLY, said the Voice), then down at her
feet to see if they might make the decision for her,
but her feet just stood there doing nothing. Ever
since they had stopped dancing, Katya's feet had
become much less spontaneous.

At the end of the road was the pond where Katya used to catch salamanders and minnows, before The Voice told her they carried terrible diseases that could make her terribly sick.

TERRIBLY SICK, said The Voice.

Katya thought about all the wonderful times she had passed at the pond, back when she didn't think twice about dipping her hands into the murky water or flipping over a slimy stone in search of a salamander. Some days the ducks would come by for a visit. Other days the kids who lived across the pond would throw sticks at her, or let their dog loose on her.

EXACTLY! said The Voice. ANYTHING COULD HAPPEN TO YOU AT THAT POND!

And Katya, walking for the pond, adding a skip to get there just a little faster, agreed. "YES. ANYTHING."

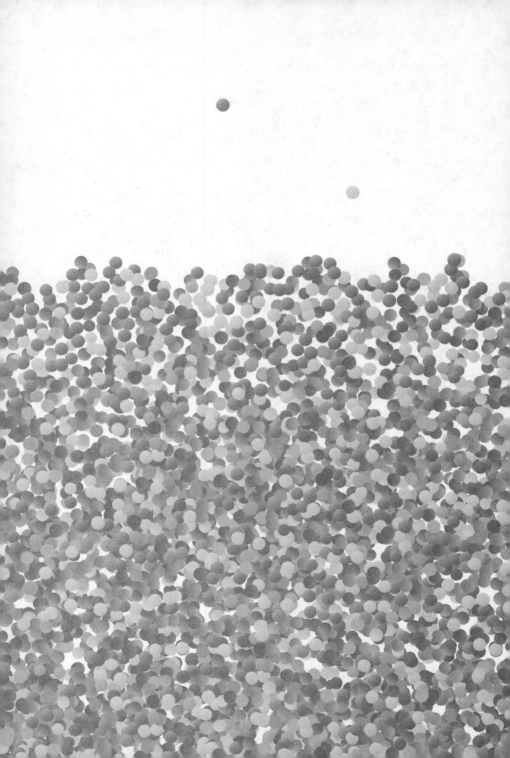

Goodbye and thanks
for coming

So long, soda spiller

cat tripper

chip choker

Glad you could make it,

clumsy dancer

nervous laughter

thought it was a costume party

See you next time,

lost every game

wish you never came

The party has ended

The ice cream has melted

The dog has made off with the last Lil'
    Smokey

So grab your party horn and your
    worries

Pick the gummy lizards from your braces
Brush the crumbs from your
  punch-stained grandma shirt
And go on out there and be the
totally awkward
anxious
odd
normal
lovable
singular
human that you are
Because that party
the real party
the you *party*
is the only
place to be

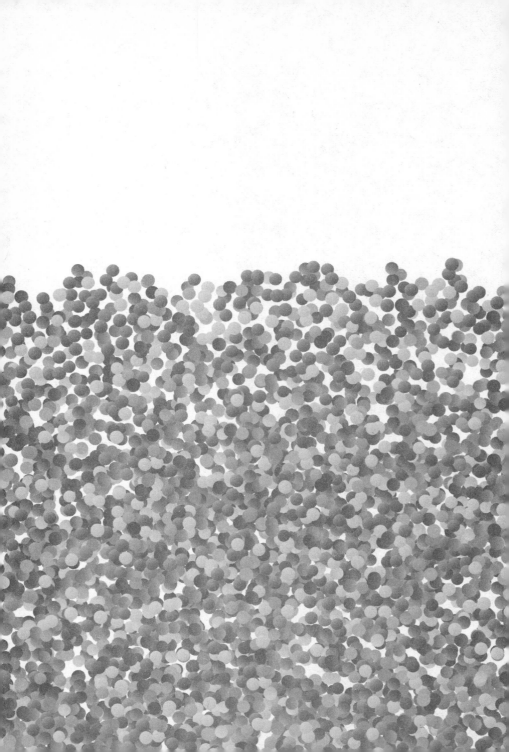

Thank you

To Agatha, Amalea, Amanda, Athena, Atticus, Bella, Cassandra, Colia, Connor, D'Angelo, Destiny, Dustin, Efi, Elenor, Ema, Emma, Eric, Frankie, Hadley, Hayden, Hazel, Isabella, Jade, Jaylah, Jazlyn, Joe, Jonah, Kaitlyn, Lauryn, Leo, Lev, Lexi, Loretta, Mason Coe, Master, Maya, Meredith, Milly, Milo, Neely, Paige, Payton, Quincy, Robert, Sabine, Sadie, Sammy, Sans, Sydney, Tashi, Titus, Trixie, Tucky, Violet, Will, Zane, and all the other young people whose wisdom, courage, heart, and humor have filled me with inspiration and joy.

And to my truly brilliant editor, Susan Rich.

KATHLEEN LANE

lives in Portland, Oregon, where she writes, teaches, cohosts the art and literary event series SHARE, and runs *Create More, Fear Less*, a program that inspires young people to connect with the creative potential of their anxious minds.